THE BOX OF DEMONS

DANIEL WHELAN

MACMILLAN CHILDREN'S BOOKS

First published 2015 by Macmillan Children's Books

This edition published 2016 by Macmillan Children's Books
an imprint of Pan Macmillan
20 New Wharf Road, London N1 9RR
Associated companies throughout the world
www.panmacmillan.com

ISBN 978-1-4472-7373-8

Copyright © Daniel Whelan 2015

The right of Daniel Whelan to be identified as the
author of this work has been asserted by him in accordance
with the Copyright, Designs and Patents Act 1988.

1 3 5 7 9 8 6 4 2

A CIP catalogue record for this book is available from
the British Library.

Typeset by Ellipsis Digital Limited, Glasgow
Printed and bound by CPI Group (UK) Ltd, Croydon CR0 4YY

This one's for Alex,
and for Lynne,
but above all . . .

for Sylwia

Contents

Chapter One

Come, Armageddon! Come!

The Apocalypse began in Rhyl, during the second-to-last weekend of January. It was the perfect place for the world to end: a neglected seaside resort on the North Wales coast, its best days far behind it. The sort of town where a cataclysmic global event could unfold unnoticed by the locals and ignored by the world at large.

The weekend started, as all weekends should, at some point on Friday afternoon. Freezing rain lashed down in the early evening gloom whilst the wind howled through the shuttered-shop streets, spraying water from the murky expanse of the Irish Sea on to the deserted promenade. Discarded chip papers and crisp packets were tossed around like tumbleweeds, the only evidence that the empty streets had recently been full of schoolchildren on their way home.

It was the beginning of the dead time between the closing of the shops and the opening of the nightclubs, and it was utterly miserable.

It suited Ben Robson's mood perfectly.

He walked as quickly as he could, the rain soaking through his hand-me-down anorak, chilling him. He was late for tea, and knew his grandparents would be waiting. He turned off the road and into a side alley, intending to cut across the muddy patch of waste ground that lay between the street and his road. He managed to get a quarter of the way across before plumes of blue smoke started to slowly rise out of his schoolbag. After a full minute of billowing, during which the rain managed to discover previously unknown parts of Ben to soak, Djinn finally materialized, gasping as if he had just climbed several flights of stairs. He ran a gaseous finger around the stone collar on his neck, as though it were a tie he sought to loosen.

'Bennnnnn,' he whined, 'can't we go the other way? I'm hungry.'

'So?'

'Want food.'

'What for? You can't eat it.'

'Yeah, but still. Can't we get chips? I like chips,' he said, licking his lips.

'You've never had chips.'

'It's the smell. Can't we just walk past the shop?'

Djinn was the largest of the three demons that lived in the Box: completely without corporeal form (and so impervious to, say, rain), he looked like he weighed at least fifty stone, which is quite a feat for a creature made entirely out of blue gas.

'Please, Ben. Pleeeeease?'

Ben looked out at the muddy field. If he ran across, he'd only have to duck down the alley and he'd come out on to Fford Heulwen. A hundred metres more and he'd be out of his wet clothes and safely ensconced in his room, working on the latest recruit to his undead army. Alternatively, he could turn round, tramp down several dreary roads with (depending on whether you spoke Welsh or not) either bafflingly unpronounceable or laughably ironic names, in order to stand outside a chip shop for the benefit of an invisible demon.

He hardly had time to consider it before he felt a kicking from inside his bag.

'That's great, Djinn, just great,' he said, putting the satchel on the ground, 'because you know who's getting out now, don't you?' He hunched his body over the bag as he undid the straps, hoping to protect its contents from the elements. Immediately he felt a whoosh of heat on his face, as if he had just opened an oven, and instinctively took a step back. Kartofel scuttled out, his short furry spider's body scurrying away lest the flap be shut again before he could escape. His talons, eight sharp little claws which were all he had in place of legs, left small dents in the soft mud as he skittered about, and the crimson and yellow flame that formed his head flickered with each gust of wind, causing the position of his eyes and mouth to sway with the movement of the fire. He too wore a collar, though for him it could just as easily be called a belt.

'Get back in the Box,' said Ben. He had already been out in the rain for too long, and was not looking forward to having to placate two demons.

'Get lost,' sneered Kartofel. 'It's bobbins in there. I could put up with it if you had anything good in your bag, but you don't. Too many books. You're nearly fifteen years old. You should be out vandalizing bus shelters or something.'

'We're going to the chippy,' said Djinn, with a big, infantile grin on his face.

'I never said that,' said Ben quickly.

'Oh right, so that's it, is it?' said Kartofel. 'You were going to give Porkins here a treat, but there's nothing for old Kartofel. Forget him – he's a pushover, he is.'

'Do we have to do this now? Can't we just get home? I've had a rubbish day.'

'All your days are rubbish.'

'And whose fault is that?'

Kartofel rolled his eyes.

'I'm hungry,' said Djinn, and began to do a strange hopping dance, like an excited dog waiting to be fed.

'Shut up, Fatso,' said Kartofel.

'I'm not fat. I'm big-boned,' said Djinn. 'Tell him, Ben.'

'You haven't got any bones,' snapped Ben. 'Look, both of you, just get back in the Box, OK?'

'Make me,' said Kartofel.

'Fine,' said Ben, picking up his satchel and starting to walk away. 'Get stretched. See if I care.' Kartofel's flickering eyes looked nervously towards Djinn, who was again playing with his collar. Ben smiled.

'You wouldn't dare,' said Kartofel.

Ben shrugged, and put the bag on his back. Djinn made a whining, whimpering noise. 'It's not fair,' he said. 'I haven't done anything. It's him.'

'Shut up, idiot. He's bluffing,' said Kartofel. Ben increased his walk to a slow jog.

'No, Ben. Wait. I'll be good. Please,' called out Djinn. 'Anything but the stretching.'

Ben stopped, put the satchel on the floor, and stood with his arms crossed, waiting. Djinn bowed his head and wisped his massive bulk over to the satchel.

'Judas,' said Kartofel.

'I don't want to get stretched,' said Djinn, sucking himself back inside. Ben found himself wondering how it was possible for gas to slosh and wobble like that.

'You weren't going to really do it,' said Kartofel when Djinn had gone. 'Were you? Because it would be so easy for me to accidentally-on-purpose knock paint over your little toys while you're downstairs having your tea.'

Ben sighed. 'Kartofel,' he said, 'if I stay out in this any longer, I'll catch a cold. And you know what Gran's like when I'm ill. I'll be confined to bed all weekend. No visit to Drylands Hall. Do you want that?'

Kartofel's flames flickered for a moment as he thought about it. He grunted, and scurried over to the satchel. He climbed up the side deliberately slowly, his claws digging into the stiff leather. It was covered in little pockmarks from years of him getting in and out.

'Just get back in before Orff gets out,' said Ben. 'Or do you want to have to stand here and listen to what the rain does to his lumbago?'

'Tch, that old bore.' Kartofel flopped over the top, his flame dimming as he fell. As Ben did up the buckles, he heard a low, dry groan from inside the Box, followed by a loud expletive from Kartofel. Orff was awake, and, as usual, in pain, which meant that the others would be stuck listening to him complain all the way home. Suddenly, even though the rain was still coming down hard, Ben felt like taking his time crossing the few hundred metres between where he was standing and his house.

Tea had been ready for a good quarter of an hour by the time Ben got home, and it was not the only thing waiting for him: as soon as he got through the front door, his grandmother appeared in the hall, wiping her hands on her apron.

'Benjamin Gabriel Robson,' she said, waving a spatula at him, 'where have you been? Look at you – you're soaked through. And covered in mud. If you were younger I'd put you over my knee.'

'It's raining,' said Ben.

'I can see that. Get upstairs and get changed. Your grandad's waiting.'

'I need to feed Druss.'

'You can do that later. Humans come first in this house.'

That's easy for you to say, thought Ben as he stomped up to his room. He closed the door and tipped his satchel out on to the bed. Anything that was made of paper had water damage, including his exercise books, and – more importantly – his well-thumbed copies of the latest *Fantasy Miniatures* catalogue and the *Warmonger* rulebook. He threw his games kit into the corner of the room where it would eventually be joined by his wet clothes, and picked up the Box.

He had never treated it with any care whatsoever. Not that it mattered, for the Box was always pristine. It regularly got dropped, bashed or slammed into walls (mostly while the satchel was still on his back) but it looked, as it always did, brand new. It even had that freshly cut new-wood smell, which it had not lost in all the years he'd been carrying it around.

As he handled it, its music swelled in his head: a warm, comforting melody that purred with satisfaction like a well-stroked cat. It was solid wood, with a natural bold red colour, and perfectly rectangular. The joints and corners were reinforced with iron brackets that were always cold to the touch, and the hinges were made of the same bizarrely rustless metal.

The lid was carved with four strange rune-like symbols that were duplicated on the demons' collars. As Ben ran his fingers over them, he felt a tingling sensation, and the Box responded positively; he spent a few seconds in this reverie before the sound of his grandmother calling caused him to snap out of it. He tossed the Box on the floor, kicked it into its default position under the bed, and quickly changed before heading downstairs. The Box protested meekly at its rough treatment, before resuming its usual background refrain once Ben was out of the door.

Downstairs, Ben's grandad was already sitting at the dining room table, hunched over the *North Wales Weekly News*. He barely looked up when Ben entered. As the reheated dinner was brought from the kitchen, and the smell of it wafted through the hall, the music of the Box changed. The scent had clearly reached his room where, he now knew, Djinn was greeting it with open nostrils.

After dinner, Ben barged through his bedroom door and straight into a cloud of fetid blue gas. An unpleasant smell filled his nose and left a horrible rotten-egg taste in his mouth. 'Djinn!' he yelled between retches. 'How many times have I told you not to hover behind the door?'

'Was it nice, Ben? Was it? It was sausages, wasn't it? I know it was, it was sausages. From the market.'

'I did try and tell him Ben, but no one listens to me,' said a dusty old voice. Orff was lying stretched out on the bed, perfectly straight, as if he had rigor mortis. His gaunt humanoid body was swaddled in rotting bandages, although patches of yellowing translucent skin peeped out, decorated with lesions, liver spots and bruises. His head was made of sackcloth, which fused to the skin around his shoulders. He had two deep round onyx eyes and a long yellow beak which curved down towards his collar: he was part plague doctor, part hooded falcon.

'Don't lie on the bed, Orff; I've told you before. You make it smell old,' said Ben.

'Well, I'm sorry if one of the inconveniences of being old is

7

that you smell old. My sciatica was playing up, and I needed somewhere soft. Would you begrudge an old man that?' He spoke slowly, as if moving the necessary muscles to make speech was a great effort.

'No, I wouldn't. But you're not an old man. You're a demon. So get off the bed.'

'I am, at the very least, thousands of years old. I can't just get up and go. Especially with my eczema and my psoriasis as bad as they are. I never know how much of myself I'm going to leave behind.'

'Just do it, OK?' snapped Ben, and sat down at his desk. He swung his mounted magnifying glass over the workspace, picked up a paintbrush, and started work on a new skeleton soldier for his army, although 'army' was probably too grand a title for his collection of die-cast miniatures. His forces were too meagre to win any respect on the local wargaming scene, but that didn't stop him taking great pride in their upkeep. It took intense concentration to complete each figurine, and while he was working on one he was able to block out the overwhelming rubbishness of his life and lose himself in the world of Warmonger.

Kartofel belched loudly and Ben's hand slipped, painting a thick brown stripe across the chest of the standard bearer he was working on. He cursed, thrust the brush into a jam jar of water and swivelled his chair round in time to see Kartofel creeping out from under the bed.

'What are you doing?' Ben said, dabbing at the skeleton with a cloth.

'I was looking to see if you'd stashed anything exciting under there. You haven't. You're the worst teenage boy in history. Not so much as a catapult or an illegally procured firework.' He crawled up the bedpost and scampered on to Orff's chest, digging his claws in like a smug cat; Orff's sores seeped into the musty bandages, releasing a stale odour. Djinn involuntarily took on a pus-coloured hue at the smell of it.

'It's going to be very hard for me to get off the bed with him doing that, Ben, what with my myalgic encephalomyelitis,' coughed Orff.

'You see, all these monsters and dragons and things, they're not good for you,' said Kartofel, dancing a little jig. 'You should get interested in the proper army instead. You might even get to blow something up. Them Territorials, they'd take you. It'd be fun.'

'For you.'

'Of course for me. Why the hell else do you think I suggested it?'

'I'm not joining the Territorial Army, Kartofel.'

'Spoilsport. What about the Cadets then?'

'No.'

'Look, all I'm saying is that your little hobby might be the cause of all your social problems, that's all. No one else at school bothers with all this, do they?'

'No one else has you three to deal with,' said Ben.

Chapter Two

The Furies

The next day, after Ben had eaten his breakfast and done his chores, he returned to his room to find Kartofel and Orff engaged in a game of Scrabble. Or rather they were engaged in an argument about a game of Scrabble, since the board had been turned over and the tiles were spread out all over the floor.

'You can't just upturn the board if things don't go your way,' said Orff.

'Who says?' said Kartofel. 'Does it say that in the rules? Bet it doesn't.'

'Some things don't need to be written down. They're common decencies.'

'I'm telling you, "idioty" is a word.'

'Use it in a sentence then.'

'Orff is really idioty.'

Ben grabbed the copy of *The Elfstones of Shannara* he'd taken out of the library, and headed for the door.

'Oi, oi, oi! Where do you think you're going?' said Kartofel.

'The garden. I've got to feed Druss.'

'Tch. Someone should skin that thing and put it in a stew. It eats books now, does it?'

'I might sit out and read while I'm there.'

'Did someone say stew?' said Djinn, billowing out of the Box.

'We're talking about the blasted bunny,' said Kartofel.

'Oh,' said Djinn, crestfallen.

Druss was the large, lazy angora that lived in a hutch in the garden. He was also Ben's only friend. He was the latest in a line of rabbits that had been recruited into the family after Social Services had first taken Ben off his mother and put him in the care of his grandparents: he could hardly remember the first, a brown lop called Dandelion, but Dandelion's successor, Muffin, had lived to the ripe old age of four. Druss had joined them shortly before Muffin's death and had become the first rabbit Ben had taken care of on his own.

'I hope you're not staying out there all day,' said Kartofel. 'It's Saturday. We should do something.'

'I am doing something,' said Ben. 'I'm going to feed Druss and then I'm going to read my book.'

'That's nutty. It's flippin' freezing.'

'Oh, you don't need to tell me,' said Orff. 'I can feel it to the very marrow of my bones. I do suffer so when it's chilly. You're not going to spend the whole day out there, are you?'

'So what if I am?' said Ben. 'What are you going to do about it?'

'Just remember to wash your hands after you handle that rodent, that's all. A dose of myxomatosis is all I need.'

The weather outside was crisp and dry, and so once Ben had changed Druss's food and bedding, he settled down in a deckchair to read. At his feet, Druss lazily hopped around the special wire enclosure that been erected to prevent an assault on the vegetable patch.

The garden was as far away from the Box as Ben could go without provoking a reaction: if he went too far, the music would get hectic and impatient, missing beats and hitting bum notes, until it filled his head with an unbearable maelstrom of noise. Happily, it was also too far away for the demons to be able to follow him, and so the garden was his sanctuary, the only place he felt truly safe. It had high brick walls and a solid white wooden gate, and it was populated by an array of plants and vegetables, all lovingly planted by his grandmother.

He spent most of the day there, and would probably have stayed longer were it not for his grandmother calling him inside as evening approached. He scooped Druss up (frustrating his attempt to strip the garden of dock leaves) and returned him to the hutch. At the back door, having had it drilled into him at an early age, he started to take his shoes off.

'I wouldn't bother if I were you,' said his grandmother.

'What?' said Ben.

'Pardon. We don't say "what", we say "pardon".'

'Pardon?'

'Don't take your shoes off. Your grandad is going to be late back, so I need you to go to the chip shop.'

'Aw, Gran . . .'

'You can go out the back gate. It won't take you twenty minutes.'

Ben took the money she offered, retied his shoelaces, and stomped back outside. He drew back the bolt on the gate to the front yard and lifted the latch. The Box began to protest, a resentful shift in its default melody.

All right, all right, he thought. Keep your hinges on.

He walked round to the front door, took his shoes off, and ran up to his room. He walked coughing through a cloud of Djinn, who was clapping his hands in excitement.

'Are we going, Ben? To the chippy? Are we? Are we?'

'Yes. Get in the Box. And stop hiding behind the door.'

Djinn dissipated, his gaseous form rolling across the floor and into the Box. Kartofel and Orff were nowhere to be seen, but the evidence of them having been out was all around him: books and clothes were strewn across the floor, and the all-pervading musty smell was proof that Orff had been lying on the bed. Ben grabbed the Box, shoved it into his satchel, and bolted down the stairs. With a grunted, 'See you, Gran,' he was off out the door.

The chippy was busy, as was to be expected on a Saturday night, and Ben found himself at the back of a long queue. The moment they had arrived, Djinn had squelched out of the satchel and set up home on top of a small circular table that was crammed into the recess of the shop's bay window. He was now breathing in the aromas and sighing happily; every time he took a 'breath', he turned a pale watery brown colour, not unlike vinegar on a chip.

A rat-faced young man in a red tracksuit came in, looked at the queue, and pushed in with a glare that dared Ben to protest. Ben waited for the man to turn away and then started mentally punching him in the back of the head. Kartofel scrambled out of the satchel and perched on Ben's shoulder.

'I wouldn't let him get away with that, no way. Taking the mick, that is.' Ben tried to ignore him, but he felt the heat on his left cheek and needed to fan himself. 'I wish you weren't such a wimp. I wish we were stuck with someone else. Someone in the Cadets who wouldn't let some scumbag push in.'

'Shut up,' said Ben under his breath.

'What was that? I didn't hear you,' said Kartofel.

'Shut it, OK?'

'You say something?' said the man in the tracksuit.

'Yeah, bog off, bumface,' said Kartofel.

'Um. No. Sorry,' said Ben with a weak smile. The man turned round, and Ben flicked Kartofel off his shoulder. He landed on his claws, his little talons clattering on the tiled floor. There, he scuttled around cursing to himself.

The queue moved slowly towards the till until Ben was next in line, which was when he heard the grating, high-pitched giggle. He knew what it was even before he turned around. It was usually his cue to run away, or to throw himself into the nearest hedge.

It was the call of the Furies.

It was typical that of all the potential bullies in school, he'd ended up with three twelve-year-old girls. It relegated him to the second string of victimhood, as if he was so pathetic that the top-tier idiots didn't even consider him worthy of their time. The ringleader of the group was Smelly Jenny: an aggressive, greasy-haired gorgon with an addiction to eyeliner and an acne problem. Her best friend, and second-in-command, was Sally, a clenched fist in the shape of a girl, and the unholy trinity was rounded off by Nikki, a nervy, slight redhead who was the source of the annoying giggle.

Jenny was pointing at him and saying something to the others. Ben turned back quickly, pretending that he hadn't seen them. He felt the heat rise in his cheeks, and stared intently ahead. The Tracksuit paid and left, and the hairy man behind the counter took Ben's order and set to work.

'Three more of them, please, Mr Chipsman. We're with Bendy here,' said Jenny, draping a chunky arm around Ben, who almost buckled under the extra weight. Sally and Nikki moved behind him, pinning him to the counter. The combined smell of cheap perfume on the three of them threatened to drown out the stench of Jenny. It was a valiant attempt, but unsuccessful nonetheless. Out of the corner of his eye, Ben saw an anxious-looking Djinn turn a murky brown colour.

'They're not with me,' said Ben quietly.

'That's not very nice, is it, Bendy?' said Jenny, and cuffed him on the back of the head.

The man behind the counter had assembled Ben's order on a kind of autopilot which allowed him to keep his eyes firmly on the teenagers. 'Sol' vingar?'

'No, thank you,' said Ben. 'Can I have them wrapped, please?' Behind him, Sally sniggered. The Chip Man shrugged and began wrapping the portions.

'What, no sol' vingar?' said Jenny, grabbing the salt off the counter. She shook it all over the food, covering the Chip Man and the counter in the process.

'Right, that is it,' said the Chip Man. 'Out. Get out. Ruddy kids.' The girls burst out laughing and started mocking his accent. Ben got out the money his grandmother had given him and offered it to the Chip Man.

'What, you no speak English? You ruddy slow or something? Get all of you out or I call the police.'

Ben looked longingly at the fish suppers lying on the counter. He began to protest, but the Chip Man waved his arms in the air and started saying how he would not serve anyone else 'till these ruddy kids disappear'.

The Furies were in hysterics. Ben stared at the fish suppers, then at the laughing Furies. He screwed up his face.

'Urgh,' said Kartofel, peering up at Jenny. 'Can you smell that? Satan's chisel! If had a nose, I'd hold it. If I had arms.'

'Oi,' said Jenny, 'are you eyeing me up, Bendy?' Nikki began to laugh so hard she could hardly breathe. 'He is, isn't he? Do you fancy me or something?'

All three Furies made noises of mock disgust, followed by more howling. Ben felt the eyes of the other customers upon him. Embarrassment flushed in his face.

'Idiots!' he yelled. 'You . . . *idiots*!' He grabbed the vinegar bottle from the counter and squirted it at them, shaking out every last drop like the winning driver at a particularly low-budget Grand Prix.

'Awesome,' said Kartofel, dancing a mad samba in excitement. Djinn started clapping his hands together and hyperventilating from blue to yellow to green, sucking in the flood of smells as vinegar was splashed around with wild abandon.

Ben let go of the empty bottle. There was a moment of silence.

Jenny wiped her hands on her hideous neon-pink skirt and looked him square in the eye. Her skin looked waxy, like a walrus just out of water.

'You,' she said calmly, 'are a dead man, Bendy.'

Kartofel squealed in delight. Ben turned back to the Chip Man, slammed the money down on the counter, and yoinked the chips from under his nose. And then he did the most athletic thing he had ever done in his life. He tucked the fish suppers under his arm, turned back to face the Furies, and charged towards the slight gap between Sally and Nikki. Djinn tried to scramble up, causing the table to wobble. Ben burst through, knocking Nikki to the ground, and shot out of the door. Djinn dived for the Box as Ben passed, but missed, splatting into the opposite wall, condensing into little droplets and sending the table crashing across the exit. Kartofel tried to scurry past, panicking, hoping to avoid the stretching, but Ben was already away, curses from the

Furies and the Chip Man ringing in his ears. The Box started to play a joyful air, but as Ben pulled away it was abruptly replaced with a familiar scraping sound as Kartofel and Djinn were drawn up out of the shop and back inside the satchel.

He ran, though it hurt his lungs, and only stopped when he thought he was far enough away to have escaped. At the bottom of Fford Heulwen he sucked in long lungfuls of air, taking deep, desperate breaths. It would have normally been a painful sensation, but it wasn't now. All he felt was elation. Slowly he caught his breath, and then walked triumphantly towards his house, his over-salted prize tucked under his arm.

Chapter Three

Bedlam

When Ben was small, he thought everyone had music in their heads. So when he first heard his grandparents' ancient radio, he could not understand the point of it: it clashed with his head music. When he tried to ask his grandmother about it, it had led to visits to specialists, who had asked him questions about what he could hear, and then about his 'imaginary friends', and whether or not he knew they weren't really there, or if they told him to do bad things. Eventually Ben had learned that the music was something to do with the Box, and that as other people couldn't see the demons, and the demons lived in the Box, it was for the best if he pretended to the doctors that neither existed at all.

Ben's grandmother had good reason to be concerned, and that reason was Ben's mother. While she was having Ben, she had started to believe that she could talk to angels, and that one day they would be coming to take her away. This was not something she had felt able to keep to herself, and so before she moved to Drylands Hall she could often be found outside the Job Centre in town, preaching to the unemployed, the shop workers on their lunch breaks, the seagulls and – if any of them ventured that far from the sea – the tourists. Anyone who would listen, and more often than not anyone who wouldn't listen and ran hurriedly past.

Ben's mum was the local weirdo. This is quite some feat in Rhyl.

Ben's grandmother had always been frank about her daughter's illness, which had made it easier for Ben to cope. He knew that his mother had been at university the year before he was born, and that things that happened there had made her the way she was. He also knew that it wasn't her fault, and that she would probably never get better.

Once it emerged at primary school that Ben's mum was 'Hail Mary' his classmates had tried to use it torment him, inventing a game that involved 'accidentally' bumping into him before running away screaming. A game of tag would develop, as the other children frantically tried to pass the 'germs' on to somebody else. It was a game Ben could never join in, and one for which he was always 'it'. His grandmother's honesty meant that they never got a rise out of him, and the game was eventually adapted to fit some other victim.

Before Ben's mum had gotten really sick, the Robson family had been religious. Ben's grandmother had even kept it up for a short while after her daughter had been sent away. However, once his daughter had been committed, Ben's grandad refused point blank to set foot in a church ever again, and had been a firm atheist ever since. Ben's grandmother remained a believer – she had insisted that Ben go to St Elian's rather than a secular school, for example – but over the years her attendance had waned. Now the family's Sunday-morning ritual did not involve visiting a church, but the asylum.

'Same thing,' Ben's grandad would mutter, 'same damn thing.'

Drylands Hall was in Abergele, an old Roman town less than five miles from Rhyl. The Hall had, at one time, been the home of some long-forgotten local squire, but since the First World War it had been in use solely as a hospital for the mentally ill. The exterior was immaculately maintained, as befitted its listed status: wrought-iron gates opened out on to a long gravel drive lined with weeping willow, leading up to a malfunctioning fountain featuring a school of fish dribbling liquid into a central pool.

The house itself was an imposing Gothic mansion in sandstone, all sharp angles and straight lines. There were plinths all around its ramparts where once gargoyles had perched: they had been removed lest they disturb the inmates, and now took pride of place in the local historical society's museum, alongside some grubby Roman coins and a signed photograph of the actor Timothy Dalton, who was from nearby Colwyn Bay.

Ben hated going to Drylands Hall. He hated the building, he hated being trussed up in his Sunday best, and he even hated the stupid fountain. He hated the other patients twitching and talking to themselves, fussing and fighting over what was on the television in the day room. He hated the staff, hated the jolly way they patronized the patients. But most of all, he hated the anticipation.

He would never know which version of his mother would be waiting for them in the day room. Would she have cut off all the elbows and shoulders of her clothes, or drawn symbols on her face with poster paints? Would she have had her medicine, and so spend the visit staring out of the big bay windows? Or would she be normal, like other people's mums? Those times were rare, and Ben dreaded those most of all, for when they came it was like they were a proper family; they would sit together, the four of them, and they'd watch the telly or do a jigsaw – the sort of thing Ben imagined normal families did on a Sunday, though having no friends he had nothing to compare it to. Those times were hard because they gave him hope. The promise that each Sunday would be one of those Sundays, and that one day they could be the norm, was too cruel.

The hospital visits were the demons' favourite part of the week. To them, Drylands Hall was a massive playground. Orff got to indulge his hypochondria; Djinn adored the smell of Sunday lunches being produced on a massive scale; and Kartofel had the opportunity to cause chaos. There was a pyromaniac who lived on the second floor that he had a special place in his charred heart for, but mostly he enjoyed 'magically' moving objects when nurses and orderlies weren't looking and tormenting the patients by running up their pyjama legs. And because they loved it, Ben always left his satchel in the car.

There had been times, when he was small, when he had taken the Box inside. He'd had it out on the table, or had sat on the floor playing with it, and the demons had behaved themselves. There were no embarrassing demonic incidents in those days. It was only as Ben had gotten older that they had become harder to handle, and so in the car they stayed.

The day room was large, well lit, and had been the victim of an NHS refurbishment at some point in the past three decades. The walls were painted a faded yellow colour and bore the wounds of generations of patients throwing food and attacking them with crayon. The carpet, once thick, was now threadbare and covered in trodden-in Blu-Tack and dried glue.

It took a little while to spot Ben's mother amongst the dressing-gowned throng. They found her on her own in the corner, sitting on an old armchair which, like all the chairs there, was covered with plastic in case an inmate had an 'accident'. When she saw Ben, she leaped up from her chair and waved enthusiastically, like an American in a Mickey Mouse costume. Ben smiled and waved back timidly.

'Hello, Mary Rose,' said Ben's grandfather. He nodded at her before taking the seat furthest away. Now that they were closer, Ben could see that his mum had received – or more likely given herself – a haircut since their last visit. Her deep-brown hair, which had been shoulder length, was now cropped short, with 'interesting' patches where it had been cut too close to the scalp, battling it out with odd tufts that sprang up here and there.

'Annette! Paul! Ben!' Mary Rose greeted them with wide-open arms, as if the day room was alive to the sound of music. That she had called her parents by their first names was not a good sign. Ben gulped as she clambered over the other chairs to reach him.

'Benji!' she said, hugging him warmly and for a little too long. 'Happy birthday!'

'It's not my birthday, Mum.'

'Really?' She looked unsure.

'Yes, darling,' said Ben's grandmother. 'Ben's birthday is in April, remember?' She hugged her daughter, and they sat down. Mary Rose looked disappointed.

'I suppose he doesn't look any older,' she said. 'Does that mean there's no cake?'

'We've brought cake for dessert, but not because it's Ben's birthday. We always bring cake, don't we? Sweetheart, what have you done to your hair?'

'Oh, it's these people, Annette, they made me cut it. These people here, the minions' – 'minions' was Mary Rose's name for the staff at Drylands Hall '– they're not good people. They don't want me to get the messages.'

'The messages?'

'From the angels. I was worried that they weren't getting through, so I needed something to boost the signal. I thought, milk bottle tops, they'll do the job, and so I spent all day gluing them to the right strands of hair, and then the minions came and cut them all off. They're real so-and-sos, Annette. Devils.'

Ben's grandfather rolled his eyes.

'That's nice, dear,' said Ben's grandmother. 'Shall we see if there is anything on the television?'

After lunch, it was time for the cake that Ben's grandmother had brought. It was Mary Rose's favourite: a home-made lemon sponge with white icing. Ben's grandmother fished the old Quality Street tin out of a carrier bag, and set it down on the table. She then produced four paper plates, and finally a small metal cake slice.

During the preparations, the day nurse – Pat – had been hovering in the corner of the room. She was a rotund, middle-aged lady with short dyed hair, round spectacles and silly hooped earrings, whose default setting was a put-on joviality which disguised a deeply selfish nature. As soon as the cake slice appeared from out of the bag she swoop-waddled over, like a fat owl spying a lemon-curd-flavoured mouse.

'Are you having cake, Marie Celeste? That's nice, isn't it?' she said. Mary Rose stuck out her tongue, but Pat had already turned to address Ben's grandmother in her most sincere tone, the effect of which was total insincerity: 'I'm so sorry, Mrs Robson, but we don't allow blades in the day room.'

'It's only a cake slice,' muttered Ben's grandad.

'Is that right, Pat?' replied Ben's grandmother, a little louder than she needed to. 'Do you know, I did not know that. I should have pre-cut it, shouldn't I? Oh well. What a shame. I was just going to send Ben to ask if you'd like a slice too.'

'Ooh, well, I really shouldn't. Weight Watchers, you know,' said Pat, unconsciously running her tongue over her lips. 'But I suppose I have been good this week . . .'

'Mmm,' said Ben's grandmother. 'But however would we cut it? That's the problem.'

Pat looked worried for a moment, before a knowing smile passed over her face. 'I'm sure we can make an exception just this once.'

Ben's grandmother took another paper plate, and served Pat a generous slice. 'Will you sit with us, Pat?'

'I'd like to, Mrs Robson, but as I was telling Marie Celeste this morning . . .'

'Mary Rose,' coughed Ben's grandad.

'. . . I have such a lot of paperwork today. I'll have to head back to the grindstone sooner rather than later. But I suppose it can't hurt to take the weight off my feet for a bit.' She picked up her plate, and held it under her downy chin as she took a generous bite of the generous slice. 'Did you tell your mum and dad about our silly accident with the bottle tops, Marie Celeste?' she said through a mouthful of crumbs.

'Mary Rose,' mumbled Ben's grandad. 'Stupid woman.'

'Oh, Paul,' said Ben's grandmother, raising her voice, 'I've left the pop and the paper cups in the car. Can you go and get them for me? Would you like a cup of pop, Pat?'

'Ooh, why not?' said Pat. 'In for a penny, in for a pound. If you're going, Mr Robson.' Ben's grandad sighed, muttered something under his breath, and got up from the table.

'Can you bring my magazine?' said Ben, seeing how things

were about to take a turn for the boring. '*Quest*. It's in my bag.' His grandad nodded, and slowly walked away, still muttering to himself.

The novelty of Pat sitting with a patient had attracted the interest of the other residents, and they began to edge closer to the table, either to eavesdrop or in hope of also being offered cake, and so Ben did not notice his grandad's return until his satchel landed in his lap, and the music of the Box played an expectant trill. 'I didn't know which one you wanted, so I brought the bag,' said his grandad. 'Don't know why you're carrying that old jewellery box of your mother's around with you.'

'Um, I keep my models in it. And some paints,' gulped Ben. He looked round the table. His grandmother was pouring a glass of cola for Pat. His grandfather had settled back into his seat and was now 'watching' the television, even though it was halfway across the room and muted. His mother had dipped her finger in a droplet of spilt cola and was drawing fishes on the plastic tablecloth.

The Box's music changed subtly, and Ben quietly lay his forearm over his bag to still the demon beneath. A pair of pale yellow hands appeared on either side of the flap and began to hoist themselves up. Ben gently pushed his chair back, and set about undoing the buckles. His mother stopped swooshing her finger about and stared at him. He smiled at her, opened the bag, and pretended as best he could to be looking for his magazine.

Orff made a deep, wheezing noise as he pulled himself out. The other patients, Pat, the orderlies, and Ben's grandparents did not notice a thing, not even Ben's fidgeting.

Ben's mother, however, screamed.

'Devil! Give me thy name, that I might send thee back to

Hell!' She stood up, knocking the armchair backwards, and pointed at Orff. Around them the room erupted with noise and laughter.

'Come on, Marie Celeste,' said Pat. 'There's no need for that, is there? That's Brian, isn't it? Your son.'

'What's all this shouting? I suffer with migraines, you know,' said Orff. 'Can she see me?'

'Aye, demon, and hear thee too. I know thee. Back to Hell! Back to Hell!' Mary Rose made a cross with her fingers and waved it at Orff.

'Well, I've never been so insulted in all eternity,' said Orff. 'All I wanted was a stretch of the legs. Fine greeting this is.'

'Shut up!' said Ben.

'Ben!' said his grandmother. 'Don't talk to your mother like that. It's not her fault.'

'Flippin' heck, Annette,' said Ben's grandad. He took hold of Mary Rose's arm and tried to force her to sit down. Blue smoke began to rise from Ben's lap.

'Ow ow ow,' said Djinn. 'Have we moved? Ooh, the day room. Not been in here for ages. Cake!'

Mary Rose switched her makeshift cross towards Djinn, who was now hovering in front of Pat. 'No cake, demon. No cake for you!'

'Don't be silly, Marie Celeste. We don't want to call the orderlies, now, do we?' said Pat.

'It's Mary Rose, you stupid woman. Mary Rose!' shouted Ben's grandad.

'Paul!' said Ben's grandmother.

'Can she see us then, Ben?' said Djinn.

'It knows your name?' Mary Rose shrieked, the tendons in her neck straining. 'I always knew you were hellspawn. Devil child, repent! Repent!'

'That's enough now, Marie Celeste,' said Pat.

'Mary Rose!' said Ben's grandfather.

'I don't think that your aggressive attitude is helping the situation, Mr Robson,' said Pat in an infuriatingly calming tone.

'Hellion!' yelled Mary Rose.

The combined commotion of Mary Rose's shouts and the chorus of the gathered inmates – including a man in pyjamas who had started joyously repeating the words 'devil child' over and over – had brought a pair of burly male orderlies in from the nurses' office. They started shifting their way through the crowd of patients to get to Mary Rose.

'I'm – I'm – I'm sorry,' said Ben, shaking. His grandmother rushed to his side, putting a comforting arm around him and rubbing his back.

'It's OK, it's OK,' she said. 'She doesn't mean it. She doesn't know what she's saying.'

'Yes I do. Succubus!'

It was that moment that Kartofel chose to poke his head over the top of the satchel. At the sight of a fireball apparently rising from the depths of Hell, Mary Rose grabbed the blunt cake slice and thrust it towards Kartofel, who was positioned directly in front of Ben's stomach.

Ben's grandad shoved her to one side, causing her blow to skew to Ben's left. The momentum of it caused her to fly forward, toppling the table as she did, sending the food flying. The orderlies barged through, descending on Mary Rose, twisting the slice out of her hand and restraining her while Pat prepared a sedative. Ben's mother thrashed around, calling out names: fiend, shaitan, cacodemon. The needle ready, Pat worked quickly: Mary Rose struggled for a few seconds more before limply succumbing.

'And that,' said Pat, triumphantly wiping sweat from her now ruddy brow, 'is why we don't allow blades in the day room.'

The demons, seeing the state of Ben and hearing his broken sobs, wisely decided to get back in the Box. Ben's grandmother hugged him tightly, whispering assurances into his ear, until his breathing calmed, and the sobbing abated.

'I think we should go home,' she said.

Chapter Four

Paradise Lost

While all that was happening to Ben, Lord Druss of the Great Leporine Kingdom was enjoying his Sunday. Naturally he had no idea that it was 'Sunday', on account of his being a rabbit. He had no concept of the division of time. For him, a day was judged by how light or dark it was; a season by how hot or cold. That, and the frequency of his meals, was all he had to mark time by.

He had been awake since first light, nestling in his straw, watching over his garden kingdom through the bars of his splendid wooden palace. He had been keeping an eye on a particularly cocky black butterfly that had taken it upon itself to flutter about like it owned the place, when the Boy – current Protector and Mucker of the Royal Quarters – arrived and released the front wall of the palace. Lord Druss hopped forward a little to better facilitate the Boy's tasks, and deigned to allow himself to be handled, that he might be groomed, or else be set down to roam his kingdom.

The Boy brought Lord Druss close to his head, nuzzling his face in the King's fur, and whispering what were, Lord Druss had no doubt, devotions into the Royal ears in Humanish. He had never had much of an ear for the Human languages, but had picked up the odd word like 'tonight' (less than a day) or 'lettuce' (food). He considered learning any more than that beneath him. It didn't do to fraternise too closely with the servants.

Once the Boy was finished, and he had the reassuring feel of soil beneath his paws, he began to survey his Kingdom. Rabbits were meant to be on the ground. If they were meant to be at great heights, they would be men, and who would want that? He tolerated the Boy grooming him in mid-air as it seemed to offer him some comfort, but in truth Druss didn't much care for being separated from the ground. The palace he lived in towered above the Kingdom on long wooden legs, and let anything that breached his borders know exactly who was in charge. But the hollow sound of the floor could not be disguised, reminding him that he was apart from the earth: such is a King's lot. As Druss lumbered slowly around, stopping every now and then to snack on a leaf or just to rest his ageing muscles, the Boy began the changing of the Royal bedding, the replenishing of the Royal water, and the removal of the Royal excrement.

He had expected to see the butterfly, but clearly it had been startled by the pomp of his coming, and had wisely retreated to the kingdom of some other rabbit, one less awe-inspiring and mighty than Lord Druss. After he had hopped once around the boundary fence, he stopped to rest, content in the knowledge that all was well in his Kingdom, and that it was safe.

The Aged Girl came out from the humans' hutch and shouted something in Humanish. Lord Druss understood the word 'later' which he knew also meant 'less than a day', and wondered why humans needed so many words for the same things. The Boy called back, stooped down to quickly run his hand through the King's magnificent fur, and then ran back to their hutch.

Forgetful, stupid boy, thought Lord Druss. He hasn't realized that he has left me here unguarded. It is fortunate that I am such a resourceful and hardy king. I shall just have to return to the palace on my own. Perhaps I will produce extra droppings for him to clear as punishment.

He turned in a wide circle, feeling every day of his reign as he did. He knew he was becoming cumbersome, and that it was only a matter of time before he ceased to be warm. He still had what it took to deal with trespassers though. He did not intend to be the rabbit who let the Leporine Kingdom fall.

He had barely made it a quarter of the way when the Boy returned. Clearly he had realized his error, and had come rushing back to beg forgiveness, for he brought with him a bounty of delicious greenery. The Boy stuffed the feast through the open palace wall, and then gathered Lord Druss up in one hand. Insulted at being so roughly handled, he instinctively gave a scurrying kick, but soon stopped when it became obvious the Boy was struggling to keep his grip. He had always assumed, rabbits being so vastly superior to cats, that he would be able to survive such a fall and land on his feet. But he had no desire to find out, and so allowed the Boy to move him without further protest. Once he was delivered safely back to the palace, the Boy leaned down, lowering his face so that their eyes met. He put one finger to the bars, at the place that was nearest to the King's muzzle, and said that strange Humanish word again: 'tonight'.

He awoke a little later to the sound of a butterfly beating its wings. A black wisp flitted merrily across his field of vision. Just you wait, he thought. You'll pay for this arrogance. He took a long drink from the metal tube that delivered the Royal water, and then shuffled back to the food the Boy had left. He ate much of it, and with his strength up, shuffled back to watch out for the butterfly. It had gone.

He took refuge in the warmth of the palace, hunched up in the straw. Brief smatterings of rain drummed down on the palace roof, echoing around his quarters. He wanted to sleep through them, but could only drift in and out according to the whims of the weather. Mostly he dreamed of great battles and swift running, the ancient tribal memories of his kind, from the time before they had civilized the humans and made them their slaves.

When he woke for the final time, it was late in the afternoon: the day was losing its light, and a greyness had spread across the kingdom. 'Tonight', he knew, drew near.

He had been woken by the sound of whispered Humanish from beyond his realm. He thought at first that the Boy and the Aged Boy and the Aged Girl had returned, but as the wall squeaked open, three Girls entered. These were humans that Lord Druss had never seen before, and he could not understand how they were using his humans' wall to enter his kingdom. It should have been sealed from the inside. The Girls whispered to each other, and one of them, clearly the runt of the litter, giggled at such a pitch that it set Druss to grinding his teeth. They were a monstrous sight, like the legendary Ogres of Petshop. They were huge, and they stank of sweat and human food, a terrible stench that threatened to overpower the radiant aromas of his kingdom.

Once inside, they became more confident. They began to chase each other round the kingdom, running through flowerbeds and kicking over pots. One of the Girls, the one that smelt the worst and had disfiguring yellow markings pitted all over her face, produced something that looked like the Royal water tube, shook it, and began squirting liquid on to the walls of the humans' hutch. Whatever was inside, it wasn't water. The tube made a sound like a snake, and what came out of it was the colour of blood. This Pitted Girl – who appeared to be the leader of the herd – made markings all over the hutch until she tired of it and started to spray one of the other Girls instead. Lord Druss quietly backed into the darkest corner of the palace.

The Runt Girl giggled. She had discovered the vegetable patch beyond the palace grounds. She rudely plucked out a handful of carrots, swinging them round her head before throwing them at the third Girl, who was like a great shaven hamster. The Hamster Girl took hold of the Runt's head, and forced it under her right arm before using her left to roughly rub the Runt Girl's head-fur. This led to a struggle, which brought them both to the ground. Together they wrestled on the floor, laughing all the time. In the melee, they rolled over the boundary fence into the palace grounds. Lord Druss's eyes widened. A long-forgotten tribal reflex kicked in, and he stamped his foot rapidly on the wooden floor, beating out a tattoo of warning and distress to any rabbits nearby. It was done before he knew he was doing it, and the sound echoed around the palace, out into the kingdom beyond. It seemed to Lord Druss to be the loudest sound ever made.

The Girls stopped fighting at once, and turned their heads towards the palace, their faces lit with joy. The Hamster and the Runt scrambled to their feet, and the Pitted Girl ran to join them. Lord Druss heard the Humanish word 'rabbit', which meant both 'person' and 'King'. Perhaps now that they had realized whose presence they were in they would show respect. In moments they were at the palace, clumsily clawing at the bars until they had their hands inside and their huge faces pressed up to the open door. Lord Druss twisted and turned, hoping to avoid the Girls' grasps, but soon found he had nowhere to go. The palace, which had always seemed generous and spacious, was now cramped and confined, a cage.

Soon the Pitted Girl had hold of him, roughly, and had raised him above her head, like he was the spoils of some war. He tried kicking out at her, but she had him at arm's length, held firmly by his middle. His heart beat wildly, blood pounding out a rhythm of fear that filled his ears, screaming *run, run, run*.

He felt sick, and scared, and he began to hear the strangest noises, lapine noises for sure, but he could not tell from whence they came, at least not at first. Disorientated, it took him a while to realize they were coming from his own mouth. He was screaming.

The Pitted Girl brought him down from the sky, and held him close to her body. He wheezed as he tried to suck in enough air to still his heart. The Girl ran a huge greasy paw over his head, flattening his ears. The other Girls bent down to his level, their big faces filling his vision as they made shushing noises. Lord Druss's heart refused to calm, and so he started to wriggle and kick. He needed to be on the ground. He twisted his head round to better escape the Pitted Girl's paw, but still it kept coming, pulling his fur back again and again. He lashed out with his head and bit her hand. His mouth filled with the taste of her horrible bloody meat and suddenly he was running towards the grass at a speed not even his swiftest ancestor could have reached. He hit the earth with a heavy thud, pain shooting through his feet as he landed.

Silence fell over the garden.

Druss tried to get up, but he did not seem to be able to move.

One of the invaders shouted something in Humanish, and they ran off, bursting out of the white wooden wall. Lord Druss tried to stamp a warning, but found that his hind legs were no longer listening to him. With great pain, he dug his front paws into the rain-softened earth.

He had fallen amongst a patch of pale green blooms. He tried to drag himself forward, but only succeeded in turning himself round in a half circle, scraping what was left of the flowerbed around with him.

He thought that it would not hurt, or would at least hurt less, if he took a little nap where he lay. The funny human word, 'tonight', was stuck in his head. Perhaps the Boy would not be much longer. Perhaps 'tonight' would be soon, and the Protector would return.

He kept trying to open his eyes, each time with increasing difficulty. He felt his breathing begin to slow, and the pain in his joints that he had felt for so many days began to ebb away. It dawned on him that this was the end of the Great Leporine Kingdom, but he did not feel as sad or as ashamed as he should. He felt free.

It had begun to rain again. He heard it, and saw it, but hardly felt it at all. He did, however, feel something land gently on his nose. His eyes opened, and he saw a flash of black before him. It was the butterfly, and it lay still. It seemed so unimportant now. He exhaled. He closed his eyes. He slept for the final time.

Chapter Five

The Tide Turns

Ben remembered the car journey clearly: his grandfather, silent as usual; his grandmother constantly turning round to check if he was OK. He also remembered pulling up to the house, and getting out of the car, but after that it was all a jumbled mess. Policemen; trails of loose earth; the open gate; the plants and vegetables strewn around the garden; the graffiti.

Druss.

The image of Druss was the hardest to shake. If he closed his eyes, and tried to escape the horrors of the day, a picture of Druss would snap into his brain, and it would set him crying again.

He retreated to his room, sat on his bed, and did not move for a long time. A tray of tea and toast lay on the floor untouched. His grandmother would check in on him periodically. He felt deeply helpless, numb with sadness and anger and the unfairness of it all, and the Box did not like it. It became rough, like sandpaper, and tried to smooth out his feelings with abrasive music. He yanked it out of his satchel and hurled it across the room. It made a loud clanging noise as it hit the radiator, then landed the right way up. It always did.

Ben's grandmother called up the stairs to see if he was all right. He managed to summon up a 'yes' from somewhere within himself, although the word grappled with his throat on the way out, and he did not recognize his own voice.

The lid of the Box squeaked open. It was a timid, toe-in-the-water sort of sound, and one by one the demons spilt out.

'Go away,' said Ben, quietly. It was easier now, his voice less alien to him. The demons said nothing. They just stood – or hovered – around him. Kartofel fidgeted, uncomfortable with silence.

'We have to talk,' said Orff. He looked less stooped than usual. His voice was reasonable, less indulgent.

'No,' said Ben. Speaking was easier still.

'Your mother saw us, Ben. No one has ever seen us before. Don't you think we should discuss it?'

'Not really.'

'I'm scared, Ben,' said Djinn.

'So?'

'Tch,' said Kartofel, 'I told you we should have waited. He only cares about the bunny carking it. Don't matter that everything went weird all of a sudden.'

Ben laughed. 'When has anything ever been normal?'

'It's not our fault you're a weirdo with no friends who gets bullied by Year Eight girls.'

'Year Seven,' corrected Djinn.

'Look, just shut up, all of you,' said Ben. 'We don't need to talk. Leave me alone.'

Amid the shouting, his grandmother's voice floated up the stairs. 'Ben, will you come down for some tea? You should try and eat if you can.'

'Maybe it's Welsh Rarebit,' said Kartofel.

'Arrgh!' shouted Ben. He was hot with anger, his cheeks crimson. He got up off the bed, and marched towards Kartofel, his fist raised.

'And what you gonna do with that?' smirked Kartofel. 'Reckon you can punch fire, do you?'

Ben let out a frustrated howl. He punched out at the air above Kartofel, prompting the demon to cackle. Enraged, Ben took a step forward with his left leg, brought his right back, and punted Kartofel into the radiator. The resulting clang was even louder than the one the Box made.

'Are you sure you're OK up there, Ben?' his grandmother called again. 'Do you want me to come up?'

'Just leave me alone, Gran,' shouted Ben, 'God!' He stomped over to where the Box lay, thrust it into his satchel, and stormed out of the room.

'What you doing, Ben?' Djinn called after him as he ran down the stairs and out of the front door. 'W-w-where are you going?'

'I'm going for a bike ride,' he shouted. He pulled his old yellow Raleigh Chopper – a hand-me-down from his mother – out of the garage, and set off into the darkness. By the time he reached the end of Fford Heulwen he could look over his shoulder and see a stream of colour flowing into his still-unbuckled satchel: a rainbow of blue gas, crimson flame, and yellowy skin.

He cycled towards the East Parade, to where Tynewydd Road met Marine Parade; it was a quieter stretch of promenade, somewhere he was less likely to be disturbed. There was a small viewing area there, a stone semicircular turret that looked out to sea. He skidded the bike to a halt, abandoned it next to a litter bin, and headed down a short winding path. He fished the Box out of his bag, and dumped the satchel. The demons burst out, and Ben carried on to the slippery green sea defences.

He felt ill looking out over the tempestuous waters, a mixture of his own terror and the torturous sounds the Box was making.

'This really isn't good for my kinetosis,' called Orff from the path behind. The roar of the waves made it hard for sound to travel, and so Ben had to turn round to hear. 'What are you doing?'

'What does it look like I'm doing?'

'Is he going to jump in?' asked Djinn.

Ben laughed. 'I'm throwing the Box in. Let the sea decide where you go. I don't care any more.'

'Why's he doing that?' said Djinn worriedly. 'How will we get home?'

'He doesn't want us to get home, idiot,' said Kartofel. 'He's casting us out to sea.'

'Don't do it, Ben!' shouted Djinn. 'I'll be good. I promise. I'll never ask to go to the chippy again.'

'He won't do it,' said Kartofel nonchalantly. 'It's a bluff. It's always a bluff.'

Ben stretched his arm over the sea. Djinn wisped behind Orff, his gassy bulk shivering.

'Do it then,' said Kartofel. 'It'll hurt you more than it hurts us.'

'I can live with it,' said Ben.

'You'll get nosebleeds,' said Orff.

'I'll heal.'

'What if you don't?'

'I don't care.' He raised the Box high above his head. The waves crashed against the rocks, stretching out their arms, begging to take the Box from him. The wind whipped water at him from all directions, sea spray splattering what the rain could not. The music of the Box mirrored the sea, turbulently stabbing from one octave to another, a rolling, seasick variation on its default theme.

With a huge grunt of effort, Ben cast it down into the water.

'No!' said Djinn, dashing forward. In his panic he overshot the water's edge, and found himself hovering above the sea for a moment. He looked down, gasped, and then zipped back to almost-dry land, breathing heavily.

Orff groaned. 'This does not agree with me. Not at all. I feel queasy already.'

The Box bobbed on the surface for a while, playfully tossed about by the grateful sea. A great wave surged over it, shoving it back towards them before receding, taking the Box a little further from the shore.

The pain started in Ben's stomach: an uncomfortable constipated gnawing at his innards that made him feel hungry and full at the same time. He knew that he needed to get off the rocks and back to the path before it became too much and he was unable to move. He stumbled on to the tarmac, managing not to slip on the rocks as he clambered over them, and fell to his knees when he reached safety.

At the top of the path, a dog began to bark; a slushy, sibilant sound somehow both high- and low-pitched. Ben was on all fours now, at Orff's feet. Kartofel scuttled up to him.

'I told you so,' he said.

The barking continued, becoming more insistent. Ben looked up towards the viewing area, and saw a small, round, canine head pop over the top of the battlements and disappear.

Orff's legs became a blur. The stretching was beginning. The barking grew louder, and as Ben looked back up to the path he could see that a short, tubby man was hurrying down it. He felt a rush of air as Orff passed under him. Streaks of colour whooshed by as Djinn then Kartofel followed.

The man – who was dressed in an ill-fitting brown suit and suede loafers – was almost upon him. The strange canine sounds were now all around, and as Ben reached out a hand he noticed the first drops of blood fall from his nose.

It was only as the man passed him that Ben realized that the source of the dog noises and the man in the suit were one and the same. It was not a man at all, but rather some kind of scarred dog-creature. It tore past him, out on to the defences, and then leaped from the rocks into the sea. Ben writhed in agony. Blood streamed from his nose, and his gut felt like it was burning. Although it was getting fainter, the Box was producing the hardest, nastiest sounds it could, as if it were struggling to hang on.

The Creature was swimming out to sea at speed. It seemed futile: the distance was surely insurmountable for such a wretched, pathetic thing. Undaunted, it launched itself forward with great strength, kicking and splashing its way towards the bobbing Box with a ferocious doggy paddle. It drew level, then lunged for it.

Ben heard a squealing in his head. The Box did not like being handled by the Creature, and it appeared the feeling was mutual – the Creature yowled in pain as it touched it, and the water around them began to bubble, as if the sea was being brought to the boil.

With great difficulty, the Creature tucked the Box under its arm, and began battling back to the shore. Its progress was hindered by the turning tide, but the Creature was tenacious and powerful, and it cut through the turbulent sea as if it were a paddling pool. Ben felt better with every stroke, and as the Creature drew closer the nosebleeds stopped, and the sharp stomach pain eased to a dull ache.

The Creature climbed back on to the rocks, and shook itself

dry. It was a hideous thing, unmistakably canine, although it was so disfigured it was impossible to say which breed. One of its eyes was too big for its socket, and it bulged, bloodshot, out of its head. The other was swollen shut in a permanent black eye. It had no lower jaw, and so its thick, lolloping tongue lashed around beneath its upper incisors according to the whims of the wind. It was a rotting-pumpkin excuse for a head, and it was attached to the business-suited body by means of four exposed vertebrae.

The Creature threw the Box down at Ben's feet, and began to scratch at its paws. Its hands were smoking, and Ben could smell barbecue. All along the Creature's side was charred: burned fabric was fused to bleeding flesh. It gave a slobbery, gargling growl of pain, as if a snake had suddenly decided to try barking. It staggered closer and closer to Ben, who tried to crawl away backwards, but like a horror-film mummy, it kept coming.

'NEVER. AGAIN.' Words were clearly difficult for it, and they came out ill-formed. All Ben could do was nod frantically.

'UNDERSSSSTAND?' It tilted its head to one side, and perked up its right ear.

Ben nodded.

'SSSSAY. IT. THEN.'

'I do. I understand. Never again. I won't try to throw it away again.'

'GOOD. NECKSTIME. YOU. DEATH.' It moved on to all fours. 'WHEEL. BEE. WATCHING.'

Ben watched it race back up the bank, using its unburned legs to propel itself. Its injuries didn't seem to affect its speed at all: it was off up the path and out of sight in no time.

Alone, Ben dragged himself over to the Box, and put his left hand on to the lid. Slowly he began to feel better: his injuries healed, as if they had never happened in the first place. He took the Box in one hand, got to his feet, and headed back up the curving path, stopping only to collect his satchel before cycling away.

At home, he did not receive the expected reprimand for running off, or for coming home soaking wet. There were no questions about where he had been, or what he had been doing. Instead, his grandmother tried to pamper him. She ran him a hot bath, and made him cheese on toast. Before he went to bed, she gave him a hug, and told him how much they all loved him, his mother included. And then, when he was in bed, she brought him warm milk and honey to help him sleep.

He woke with a start. His eyes snapped open and he took a snatched, gasping breath. It was still dark, and his alarm clock read 4.48 a.m.

He never woke up in the night. Never.

Something was wrong.

He lay there in the dead quiet, too scared to move, eyes wide open, breathing heavily.

The dead quiet.

The Box was not singing. The fear seeped away, replaced by a sense of wonder. This peace, he thought, is this how everyone else hears the world? If it is, then how is anyone ever unhappy?

He tumbled out of bed, scrabbling around for the Box. He put his hand on it, and it didn't make a sound. Anticipation building inside him, he took it out and tried to open it. He could not. It was shut tight, and no amount of prising could budge it. He shook it hard, putting it to his ear to listen for signs of afterlife, but he could hear nothing. The Box was dead. It was just a box.

He hardly dared imagine a new life without the demons. Excited, he rose from the floor to turn on the light.

'Are you enjoying it, Ben Robson?' whispered a voice. 'The silence?'

Ben spun round, a little too quickly for his still-sleepy arms and legs, and promptly fell face down on the carpet. He turned his head to look up at the source of the voice, and as he did, the far corner of the room began to emit an orange glow. A figure emerged from the darkness. He was taller than anyone Ben had ever seen, and wore a long dark robe the same colour as the night. The light streamed from him, and as he moved closer Ben could see him more clearly: his arms, his face, and finally, his wings.

Standing in front of him, in his little bedroom in North Wales, was an angel.

Chapter Six

Thus Spake The Seraph

It had never occurred to Ben that angels might actually exist, which seemed unbelievably stupid now that he had one standing in front of him. It stood to reason that if there were demons, then there would be angels too; maybe if his mum hadn't been the way she was, he would have come to that conclusion sooner. Instead, he was only getting used to the idea now that the one in his room was at its most radiant.

In silhouette, the figure had appeared to be the classic statue-on-the-side-of-a-building sort of angel. He wore a sleeveless cassock, tied at the waist by a long tasselled cord. Huge feathered wings sprouted from his shoulders and a halo of light encircled his head, like a saint on a stained-glass window. But as the orange light grew warmer and brighter, filling in and defining each feature, it became clear how different he was. This angel was the colour of perfect darkness: were it not for the orange glow, Ben would not have been able to see him at all.

'It is pleasant to finally meet you, Ben Robson,' said the angel.

'How are you doing that? Making it go all quiet?'

'Alas, it is only temporary. My time here is short, and we have much to discuss.' His voice was quiet and breathy, with a warm tone quite at odds with the cold remoteness of his eyes: he had white pupils and red irises set in tar-black eyeballs. They bored into Ben in the most unsettling way, as if he were being weighed and judged. 'I am the Holy Seraph of the Strident Blasts, First

Oblate of the Cult of the Four Winds, Celestial Lord of the Skies.'

'Oh,' said Ben. 'Right.'

'I am also your Guardian Angel.' The Holy Seraph of the Strident Blasts gave a slight bow, followed by a long pause. He shot Ben a quizzical look, almost affronted.

'Um . . . OK?' said Ben.

'Forgive me. I am accustomed to a little more awe when interacting with the children of Men.'

'I've had a bit of a strange day. What do you want?'

The Holy Seraph of the Strident Blasts opened his mouth as if to reply quickly, before promptly closing it again. 'I have come to ask for your help in the name of the Prime One,' he said after a moment. 'The fate of the Creation is in your hands, Ben Robson.'

'Right,' said Ben.

'You attempted to dispose of the Box today, did you not?'

'Yeah.'

'And you were prevented by a demon, were you not?'

'It was a sort of a dog creature,' said Ben. 'Why are you talking like that?'

'I'm sorry?'

'Like we're in a courtroom drama or something.'

'Forgive me,' said the angel, with a stretched smile. 'It has been generations since I was able to enter into discourse with one of your kind. I am disinclined to learn the latest colloquialisms.'

'Oh,' said Ben. 'What does that mean?'

'It means the Veil which separates the Worlds is shifting, and the Creation is in flux. My kind believe The Adversary means to take advantage of this perilous state to steal back the powers stripped from him after the Grand War.'

'I meant what does "colloquialisms" mean, but that's nice to know as well.'

'I see.' The Holy Seraph of the Strident Blasts shook out his wings, and sat down beside Ben on the bed. 'Henceforth I shall endeavour to speak as plainly as angelically possible. You are familiar with the story of the war in Heaven? It is well known on Earth?'

'Not really.'

'It was eternities ago.' The angel suddenly appeared distant, sorrowful even; he stared straight ahead. 'The Adversary led an uprising of the infernal against us, and we, the Prime One's chosen, smote them with His wrath. We did not smite them enough.' He shook his head ruefully. 'We showed mercy. As punishment for their blasphemies, the worst of their powers were stripped from them and sealed in a prison here on Earth, safe on the other side of the Veil. Until now.'

'Why? What's so special about now?'

'Fluctuations in the Veil are rare. It has been nearly seventy years since it was last safe for angels and demons even to attempt to traverse it.'

'Oh,' said Ben, disappointedly. 'It's just that my mum saw the demons today, and she's always talking about angels and—'

'She is gravely ill, I know,' interrupted the angel. 'I can only assume that it is this sickness, combined with the tumult in the Veil, that allowed her to glimpse the infernals. I am sorry to say that she could never have met one of my kind. I would counsel you not to broach the subject of my coming, lest you agitate her, or worse, join her in that place.'

Ben bit his lower lip and bowed his head. The Holy Seraph of the Strident Blasts tentatively placed a comforting arm on his shoulder. It was an awkward gesture, as if he had only ever seen it done and never tried it.

'I did not intend to upset you, Ben Robson.'

'That's OK. But do you think you could call me Ben? Just Ben?'

'As you wish.'

'And what can I call you?'

'I am The Holy Seraph of the Strident Blasts, First Oblate of the Cult of the Four Winds—'

'I'll call you "The Seraph", then.'

The Holy Seraph of the Strident Blasts paused for a moment. His red eyes narrowed, and he pursed his lips. 'As you wish.' He stood up from the bed and crossed over to the window, resting his hands on the sill. 'If The Adversary is successful, he will unleash the Apocalypse. Chaos will reign. My kind mean to prevent it, which is why I have come to you.'

'Me? Why me?'

'I would have thought it obvious.' The angel stared intently into Ben's eyes for a moment. 'But I can see it is not. You are the keeper of the Box.'

'So?'

'It is the prison of which I spoke.'

Ben laughed. 'I think you might have the wrong Box.' The demons were annoying, and he hated them, but they weren't evil. They certainly didn't have the power to start the Apocalypse, that was for sure. Orff could barely walk.

'It is no laughing matter,' said the angel, and his sombre expression was enough to make Ben agree completely. 'Towards the end of the Grand War, Pestilence, Famine, War and Death were made flesh. The Adversary summoned them to his aid with a promise that they could divide Creation between them when the battle was won. Fortunately we prevailed, and were able to seal them inside the Box. The wretches that torment you are little more than collateral damage. Its true prisoners are the Four Horsemen of the Apocalypse.'

'I think the demons would have said something if they had been sharing with the Four Horsemen of the Apocalypse,' said Ben.

'How would they know? The Horsemen can only take form when they are released from the Box. Until then, they exist only as potential energy. Why do you imagine The Adversary sent his personal herald to stop you destroying it?'

'Then why didn't it just take it? It had it in its hands.'

'And I imagine it suffered for it, did it not? The Box cannot be touched by celestial hand or infernal claw without grievous injury. It is the only thing that has the power to erase either from the Creation. If The Adversary plans to release the Horsemen, he will need a human to accomplish it. He will need you. I mean to prevent it.'

'How?'

'I will use the will of the Prime One to divorce you from the Box and banish the demons to Hell. Then I will destroy it, and the Horsemen along with it.'

'Great,' said Ben. 'Where do you want me to stand?'

'Patience,' said The Seraph. 'The Veil will soon shift again, and I must depart. The next fluctuation will be during the dying hours of the twenty-fifth day of January.'

It took Ben a little time to work out what The Seraph meant. 'You mean Thursday? This Thursday?'

'Yes. You will have to guard the Box with your life until then.'

'Pardon?'

'The Adversary will stop at nothing to possess it. The rites we will perform require a sacred place. There is a neolithic burial ground not far from here: the Box was interred there when it was first forged. It is known as the Greyhound's Lair, and it lies atop a limestone crag. A place where feral goats roam among white horehound.'

'That sounds far away. And dangerous.' Ben wasn't sure which bothered him more, the feral goats or the white horehound.

'It is not. In the current vernacular, the place is called Llandudno.' He pronounced it precisely, as if he were a native. 'The crag is known as the Great Orme. Bring the Box there at midnight on Thursday, and I will take care of the rest.'

'Llandudno?' said Ben.

'Yes.'

'That *is* far away.'

'It is only fifteen point seven three miles to the west of here, as the angel flies.'

'But I'm not an angel.'

'There are other forms of transport, are there not? Thursday. Midnight. That is when the conditions will be perfect.'

An urgent whispering in an unfamiliar language filled the room. It seemed to be coming from all around them, as if it were being transmitted from the very particles of the air.

'What's that?' said Ben.

'It means my time here draws to a close.'

'Wait. How am I supposed to find this place?'

The Seraph opened the window. As he did, the orange glow around him began to fade, and the whispering became quicker, more intense. 'The Prime One will provide.' He hoisted himself through the window, and with a beat of his giant crow wings he once again faded back into the darkness. 'Creation is in your hands, Ben Robson. I mean Ben.'

Ben felt a sudden gust of wind on his face, and ran to the frame. There was nothing to see, save the freezing dark of Monday morning stretching out across Rhyl. The whispering noise cut out as abruptly as it began, and it was quiet once more.

He shut the window. The Greyhound's Lair didn't sound like somewhere that would be clearly signposted. And even if it were, it would be dark when he was looking for it. As he stumbled towards the light switch, arms outstretched in the angel-black gloom, the Box crept back in. It began to clatter beneath the bed, and the music grew stronger until it was clear and confident, as if he were a radio that the Box was tuning in.

Kartofel tumbled out on to the floor with a thud.

'What in Asmodeus's name is going on?' he said. 'I was sleeping, right? And then the lights come on, and I think, righto, Ben's up, let's go. But I can't. I'm only chained to the flippin' wall, aren't I? So I shouted over to Bulk and Skeleton, and I said "can either of you move?" and Chunk starts crying, so I know he can't, and the Old Fart starts up with the creaky door sound he makes in the morning, so I know he's awake too. And so I start to think, something ain't right here, it's too quiet. No music. But then it starts, and pfft, the chain is gone and I can move again, so I think, I'm getting to the bottom of this. And I go to get out, and the lid won't open. I had to give it a shove, which takes some doing when you're built like I am, just to get it open a crack. And then pow, it swings open, and I come rolling out. So, I ask you, what the clanging bell is going on?'

'I don't know,' said Ben. 'I don't know how the Box works, do I?'

'It's damn weird if you ask me.'

'Go back to bed, or the abyss, or wherever it is that you go,' said Ben. 'I don't know anything about it, all right?'

'Bloomin' cheek,' grumbled Kartofel, but went all the same, muttering obscenities. Ben waited for the lid of the Box to fall shut, and then got back into bed.

His last conscious thought of the night was not of his mother, or Druss, or any of the day's traumatic events. It was this:

Llandudno. How the hell am I going to get to Llandudno?

Chapter Seven

The Broken Forge

Ben was usually a reluctant riser, but the next morning his head was too full of white horehounds, apocalyptic battles, and angels the colour of night for him to stay in bed. When his grandmother came to knock on his door at seven thirty, as she did every morning, he was already up and dressed. She eased the door open and crept into the room almost on tiptoes, as if the tiniest disruption would send him into a never-ending spiral of despair.

'Poor thing,' she said. She sat on the edge of the bed and pulled him towards her. 'Me and Grandad have been talking, and we've decided it might be best for you to take the day off school.'

'Hmpf?' said Ben, his mouth full of the distinct taste of old-lady dressing gown. He never missed school. Never. Despite his best efforts, he had a perfect attendance record. He had tried putting thermometers on radiators, sucking ice cubes, sleeping with the window open, talking in a 'poorly' voice. None of it had ever convinced his grandmother to keep him home before. He thought of The Seraph, and how he had said the Creation was in flux. Maybe this was the kind of thing he meant.

'You just take your time coming down now, but when you're ready there'll be breakfast waiting.' She smiled, and then ludicrously quietly, as if to avoid waking him, she shut the door behind her.

It was not long before the smell of bacon wafted up the stairs, and Ben realized that they would be having a fried breakfast. That proves it, he thought. The world is in flux.

The Box lid eased open and Djinn rose out of it nose-first. He curled once about the room then drifted down to the floor a juicy pink colour.

'Bacon,' he said. 'I like bacon.'

Kartofel scurried out from under the bed. 'What's all this then? We not going to school?'

'No,' said Ben, 'I'm staying home.'

'Nice, throwing a sickie, are we? Did you use laxatives? I told you, that's the way to do it. Nobody argues with diarrhoea.'

Thursday suddenly felt a long way off. 'Gran said I didn't have to go. And so I'm not.'

Kartofel's flame flickered, and he impatiently scratched his talons along the carpet. 'Right, that's it. There's definitely something weird going on around here. I want to know what it is.'

'As do I,' said Orff. 'The incident last night has caused havoc with my bedsores. Terrible way to treat someone in my condition. And that's before we even get to what it's done to my arthritis.'

'There's bacon,' said Djinn, dreamily.

'So?' said Kartofel. 'There are more important things than food, you know.'

'You take that back,' said Djinn.

'We can't go on pretending like nothing has happened,' said Orff. 'The sooner that something is done about it, the better. My neuralgia could strike at any moment and then I'll be no use to anyone.'

Kartofel sniggered.

'I can't talk now,' said Ben. 'My breakfast's ready.'

'Food can wait,' said Kartofel, 'I want answers. Your mum sees us, you try to drown us, we meet a weird dog-demon, and then we finish the day chained to the wall, and you reckon you can just go and eat breakfast like that's normal?'

'What do you know about normal? Two-foot talking flames aren't normal.'

'I'm as normal as the next demon, I'll have you know.'

'We can't let him miss breakfast,' said Djinn, jigging around as if he was about to wet himself.

'We'll talk about it later,' said Ben, ducking out the door. Three days, he thought. In three days I will be free.

The music of the Box had been turbulent ever since he'd woken up, as if it were unsure of what its opinions of the last twenty-four hours were. But it recognized that one thought, *free*, as familiar, and played a little fanfare to greet it.

Ben's grandad was already sitting at the breakfast table, reading the paper over a cup of tea. His grandmother was in the kitchen, supposedly cooking, but mostly making passive-aggressive clanging noises with the frying pans. Before long, she emerged with three fried breakfasts. As they ate, the only sounds were those of their cutlery as it scraped along the plates. Ben kept catching his grandmother looking at him with a concerned smile, and whenever their eyes met, she would tousle his hair or pat him on the head. Both annoyed him greatly.

The portions were huge, and Ben found finishing was beyond him. He tried to force as much of it down as he could, and as his grandmother took away his half-full plate, he winced, expecting a lecture about starving babies in Africa. She said nothing. Ben's grandad, however, peered over the top of his paper, saw the uneaten food, and tutted.

'Is there anything you'd like to do today, Ben?' asked his grandmother. 'You don't have to do anything at all if you don't want to.' Ben's grandad dropped his paper and mumbled something under his breath.

'What was that, Paul?' trilled Ben's grandmother, 'I didn't quite catch it.'

'I said, "Don't mollycoddle the boy, Annette, for God's sake."' He folded the paper up and tucked it under his arm. 'I'm going for a walk.'

His grandmother's rosy facade slipped for the briefest moment. 'Never mind Grandad,' she said after he'd gone. 'He's just upset about the garden. Nothing to do with you at all. So, is there anything you'd like to do?'

Ben certainly did not feel like staying at home. There was one place left he could go that he knew would not be subject to the shifting sands around him, one place that never changed, regardless of whether the Veil was fluctuating or not. 'I was thinking,' he said, 'maybe I could go to the Forge, if that's all right?'

His grandmother tousled his hair again. 'Do you need any money?' she said.

Creation in flux. Definitely.

War is a hungry beast. No matter how well funded or well supplied a military force is, it will always cry out for more: more money, more guns, more lives. In that respect, Ben's army of painted die-cast skeletons was no different to the US Military, except that Ben's army had fewer helicopters. But then the US Military didn't have a Zombie Dragon, which in a real-life situation Ben reckoned could probably take out several helicopters in one go.

When Ben's army needed supplies, it was to the Broken Forge

that he went. The Forge was Ben's nearest stockist of fantasy wargaming products, and it was situated in Towyn, yet another seaside resort not even ten minutes' drive from Rhyl. If Rhyl was a dog of a town, then Towyn was a length of dental floss trailing out of the dog's bum after the dog had been through the rubbish.

The shop was tucked away on a side street, although Towyn was the kind of place where you could not be sure if any given side street was, in fact, the high street. The road in question, which was hidden behind a row of candy floss stalls and amusement arcades, also housed other long-forgotten shops that were of little interest to tourists or locals. They included a taxidermist, a fruiterer 'specializing in watermelons' according to their sign, and a closed-down TV repair shop that had such an impressive cobweb display in the window that it put its near neighbour, Towyn Arachnid Emporium, to shame.

At first glance, a passer-by might assume that the Broken Forge had suffered a similar fate to the TV shop. The paint on the windowsills and door frames was cracked, and the window display – a selection of Warmonger boxes – had been touched too much by the sun, and not enough by a duster.

The run-down facade made what was inside all the more special. For Ben, passing through the rickety door was like passing into his own private Narnia: the smell of paint and glue, the rough wooden racks, and the well-stocked shelves of fantasy and folklore books were every bit as magical. The limited floor space was dominated by a huge gameboard with two opposing armies ready to fight: Feral Tigermen versus Orcs and Goblins. It was Tegwyn Price's pride and joy, and represented a small fraction of the army he had created.

Tegwyn was the shop's owner, manager, and sole employee; he

was in his late forties, bearded and bespectacled, with a messy moptop of mousey brown hair. He was a scruffy man of average build, with a prominent stomach hanging over his trouser belt, but to his teenage clientele, he was a god. A vengeful, petty, Old Testament sort of a god. He was usually to be found behind the counter squinting into a magnifying glass, or else the loud ding of the brass bell would bring him skulking out from the mysterious land of Out-the-Back, a stockroom which lay beyond the bead-curtain-covered doorway behind the counter.

Not, however, on this occasion. Instead, Ben was greeted by the sight of a girl not much older than he was. She was dressed completely in black, and was either naturally pale or had made herself up to look so. She was tall, with long, straight hair that went all the way down her back. She made Ben think of an elf, albeit one that wore cool spectacles with thick black frames.

'Hello,' she said. Her smile was warm, and kind, and completely at odds with her severe make-up. That she should smile so nicely put him on his guard: the mistrust of the terminal victim.

'Um . . .' said Ben. He knew female gamers existed: he had read about them in *Table Gamer.* But he thought they were something that only happened in places like London or Nottingham.

'Nnnn,' said Tegwyn, as he came through the curtain. He started every sentence with a vocalized sneer, as if speaking was a huge inconvenience, and conversation was only to be participated in with the utmost reluctance. 'Shouldn't you be at school? What do you want, you little turd?'

This was Tegwyn's standard greeting for the majority of his customers. The Broken Forge was the oldest wargames stockist in North Wales, but faced stiff competition from bigger stores in

Llandudno and Chester; the locals who could afford to travel, did – not only for the wider product range, but also for the pleasure of not dealing with Tegwyn. He was unable to put the same dedication into customer service as he had into learning the codexes for every Warmonger army off by heart, and so he was unable to accept that his brusque manner was the reason he had been left with the less mobile corner of the market. Instead, he blamed the success of the other stores on the government, who he suspected of trying to shut him down because he was a pagan, and therefore a danger to the established order.

'We've got a teacher-training day,' said Ben. 'What's going on?'

'This is my apprentice.' He turned to face the girl. 'What's your name again?'

'You know very well it's Lucy. And I'm not your apprentice, I'm on work experience.' Lucy stretched out her hand. Ben blushed, and was so dumbstruck that he forgot to take it. Lucy stepped out from behind the counter, picked up Ben's limp hand, and shook it.

'Very nice,' sniggered Tegwyn. 'Now if you two lovebirds are finished, there are Dark Elves to be catalogued Out-the-Back.'

'It was nice to meet you.' Lucy smiled again, and passed through the curtain.

'She is my apprentice really,' said Tegwyn after she'd gone.

'No, I'm not,' shouted Lucy.

'You wouldn't understand,' said Tegwyn in a noticeably quieter voice. 'What do you want, anyway, arsewipe? Here to buy nothing, as usual?'

'I want the Bone Lords,' said Ben. They were a regiment he had long wanted to add to his army, and thanks to his grandmother, who had given him twenty-five pounds, he could finally acquire them.

'Ooh, big spender,' said Tegwyn. 'What's the magic word?'

'Please.'

'Manners cost arse all. Nnnn, girl,' he shouted Out-the-Back. 'Look for a Bone Lords, part code nine-one-nine-two-zero-two-zero-seven-zero-one-zero.'

'Look yourself. And my name's Lucy.'

Tegwyn grunted, and reluctantly got up from his swivel chair. 'Try not to break anything while I go Out-the-Back.'

This was something Tegwyn said whenever he left Ben alone in the store, a habit that he had adopted after an incident when Ben had first started to get into the hobby. The demons had all manifested in the store at once while Tegwyn was Out-the Back, and the limited space in the poky shop had led to Orff knocking glue all over the Orc Wolf Chariot that Tegwyn had been working on at the time. Ben had been barred from the shop until he could pay for the ruined model.

As much as Tegwyn liked to believe himself a rebel, eco-magician, and dangerous threat to the system, he was at heart a businessman, which was why he soon returned from Out-the-Back with a sun-faded box containing a set of Villagers and Townsfolk. Ben immediately recognized it as the one that had sat in the window most of the previous summer.

'No Bone Lords. Buy this. They don't make it any more.' (This was because, Ben knew, models of peasants with pitchforks are not as popular as undead samurai.)

'You said you had two last week.'

'That was last week. Now I've got this. Take it or leave it.'

It wasn't an offer Ben had to think about for long. 'I think my grandad might be going to Chester next week. He can get one there.'

He found it impossible to look Tegwyn in the eye as he said it. If he had, he would have seen the older man's face drop on hearing the C-word. Instead, he just heard his reaction in the irritated, resentful tone of his reply.

'Nnnn. Forgot to check the new delivery, didn't I? The girl hasn't finished unpacking it yet. Wait here,' he said, and went clattering Out-the-Back again.

While he waited, Ben wandered over to the bookshelves. The sign above them said 'A Cornucopia of Tomes' in Celtic script. Scrawled beneath the sign was a handwritten note: 'YE CORNUCOPIA IS NOT A LIBRARY. YE MUST PAY THE TOLL.'

The shelf covered every aspect of fantasy, from novels by Terry Pratchett and David Gemmel through to Practical Model Painting Guides. Ben had either read or already owned most of them. There was also a small section dedicated to Tegwyn's other interests: there were a few volumes on folk music and real ale, but these shelves were mostly given over to pagan rituals and magic. These were books that no one ever touched, bar the occasional member of the local druidic circle. They'd turn up in battered old cars wearing knitted jumpers, and would quickly buy some book about the winter solstice or something before racing back to their vehicles. Ben had seen similar behaviour from the customers of 'The Garden of Love' (five doors down, next to the Arachnid Emporium).

These books all had bizarre titles, and seemed hell-bent on combining the magical with the mundane: *Bringing Witchcraft to the Washing-Up* was one of them; *The Moon Goddess for Chartered*

Accountants another. But towards the end of the section was a run of local-history titles, and one in particular caught his eye. It was called *Sacred Orme: Neolithic Monuments on Llandudno's Ancient Beachhead*.

Maybe the Prime One really does provide, thought Ben as he levered the book off the shelf. It was a hardback, much heavier than the books Ben was used to reading. It even had a dust jacket: a black and white photograph of what he supposed must be the Orme, with the title in large red letters. The author was called Terry Owens.

Ben opened the book and felt his heart flutter. He flicked straight to the index, and ran his finger down the G column. No luck. He moved to the letter L, hoping for 'Lair of the Greyhound'. As he looked, he felt movement in his satchel: the familiar feeling of claws digging into leather.

'He's gone, has he?' said Kartofel. 'Chubs smelt him go, so I reckoned I'd come out and have a look round.'

'He'll be back in a second,' said Ben. 'He's only gone Out-the-Back.'

'Tch. I bet he's got freezer full of corpses back there. What's that?'

'A book.'

'What's it about?'

'What do you care? Get back in the Box.'

'Nnnnnn. Talking to yourself, are you?' Ben had been so absorbed in his search that he had not noticed Tegwyn return. Startled, he slammed the book shut and looked up. He felt colour rise to his cheeks.

'No.'

'Then who were you talking to? Imaginary friend?'

'Who are you callin' imaginary?' grumbled Kartofel. 'I'll give you imaginary . . .'

'What you got there?' said Tegwyn.

'Nothing,' said Ben.

'Doesn't look like nothing. Looks like a Tome to me.'

'I was just looking up something I heard about. The Greyhound's Lair.'

'Yeah. Llety'r Filiast,' said Tegwyn. 'What about it?'

Ben did Welsh at school, but like most subjects, he wasn't very good at it: too much demon distraction in the classroom. In Welsh, the problem was Kartofel. He had taken a bizarre shine to the teacher, Mrs Thomas, who was one of the strictest in school.

'Llety'r Filiast,' said Kartofel. His Welsh pronunciation was immaculate. 'Where's that? Why do you want to know about that?'

'Llety'r Filiast,' said Tegwyn again. 'The Greyhound's Lair. You'll find it under LL. For Llety.' He overemphasized the Welsh sounds each time. Ben flicked back to the index, running his finger down the letters until he found the right entry. He flipped quickly through the book, impatient to see this mythical place.

'Ah-ah-ah-ah-ah,' said Tegwyn, tapping the 'Pay the Toll' sign. 'You know the rules.' Ben looked longingly at the book, then up at Tegwyn, who was holding a factory-sealed Bone Lords box.

'I just want to look it up. It won't take a sec,' said Ben.

'Then it'll be an expensive second, won't it?' said Tegwyn.

Ben turned to the inside cover and found the price on the dust jacket: £24.99. It was one or the other. His eyes flicked from book to box and back again. The Bone Lords looked exciting. Ben could imagine the thrill of digging a fingernail into the vacuum-packed plastic, releasing that new-box, new-figure smell. The book, on the other hand, was mostly pictures of old rocks and goats and had been written by some spotty fat bloke called Terry. It looked like the most boring book ever written.

'Just buy your little skeletons so we can get out of here, will you?' said Kartofel.

There was no contest.

'I'll take the book,' said Ben.

Chapter Eight

Pilgrim's Progress

By the time Thursday rolled around, Ben had become something of an expert on the Great Orme. *Sacred Orme* was his constant companion, and its perfect fresh pages were soon dog-eared and grubby, its dust jacket battered and torn. It was a shame that none of his lessons at school required an encyclopaedic knowledge of Stone Age monuments in the local area, because he was certain he could ace any test on the subject.

The first thing he'd learned about Llety'r Filiast was that it was nowhere near as exciting as its name suggested. He had expected flaming torches and cobwebbed catacombs, with a fearsome beast guarding the door. He was relieved (and secretly a little disappointed) to discover that white horehound was a nondescript plant of the genus *Marrubium* that had been used by druids to cure sore throats, and that the monument itself was just a pile of wonky slabs that had been dumped in the middle of the most unremarkable field in Wales. It seemed that giving boring things fantasy-style names was a speciality of ancient Welshmen: other underwhelming ruins included a lump of rock called Tudno's Cradle, and a feeble stone circle called the Place of the Deer.

The speed at which he had absorbed this knowledge was only possible because the demons allowed it. Once Kartofel had seen the book, there was no putting off talking to them about The Seraph, and so a summit had been convened and Ben had related almost everything the angel had told him (though he left out the part about having the power to unleash the Apocalypse – he thought it wise).

'You want to send us to Hell?' said Kartofel.

'It's not like that,' said Ben.

'It sounds like that. You want us to agree to go to Hell.'

'You're making it sound really negative.'

'It's Hell!' bellowed Kartofel.

'Yes, but you're meant to be there. You'll like it. See, at the moment you're prisoners, and The Seraph will set you free.'

'You want to send us to Hell AND you want us to trust an angel? We're demons!'

'Exactly. You're meant to be in Hell.'

'Bog off,' said Kartofel. 'I'm not standing around listening to this.'

He scuttled over to the Box and made a great show of letting the lid slam shut behind him. Almost immediately Ben heard a subtle change in the music as it opened again a tiny crack.

'Don't you want us any more, Ben?' said Djinn, nervously playing with his fingers. 'Because you tried to throw us away, and now you're sending us to live in Hell.'

'No, it's not that,' Ben lied. 'It's just that you were never meant to be in this world in the first place. Hell is where you're supposed to be.'

'Is it scary?'

'I don't know,' said Ben. 'Probably not to you. Lots of demons live there.'

Orff slowly cleared his throat. 'The worst thing about this existence,' he said, 'isn't that inside the Box is cold, and dank, and probably crawling with germs and allergens that bring you out in hives or give you whooping cough or rubella. It's not even that it robs you of any sense of time, so that seconds pass like hours and centuries go by in minutes, which is particularly confusing to me with my thyroid condition. It is that every now and again a green glow passes by that illuminates and warms us. And then it is gone, and we are left as before. Once you feel that glow, you yearn for it to return.'

Orff was no longer looking at Ben, or Djinn, but straight ahead, into the centre of the room. There was a heaviness in the air, as if his unburdening had infected even the oxygen molecules. 'If that is not Hell, then how can Hell itself be worse? It will be warm there, at least. It will be good for my tuberculosis.'

Djinn nodded. Inside his head, Ben heard the Box lid close completely.

Thursday brought loud and blustery winds, and Ben woke up to a Box that was as choppy as the weather. From first light, it constantly varied the speed of its music, setting Ben's nerves on edge.

At school, every class was abuzz with excited gossip about the weather: rumours spread that the strength of the winds would mean that the school would close early. It was the kind of excitement that the reluctant pupil longs for, something to break up the monotony of the school day, but to Ben, it still dragged. The hours ground against each other, churning out slow second upon slow second.

Sacred Orme was intended to double up as a rambler's guide (although no rambler worth their salt would ever lug a hardback book around with them) and so it provided directions to all the 'sacred' sites on the Orme. Ben was confident that finding Llety'r Filiast would be easy enough. It was getting to Llandudno that was the hard part. He resolved to sneak out and take the last train of the day. Although the bus ran later, and so offered the best chance of cover, it was possible to bunk the train, which is what he needed to do, having no money to pay for a ticket.

He went to bed early, to much sympathetic clucking from his grandmother. Once upstairs, he had set about fashioning a decoy in his bed out of pillows and spare blankets. It wasn't particularly convincing, but Ben thought that in the darkness it would probably be OK. Then he packed the Box in his satchel, along with *Sacred Orme* and a torch he had borrowed from his grandad's tool box. He was dressed in black, or at least as much black as he could muster: his grey trainers, his black school trousers, and a black T-shirt with a big picture of a green troll holding the severed head of a dwarf on it. He also had his anorak on, although he knew from experience that it would be little help in the rain. As ready as he would ever be, he took a deep breath, and opened his bedroom window.

It immediately blew back on its hinges, slamming against the side of the house. Ben threw his leg over the windowsill, straddled it for a moment, then swung his other leg round too; moments later he was standing on the sloping brown brick tiles of the roof. He gripped the frame tightly. The wind was strong and fast, and Ben felt that if he let go, he would probably be blown clear off the roof.

He took a series of short, sharp breaths, promised himself he would go after three again and again until suddenly and recklessly he let go. He turned round, sat down violently, and dug his heels into the tiles to slow what he was sure would be a quick slide to the gutter. Instead, the wind knocked him back against the wall beneath his window and pinned him there.

The tiles were not at all slippery. It took a lot of effort for him to pull himself into the wind, using his feet to drag himself towards the gutter. Once there, he felt elated. This, he thought, was the easy part. Adrenalin flooded his system. He placed his heels into the plastic trough. It bent a little, which was worrying, but he was still confident it would take his weight. After all, people shinned up and down drainpipes all the time in films.

He twisted at the waist and then, his feet still hooked in the guttering, tried to move into a crawling position. As he turned the bottom half of his body round, he was caught by a gust of wind which threw him diagonally across the roof, scraping him along the coarse tiles. His arms flailed wildly for anything that he could cling on to, finally finding the guttering again. He held tightly to the far corner of the roof, where the drainpipe ran down the side of the house, his legs swinging in mid-air.

He clung on, panting. Now it was just a case of easing himself down and dropping gently to the grass in the front garden below. Or so he thought. He began to feel the guttering bend where it met his belly, and before he really knew what was happening it buckled under his weight, and the plastic clamps that attached the pipe to the awning of the house cracked. The roof got further and further away, until he landed with a thud on the muddy ground, the gutter still in his hand.

The Box complained as it hit the dirt, and Ben felt a blunt pain in the small of his back where he had landed on it. Without waiting to check his injuries, he clambered to his feet, threw the guttering on to the grass, and ran. His back hurt, but he was too full of endorphins to let it bother him. He raced down the middle of the road, through the neighbouring streets, and on towards the station.

The train toilet was cramped, and bore all the signs of a full day's use. A soggy trail of toilet paper had wound itself around the base of the metal bowl, and there were a series of strangely gloopy puddles on the floor. It was not a very pleasant place to spend the forty-minute journey, but it was the only option for the ticketless traveller.

With the buzz from his rooftop escape wearing off, all Ben could now feel was pain. He stripped off his T-shirt, taking care not to touch anything in the rank cubicle as he did, and slung it over his shoulders. His chest was covered in scratches and friction burns from the roof tiles. He turned his skinny torso away from the mirror, and looked over his shoulder at the damage on his back. A large Box-shaped bruise spread across the base of his spine, a perfect copy in yellow and purple.

His left ankle hurt when he put weight on it, which made it difficult to dodge the streams of urine that were flowing along the floor in time with the train's rickety movement. He closed the toilet lid and sat on it, his feet hovering above the ground as he dabbed at his wounds with damp paper towels.

At Abergele & Pensarn station, Djinn appeared, turning a dirty amber colour as he did. He was quickly followed by Kartofel, who, on seeing the state of the floor, elected to perch himself on top of the satchel.

'It stinks in here,' he said.

'I know,' said Ben.

'It'd probably be all right if you just sat in the carriage.'

'Or the buffet car,' said Djinn.

'No one ever checks tickets on these things.'

'How do you know?' said Ben.

'Dunno,' said Kartofel. 'Demons' intuition.'

There were three hard knocks on the door. Everyone froze. The person knocked again, harder, more insistent. Ben held his breath.

He hoped it was a passenger, but dared not call out in case it was a ticket inspector.

The train pulled off, slowly getting up to speed. No more knocks came, and Ben let out a sigh of relief. The next station was eight minutes away. After that it was twenty minutes non-stop to Llandudno. He just needed to get past Colwyn Bay – then if he got caught he'd be ejected at Llandudno anyway.

'Probably some drunk,' said Kartofel. Immediately, the banging on the door began again. It was no longer a stern sharp knock, but a constant, authoritative pounding.

'Ah, get lost, you old wino,' said Kartofel.

Ben glared at him.

'What? It's not like he can hear me.'

A strange gargling noise came from the other side of the door in response. It was followed by the sound of a body being thrown against the door repeatedly. The gargling noise juddered into a familiar serpentine barking sound.

'It's that dog thing,' said Ben.

'At least it's not a ticket inspector,' said Kartofel. The door was beginning to show the signs of strain now, bending with each new slam.

'What do we do?' said Djinn 'What do we do?'

'Get ready,' said Ben. He hobbled to his feet and hid behind the door. The demon's assault continued, the little dog-man hitting the door more and more forcefully with each new pass. Ben waited for it to launch itself once more, then reached forward and undid the lock.

The demon burst in. It was wearing a ticket collector's uniform and a little peaked hat. It looked from side to side, searching for Ben, seeing only the demons. Ben thudded his satchel into the

71

back of the demon's head, sending it crashing into the rim of the toilet bowl.

'Run!' he shouted, and ducked out of the door. The demons scrambled, diving back into the Box as Ben fled down the empty carriage. It was hard to run, the movement of the train and the state of his ankle threatening his balance. He kept banging into seats as the winds and the uneven track rocked the carriage from side to side. As he reached the end, he glanced over his shoulder. The demon had come out of the cubicle, and stood growling at the opposite end. Black liquid dripped from its muzzle.

It sprang into a run. Ben crashed through into the First Class carriage, slamming the door shut behind him. It was an old train, and so the carriage was split into a series of closed off compartments. He hobbled along to the third one, tried the handle, and ducked inside.

It was empty. As he crouched beneath the door, he heard the dog-demon pad into the carriage, yapping and hissing as it stalked along the gangway outside.

The train began to slow. Ben pulled the satchel close to his body, and held it tight. The Creature's gargling got further away as it paced down the carriage. But then it stopped, and Ben heard it snuffling out his scent as it came back down the gangway on all fours.

The train was almost at a complete stop. The dog-demon was maybe half a carriage away: before long it would follow his scent to the compartment. Over the tannoy, in Welsh and then English, the train's arrival at Colwyn Bay was announced.

And then Ben had an idea.

He burst out of the compartment. The dog-demon stopped, shocked, and for a moment they stood staring at each other from opposite ends of the gangway. Ben broke first, on the sound of the doors unlocking. He dashed to the vestibule at his end of the carriage, hearing the dog-demon sprinting for the far one at the same time. He got to the exterior doors, pushed the button, and fell through on to the platform. Seconds later, the dog-demon did the same, skidding on to the concourse and continuing its pursuit without missing a step.

Ben did not move. He waited in the middle of the platform, allowing the demon to catch up with him. It tore along on all fours until it was almost within touching distance; Ben could smell the foul black blood on the Creature's muzzle, and its infernal breath as it bore down on him.

And still he waited.

The dog-demon snarled as it stalked forward, slowing as it approached its quarry.

Ben took a deep breath and shot back on to the train, pressing the door button closed behind him. The station master blew his whistle, and the dog-demon let go a ferocious burst of snake-barking.

The train pulled away. Ben staggered to his feet, pressed his head to the window, and saw the Creature frantically scurrying after the train. It was fast, but as the train picked up speed, the demon began to run out of platform until it was forced to rear up.

Ben collapsed. He was breathing rapidly, and his poor lungs burned, but he had done it. He closed his eyes, and a wide grin crept across his face.

'Tickets from Rhyl, Abergele and Pensarn, and Colwyn Bay, please.'

Ben opened his eyes. A red-faced ticket inspector with a toothbrush moustache loomed over him.

Ben laughed. A long, mad, exhilarated laugh.

Chapter Nine

The Greyhound's Lair

Ben paused at the top of Cromlech Road. According to *Sacred Orme*, Llety'r Filiast could be found in a field at the end of the street. He was surprised to see that there were houses there, and parked cars; there was even a streetlight at the opposite end, illuminating the small set of wooden steps that led over the wall and into the field. It had been difficult, climbing the steep hills of the Orme with a throbbing ankle, and it had been made all the harder by the weather: he always seemed to be heading into the wind, no matter which direction he faced. It had only gotten stronger the further up the Orme he climbed, and once he reached Cromlech Road it was all he could to do to keep his feet.

'You are early, Ben Robson,' said a voice. Two small red dots floated in the air before him. 'Allow me to escort you.'

The Seraph appeared in a dull throb of orange light. Ben blinked, and fumbled with his now useless torch. 'The Box,' he said. 'I can still hear it, in my head.'

'Yes,' said The Seraph. 'It cannot be suppressed now. But you will get your peace soon enough. Come, it will not be long before the others arrive.'

'The others?'

'The other Oblates of the Cult of the Four Winds. I cannot do this alone.' The Seraph set off down the road. 'You may find it easier to walk behind me. I do not feel the wind as you do.'

Ben slipped into the angel's wake. The difference was instant and amazing: the air was clearer, and the wind did not screech. 'The Veil is weak, and this World is vulnerable,' said The Seraph. 'The Box knows this and is trying to exploit it.'

'The Box is doing this?' said Ben. In his head, it played a little self-congratulatory tune.

'I told you it was powerful, did I not? Throughout history, wherever it has been, there has been disaster. It was in Troy on the day the horse was delivered, and it was in Alexandria when the library was sacked. It causes trouble, creates conflict. It leaks chaos and then absorbs the results, ready for the day when it can unleash the agents of the Apocalypse.'

The Seraph led the way to the wooden steps, and took the first four in one massive stride. Ben clambered up after him, then followed him down into the field beyond. There, on top of a grassy mound and protected by a poorly maintained wooden fence, stood Llety'r Filiast. It was even less impressive in real life than the picture in his book: it looked like a pile of discarded rocks with a roof on it. It barely came up to his waist.

'Is that it?'

'Yes,' said The Seraph. 'Millions of years ago, this place was on the Equator. The Box was hidden here when it was first created. This is sacred ground. You can feel it throbs with power.'

'Um . . .' said Ben.

'I would not expect a human to be able to feel it. I thought you might.' The Seraph sniffed the air, then licked his finger and held it up. 'The other Oblates will be here soon. May I see the Box?'

Ben reached inside his satchel. As soon as he touched it, the Box switched from the nauseating music it had been playing all day to a familiar comforting tune. He ran his hand over the lid in reverie. He remembered things he had long forgotten: sitting on

Orff's knee as he told stories; giggling as Kartofel switched the salt for the pepper just as his grandad was reaching for the shaker; getting Djinn to pass over his peas so he wouldn't have to eat them. These were magical memories. They were his childhood. He did not want to let them go.

'It is trying to seduce you, Ben. Do not let it.' The Seraph spoke in breathy, soothing tones, with empathy. 'Place the Box inside the stones, and I will prepare the ground for what must be done.'

Reluctantly, Ben stepped out of the windbreaker of The Seraph's body and headed for the mound. The wind had grown faster since he was last in it fully, and it wailed as it whipped through him. The jumble of rocks formed a sort of shelter. Inside it there lay a piece of stone; from the shape of it Ben could tell it had once been part of the roof. He tucked the Box behind it, and took a step back. The yearning music stopped, and the Box returned to mimicking the rush of the wind.

The lid opened, and the demons sprang out. As each left the Box, the symbols on their collars lit up, illuminating their faces in the dark January night. Djinn shone like a sun, but as Ben was admiring the pretty sight he noticed Djinn's hands move to his neck. He tried to speak, but it was as if he was choking. Bewildered, Ben's gaze moved to the other demons: Orff was on his knees, his mouth wide open. Kartofel was kicking up earth and grass, struggling like a wild rabbit caught in a snare. Ben turned back to The Seraph in panic. The angel had his arm raised, fingers outstretched, orange light flowing from each digit.

'Do not worry, Ben,' he said. 'I have them under control.'

'You don't need to hurt them,' yelled Ben over the wind.

'They are demons,' said The Seraph.

'You don't understand. They want to be here.'

The Seraph dropped his hand, and instantly the demons stopped struggling. 'They want to go to Hell?' he asked.

'Yes. To be free,' said Ben.

'How strange.'

'See?' said Kartofel, gasping from his ordeal. 'Even the angel thinks this is crackers.'

'Hold your tongue, demon,' said The Seraph. 'You will address me with respect.'

'Screw that for a game of soldiers.'

The Seraph leaped forward, his hand outstretched. Kartofel started to make the choking noise again. 'I could grind you to dust and throw you to the wind if I so desired, but instead I will let you pass into Hell. As a beneficiary of my mercy, you will respect me.'

'That's enough,' said Ben, pulling at The Seraph's habit. The angel dropped his hand, releasing Kartofel.

'Psycho,' muttered Kartofel.

'Forgive me, Ben Robson,' said The Seraph. 'I am unaccustomed to dealing with Infernals in an amiable manner.'

'I understand,' said Ben, taking the angel to one side. 'Do you think you could give us a moment alone? I know it's stupid, but, well, I'd like to say goodbye to them.'

The Seraph shrugged. 'As you wish. I have much to do.' He walked away from the stones, and began scratching something into the ground with his fingers.

'Right, just so you all know, I am on record as saying this is a bad idea, OK?' said Kartofel once the angel was out of earshot. 'So when you're complaining about how Hell stinks of sulphur or about the heat bringing you out in hives, I'm not listening. Got it?'

'I'm scared,' said Djinn.

'You don't need to be,' said Ben. 'You're going where there are others like you. You'll probably be able to touch things.'

'Will there be food?'

'I don't know. I suppose demons have to eat something.'

Djinn grinned. Ben took one last look at the demons. Orff had his palms pressed against his lower back, rubbing at his imaginary sciatica. Kartofel was hopping from claw to claw, trying to disguise his nervousness, and Djinn was licking his lips. A new motif appeared in the Box's music: it was sad, regretful. A requiem.

'Despite everything, in a funny way, I think I'll miss you,' he said.

'Everything is ready,' said The Seraph. 'I have prepared the earth.' He had carved the symbols that the demons wore on their collars into the ground at four different points around the base of the mound. They formed the points of a cross, with Llety'r Filiast at the centre.

There was a flash of lightning, followed by a roll of thunder. Malevolent black clouds gathered overhead. 'They are coming,' said The Seraph. 'The Cult of the Four Winds are coming!' He started to chant, words that Ben did not understand. The Seraph stretched out his arms, and raised his head to the heavens. He was brighter than ever now. The music in Ben's head shifted again, becoming almost triumphant: regal fanfares were accompanied by a shift to a marching rhythm.

A deep growl came from somewhere on the Orme.

The Seraph stopped chanting, and looked around. The growling became a bark, a bark Ben knew only too well. It was sibilant, and slushy, and could only have come from one thing.

'We are discovered,' said The Seraph. In his head, Ben heard the music that meant the demons were being sucked back inside the Box. Lightning flashed.

On the crest of the hill stood the dog-demon. It was on all fours, still wearing the remnants of its ticket inspector uniform. The thunder rumbled overhead, and it howled to greet it.

And then it ran.

'Protect the Box!' cried The Seraph. 'Get behind the stones!'

Ben ran towards Llety'r Filiast and ducked inside, pulling the Box from where he had laid it. Then he dived behind the stones and poked his head round to view the oncoming threat.

'You need to run!' The Seraph turned to face the Creature, his wings fully unfurled. He cut such an imposing figure in comparison that Ben wondered how he could ever lose. Surely The Seraph, who could crush Kartofel to dust, would have no trouble with this yappy little thing?

'I said run!' blasted The Seraph. Ben saw a celestial rage in his eyes. Now he was scared. Now he would run. He grabbed hold of his satchel and ran up a nearby bank. At the top, he turned back. The dog-demon had stopped running, and was cautiously pawing towards the angel, snarling. The Seraph hovered above its head, treading air, poised to attack. It was an inspiring and fearsome sight, but if the Creature was afraid, it did not show it: it was leaning back on its hind legs, like a wild animal preparing to strike.

The angel's wings beat rhythmically, blowing gusts towards the dog-demon, ruffling its mangy fur. The Creature sprang up, strong and powerful, and sank its sole row of teeth deep into The Seraph's shoulder. It hung above his breast, and wrapped its short legs around his trunk. It tore at The Seraph's habit with its grubby paws, leaving deep scratches on his chest. The Seraph shrieked.

The brawling pair fell backwards, the dog-demon pinning the angel to the ground. With its upper jaw free, it was able to swipe at The Seraph. When Ben had first seen the Creature, he had assumed that its scars were the result of centuries of torture in some dark corner of Hell, but now he could see the truth: the demon was a warrior.

But so was The Seraph. He worked an arm free and thrust it, palm up, into the beast's maw, reopening the wound it had received on the train. The angel screamed as his hand made contact with the Creature's teeth, but followed the blow through nonetheless, freeing himself, sending the demon flying backwards in an arc of black gore. It landed hard on the ground, righted itself, and came straight back at The Seraph.

This time the angel was prepared. As the Creature launched itself forward, The Seraph leaped to greet it, slamming it down into the ground from mid-air. With the Creature squirming under his arm, The Seraph went to work. The Creature's arms flailed, struggling to push The Seraph away with his short limbs, all the while taking the angel's heavy blows.

The battle was all but over. It was only a matter of time before The Seraph destroyed the Creature. It was beaten, but nobody had told it that. A paw shot up and caught The Seraph's left arm, and then another caught the right. It wriggled its small body out from under the angel, and powered up through its legs, forcing The Seraph back. They grappled for a while, until the Creature swung its neck back and slammed its face into The Seraph's glowing head.

There was another flash of lightning, and a thunderclap. The Creature pulled back and The Seraph slumped to the ground.

'No!' yelled Ben.

The Creature looked at him, a dopey grin on its face, its muzzle dripping blacks and golds and browns. It sniffed the air, and galloped up the hill on all fours. It covered the ground between them in no time at all, snake-barking all the way.

'WARNED. YOU.' The dog-demon called as it ran, struggling to slur the words out. 'I. WARNED. YOU.' Ben dropped his satchel, and took the Box in both hands. It was now playing a full-on fanfare, war music, a charge. It was vibrating. He could feel power surging up and down his arms. He let out an anguished yowl, and thrust the Box out in front of him.

A beam of green light shot out towards the demon. It missed its target, but caused the Creature to skid to one side, thrown off balance by the wind and the need to dodge the blow. Stunned, it blinked its one good eye and cocked its head before charging again.

'Back!' cried Ben, his voice surging up from deep within him, the power of the Box flooding his system. He felt it in the soles of his feet, pumping up from the ground, through his body, and into the Box.

Lightning blasted the burial mound. The thunder rumbled applause. The Box shuddered violently, and once again an intense beam of green light shot out towards the monster.

Ben gritted his teeth and shut his eyes, feeling the beam connect with the Creature, dissolving it, flooding through it until there was nothing. No resistance. No flow.

He opened his eyes. The screaming wind died down to a mere breeze. The Creature had gone, the lightning and the thunder had gone, and so had the body of The Seraph.

Ben dropped the Box, and there, on top of the Great Orme, with no shelter except the blasted trees, he curled up into a ball, and began to cry.

Chapter Ten

The Grand Druid

The day after the storm struck, the news was full of the damage that had been done. Schools and offices had been forced to shut, advertising hoardings had been thrown on to motorways, and telegraph poles had been toppled. Not that anyone in Rhyl needed to turn on a television to see evidence of the carnage: it was all around them, from the upturned rubbish bins that made the streets look even grimmer than they had done before, to the uprooted tree that lay across Fford Coed Mawr. This was an especially potent symbol of the power of the storm, for there were no trees to be found on Fford Coed Mawr before the storm, nor in any of the surrounding streets.

As Ben left for school that morning, his grandad was already out in the front garden, reaffixing the guttering to the side of the house. Ben tried to sneak past, fearing awkward questions about how the gutter could have been torn away, but instead all he got was a few grumbles about 'the ruddy storm', and a begrudging acknowledgment that, 'It could have been worse – they've lost half their roof down the road.'

Ben should probably have felt guilty about all the destruction. He was, after all, the reason it had happened. But his mind was at ease, for when he had woken up on the morning after the Battle of the Orme, the Box was empty and the demons were gone.

*

The last thing he remembered was curling up under the trees next to Llety'r Filiast. And so it was a little disconcerting to wake up in his own bed at seven thirty with no idea how he had gotten there.

Bleary-eyed, he surveyed his bedroom. His satchel had been dumped in the corner, all damp and muddy, and his 'stealth' clothes lay strewn all over the floor, soaking wet and streaked with dirt. He swung his legs out of bed and as he put his feet on the floor he suddenly remembered he'd hurt his ankle, but now he felt no pain. He wrapped his duvet around himself and shuffled over to his satchel. His copy of *Sacred Orme* was gone, and so was his grandad's torch, but the Box was still there, tucked snugly inside, safe. It had been ambling along at its normal pace ever since he'd woken up, but as soon as he touched it, it swelled. It was somehow clearer than he had ever heard it; it did not seem to be louder, and it hadn't been particularly muffled before: it was just more precise. Each individual element of the music rang out. It was as if he had never heard it properly before, and now it made sense to him.

He pulled the Box out of the bag, and set it down on the floor. It bore no sign of the blast it had emitted. He ran a hand across the top of it, a gentle gliding stroke, before easing the lid open. He was expecting the green light, or some other sign that it had changed, that it was now a demon-slaying machine; but it was no different. He let the lid flap back, and the Box yawned open.

Nothing happened.

It was empty. He could see the bottom of it, could put his hand inside and feel the wooden base. He wrapped his knuckles on it a few times. It made a hollow knocking sound.

There were no demons. In all the years that he had been carrying the Box around, he had never seen the bottom of it. Opening the lid always led to the demons manifesting, always. But now they were not there. The Box's music played a joyous tune and Ben felt a rush of happiness. It was like the Box knew him now, and there was nothing to dampen or drown out its sound. It blew a breeze of fresh air through his brain, scattering all his questions away like they were seeds on dandelion clocks.

The week that followed was the easiest week of Ben's life. Without the demons to distract him and with the Furies still safely on suspension, school improved immeasurably: he started to feel less socially awkward, less out of place. He did not become instantly popular, but it seemed to him that the disappearance of the demons had taken the edge off the strangeness that had marked him out for exclusion, and getting through each day was no longer a test of his endurance.

As the week progressed, he enjoyed a deeper and deeper relationship with the Box. Every day the music grew more complex, and every day he understood it better.

After the incident with the cake slice, it had been decided that Ben would take a few weeks off from visiting his mother and so on the second Sunday of February, a week and a half after the Orme, he was enjoying a lie-in while his grandparents were at Drylands Hall. Or at least he was, until the telephone started to ring.

The caller was persistent, and by the fifth or sixth ring Ben reluctantly hauled himself out of bed, put on his dressing gown, and sloped off downstairs, the cacophony continuing throughout. He didn't know why he was bothering. No one ever rang for him, unless it was his grandmother, calling to tell him where the jam was or to remind him to record some boring programme about cows or something.

'What?' said Ben.

'Nnnn. What kind of a way to answer a phone is that?'

'Tegwyn?'

'It is I. Come to the shop.'

'Why?'

'Because I said so. Come to the shop.'

The line went dead. Tegwyn did not like using the phone. He suspected it was being bugged by the government, who obviously have nothing better to do than to monitor the rate at which die-cast elves are bought and sold on the North Wales coast. Ben shrugged, replaced the receiver, and headed into the kitchen. No sooner had he put a few rounds of bread into the toaster than the phone rang again.

'Hello?'

'Nnnn. Why haven't you left yet?'

'I'm still in my pyjamas.'

'We know what you've been up to, you little turd. *The Weekly News*. Llety'r Filiast. I'll say no more.'

Ben raced into the dining room. He dug out the *North Wales Weekly News* from his grandad's pile of papers, and could hardly believe the front page. Taking the stairs two at a time, he ran to his room. The phone began to ring again, but he ignored it. He dressed quickly, and was out the door in five minutes flat.

The headline read:

SATANIC RITUALS ON ORME?

ANIMAL SACRIFICES ROCK LLANDUDNO

The never-dusted blinds of the Broken Forge were drawn shut, and a highly detailed drawing of a dwarf saying 'WE ART

CLOSED' was stuck to the front door. Ben pressed the rusty doorbell, and waited. It was either one of those annoying doorbells that didn't make a sound, or it just didn't work.

After a few minutes he heard a shuffling inside. To his right a gap opened up in the blinds, and an eye briefly appeared before the slats snapped shut again. Behind the door, a symphony of unlocking began as latches were drawn back, bolts were undone, and chains were lifted and dropped. The performance crescendoed with the door opening just wide enough for Tegwyn to poke his head out. He looked from left to right and then to the left again, at which point he noticed the bicycle.

'Nnnn. What did you bring that for?'

'You wanted me here quickly, didn't you?'

Tegwyn looked left-right-left again, sighed, and reluctantly opened the door wide enough for Ben to wheel his bike inside.

The shop stank of glue, even more than it did on a weekday. The Warmonger diorama had been cleared away, and in its place was a long trestle table, covered in old newspapers, with a selection of newly assembled models slowly drying on top.

'Don't touch anything,' said Tegwyn, as he completed a coda of locking up. 'In fact, don't even look at it. Stick your bike by the counter and come with me.'

Ben did as he was told, at least as far as the bike was concerned. He couldn't help but gawp at the rows of miniatures as he followed Tegwyn through the hatch in the counter. Tegwyn stopped in front of the bead curtain that separated the shop from Out-the-Back, turned to Ben, and intoned:

'Are you ready to come inside the circle?'

Ben nodded eagerly, and the Box greeted the thought with a little trill of happiness.

Out-the-Back turned out to be something of a disappointment. Naturally, it stank. Most things to do with Tegwyn stank: either of paint, glue, old paper, or body odour. Out-the-Back stank of them all. It was a cramped labyrinth of metal bookcases full of unsellable stock, lit by a dim red bulb and covered in a fine layer of dust. The spaces between the rows were narrow, and Tegwyn was forced to turn side-on in order to be able to squeeze through.

As they progressed deeper into the room, the stock got older, mustier, and less desirable. Ben had supposed that Out-the-Back would be Eden. He could see now that it was not: it was a graveyard, and an unloved, untended one at that.

After they had walked down a row of shelving that Ben could have sworn they had passed before (he would not be surprised to find out that Tegwyn had been leading him round in circles, either in an effort to impress him, or to make sure he didn't remember the way) they came to a short corridor, at the end of which was a feeble wooden door with a padlock on it. The passage was mostly taken up by a bank of old metal lockers. Most of them had their doors open, revealing discarded chocolate wrappers and crusty paint pots, but the last two were locked. One had Tegwyn's name written on it in ornate gold script. The other had a piece of white gaffer tape stuck to it, on which was written 'THE GIRL' in thick black marker. This had been crossed out with a biro, and underneath, in a different hand, was written 'LUCY'.

'What are you grinning at, you little turd?' said Tegwyn as he held open the door.

In front of them was a narrow staircase covered with ancient grey carpet. It may have been a different colour once, but it had long since been given over to crumbs, grit and house dust mites. The narrowness meant that Ben had to ascend first, as it would have been impossible for Tegwyn to pass him on the stairs. Faded, dated wallpaper covered the walls, upon which hung a variety of posters and wicker objects.

At the top, the passage opened out a little wider. The stench of incense added a new note to the chord of unpleasant smells. The carpet continued its run (or the mites continued their run with the carpet) down a dark corridor. Tegwyn took advantage of the wider space to unceremoniously barge Ben into the wall.

'Careful there,' sniggered Tegwyn, taking hold of the handle of the door at the end of the hall. 'Clumsy.' He took a deep breath, and grinned the smuggest grin that Ben had ever seen. 'Are you ready to meet the Grand Druid for the whole of the North Wales coast?'

'Um . . .' said Ben. Tegwyn did not wait for more of a reply than that, and with a theatrical flourish he threw open the door.

Inside what Ben assumed was Tegwyn's living room sat a man in his thirties. He was wearing grey tracksuit bottoms, a mustard-coloured shirt, and a black waistcoat covered in a sequinned pattern. His hair was brown, too short to be long and too long to be short, and his chin was poorly shaven. He was fleshier than in the picture on the back of *Sacred Orme*, but Ben recognized him at once as the author, Terry Owens. He got up from the knackered old settee and offered his hand.

'Benjamino! I'm the Grand Druid for this area, but you can call me Terry. Tell me, Ben, do you like *Doctor Who*?'

'Err, well . . . not really. No.'

'Yes, well, I suppose it's not what it was. Would you like a cup of tea? And a biscuit?' He gestured to what looked like a coffee table. It was piled high with books and magazines, on top of which sat a teapot, some chipped mugs, and a paper plate full of

Rich Tea Fingers. Ben took one and sat down.

'Now, you know we're druids, don't you? So you can imagine that when we – I mean the druidic community, not just me and Teg here – saw this story in the *Weekly News*, well, we became a bit worried. It doesn't look very good on us, talk of animal sacrifices and the like. So now I've got grander druids than me breathing down my neck, the council asking why there are people shedding blood on historical sites, and a lot of worried pagans asking questions. So I was wondering if you wouldn't mind helping us out. Teg tells me that you bought my book, *Sacred Orme: Neolithic Monuments on Llandudno's Ancient Beachhead*. Did you enjoy it?'

'Erm . . . yes?' said Ben.

'Splendid,' he said, clapping his hands together in delight. 'So what did you think of Llety'r Filiast when you went there? It's wonderful, isn't it? So spiritual. The ground throbs with it.'

'I didn't say I went there.'

'Don't lie, you little turd. He's the Grand Druid,' said Tegwyn.

'You didn't need to. Druidism is ancient and varied, Benjamino. We are alive to changes in the natural world, especially to the spiritual rhythms of our sacred spaces,' said the Grand Druid. 'And we have a druid who works as a copper in Rhos-on-Sea. They found your copy of *Sacred Orme: Neolithic Monuments on Llandudno's Ancient Beachhead* at the site.'

'That could be anybody's copy,' said Ben.

'Nnnn, we've got you now. That's the only copy ever sold so we know! We know!'

'Now, Teg,' said the Grand Druid, 'there's no need to crow. Look, Benjamino, we're not going to report you to the police or anything, we're not like that. We're just a bit worried about you, that's all. What were you doing up there?'

'I'd like to go now, if it's all the same to you,' said Ben, standing up.

'Well, you can't,' said Tegwyn. 'Sit down.'

'We can't keep him here against his will,' said the Grand Druid. 'If our guest wants to leave, then kindly show him out.'

Ben gathered up his satchel. Tegwyn scowled his way across the room, and held the door open. Once Ben had crossed the threshold into the corridor, the Grand Druid spoke again.

'We know about the markings on the ground in Llety'r Filiast,' he said. 'We know what they mean.'

Ben stopped. He wondered why the Grand Druid had let him get all the way over to the door before speaking and decided it was because the Grand Druid watched too much television.

'We know your pet recently passed away. The police were involved, and three girls at your school were suspended. We're wondering if that's got anything to do with this?'

'What do you mean?'

'He means why've you been sacrificing goats, you little turd?' said Tegwyn.

'I don't mean that at all,' said the Grand Druid. 'The combination of symbols you drew on the Orme are for rites pertaining to the summoning of the departed. They are ancient and powerful, as old as recorded language itself. Probably older. What we're worried about is a situation where there's a rogue druid, if you like, running around North Wales trying to bring something back. Like a beloved rabbit.'

Ben laughed, and the Box played a few mocking triads to match. 'You don't know what you're talking about.'

'Oi! You can't talk to him like that,' snapped Tegwyn. 'He's the Grand Druid.'

'You need to be careful, Benjamino.' The Grand Druid reached into his back pocket and produced a deck of business cards bound together by a red rubber band. They were curved slightly from where he had been sitting on them. He took one and handed it to Ben. 'You can always come and see us if you need to. We try to come together just before high tide, so we can connect to the sea, you know? We meet at the Old School Youth Centre in Towyn. There's a little tide table on the back there.'

The card was grubby, and had 'TERRY OWENS: GRAND DRUID, PROFESSIONAL SCRIBE' printed on it, followed by a local phone number. 'Tide table' was probably too grand a title for the biro scribblings on the back of the card: it was a list of dates and times for the next few months. Ben shoved it into his pocket, and left. Tegwyn followed behind, jangling his keys and muttering something bitter and incomprehensible.

Chapter Eleven

Death and the Maidens

Around a week later, Ben was walking home from school with as much of a spring in his step as he ever had. The half-term holidays were a week away, and he was looking forward to a whole week of listening to the Box without the annoying interruption of school. Ever since the Orme it had been making the most beautiful music, and now that the Forge was somewhere he did not want to be, it was fast becoming his only leisure activity. It soundtracked his thoughts and feelings perfectly, and each day he looked forward to being able to seal himself in his room and listen to all the places it would take him.

He was about halfway across the waste ground when he noticed a dead tree trunk belching out a yellowy smoke, and stopped. Jenny stepped out from behind it in full school uniform. She took a long drag on her cigarette, then blew the filthy smoke she had taken into her lungs right into Ben's face. He coughed. A lot.

'Awww. Are you all right there, Bendy? We've been waiting for you.'

'But you're suspended,' protested Ben.

'Not any more. Pigs couldn't prove nothing so they have to let us back. Did you miss us?'

'Yeah, did you miss us?' said Sally, grabbing his shoulders and pulling his satchel off his back. She upended it, and the Box squealed as it hit the ground.

'Oh my God, that is so sad,' said Sally. 'He's got a jewellery box.'

'Why've you got that then, Bendy?' said Jenny. 'Or should I call you Wendy? Bendy Wendy, the little girl with a jewellery box.'

Sally held the Box upside down and started to shake it. The music became juddery and unhappy, and skipped a few beats. 'It's empty. What's the point of that?'

'Give that back,' said Ben.

'Aww, ickle Wendy wants her jewellery box back,' said Jenny. 'Give it here, Sal.'

Sally launched the Box over Ben's head. It made a terrible sound as it flew through the air, ending in a wince-inducing sting when it finally thudded into Jenny's arms.

'I suppose we should thank you for getting us time off school,' she said as she threw the Box to Nikki. The smaller girl giggled as she caught it. Ben spun round, but Nikki had already thrown it back to Sally. He spun again, and again, the Box whining and stinging all the time as he pivoted to face each Fury in turn until Jenny stopped. She was panting more than Ben, even though she'd stayed in the same place.

'What you been saying to the pigs about me, then? You been telling them that I killed your rabbit?' Jenny dangled the Box out in front of her, and Ben reached forward to snatch it. He knocked it out of her hand, and ducked to catch it before it hit the ground. Jenny growled, and launched her whole body at his middle. He folded, the air rasping out of him as he hit the muddy ground. The Box flew backwards over his head. He tried to turn, but before he knew it Jenny was clawing her way up his body. She straddled him, and leaned forward so that her spot-covered face seemed impossibly, grotesquely large.

'I was grounded for two weeks. Two whole weeks,' she said. Ben could smell her foul breath, a mixture of nicotine and lip gloss. 'And what for? For nothing. No evidence. Just a little wuss and his dead rabbit.'

Ben flailed his arms in front of his face, squirming and pushing in an attempt to shift her. Her skin was clammy and cold, and he winced to touch it. She moved forward, so that she was sitting on his chest, and grabbed his arms. She caught the right one and pulled it back, bringing her knee to rest on it so that it was pinned to the ground. 'Crying over some stupid little wabbit. Like, grow up. It was practically dead when we got there anyway.'

Ben tried to speak, but Jenny clamped her hand over his mouth, squeezing his cheeks until his teeth hurt. The Box beat in time to his heart, pounding out battle music, calling him to action. He pawed wildly at her face with his free hand until he found her chin, and extended his arm as much as could, but Jenny had the advantage of her entire body weight and he wasn't strong enough to shift her. She gargled a bit, but that was all.

It became hard to breathe. He twisted his head to try to free his mouth, but Jenny held firm. The Box reacted with a loud thwacking sound, as if a wet fish had been thrown at a cello, and something changed in his head. He started to feel the power of the Box pulsating through him, just as he had on the Orme. In an instant his outstretched arm was consumed by green fire, which licked up to his hand and then spread on to Jenny's face. It slowly spread across her chin, bleaching her face with light.

'Ugh, what you doin' to me, Wendy? How dare you touch me you little . . .' gargled Jenny.

Ben ignored her, choosing instead to concentrate on the green light, watching it spread all over her chin and cheeks. He felt himself drifting away, hearing only the Box; it sang, but not in any language Ben could name, if it was a language at all. It was more a feeling, an understanding between him and it.

Jenny's face began to change. 'Hey,' she said, 'how . . . how are you doing that? How did you make your eyes change colour? Here, Sal, look at this . . .'

She turned to look at the others, letting go of Ben's face as she did. Ben took a deep breath, and let go of her chin. The light disappeared as quickly as it had arrived.

From the other end of the field, Ben heard shouting. Someone was calling for the girls to leave him alone. Jenny sprang back, and Ben scrambled to his feet. She stood heaving great heavy breaths, like a giant wounded boar.

'W-w-w-what are you waiting for? Get him!'

The other Furies looked at each other. Nikki giggled.

'What?' demanded Jenny.

''Ere, Jen,' said Sally. 'When did your spots clear up?'

Jenny's face was suddenly like rock. 'What? What spots? What you tryin' to say?'

Nikki bit her fist. Sally looked at the floor. 'I know we sort of pretend you don't have them, but now you sort of really don't.'

'What you on about?' Jenny patted her face. The skin was smooth. She looked confused. 'Mirror,' she thundered, her arm out.

Sally fumbled in her bag for her compact. Jenny gawped at her reflection, and then at Ben. 'How?' she said. She dropped the mirror and ran back across the waste ground with such athleticism that all her months of PE sick notes were instantly proved to be forgeries. The other Furies looked confused for a moment before sprinting off after her.

'That's right,' said a voice – it was Lucy, running towards him.

'Get lost, you bullies! Losers!' She was carrying two full bags of shopping that bashed her sides as she ran. 'Phew. I didn't expect that to work quite as well as it did. Are you OK?'

Ben was staring down at his muddy hands. He didn't quite understand what had happened. He wasn't really aware of the girl at all.

'You're Ben, aren't you?'

'Um,' said Ben.

'Lucy. We met at Teg's shop. Remember? Are you all right?'

'Um.'

'I hate bullies. Do you want me to walk you home?'

Ben shook his head. He didn't want to be walked home. He wanted to know what had just happened. He had healed Jenny's acne.

'OK,' said Lucy. 'Maybe you could walk me home, then.' She clicked her fingers in front of his face. 'Hello?'

'I don't know where you live.'

'That's all right. You can walk me to yours instead.' She picked up one of her bags. 'I've got animal biscuits in the other one of these. Grab it for me and I might share them.'

Ben frowned. 'Um,' he said. Again.

'Which way then?'

Ben pointed in the direction of Fford Heulwen, and Lucy nodded. She started walking. 'Come on. Animal biscuits.'

He picked up the other bag, and trailed along after her. He had only walked a few steps when the Box protested, and he turned back. He hurriedly gathered it up and thrust it into his satchel before jogging to catch up.

Chapter Twelve

Love and Warmonger

'Well, thanks for everything,' said Ben when they arrived at his house. His head was still a little muddled, though the Box seemed to understand this and was trying to be reassuring. He wanted to be on his own, to figure out what had happened and to listen to the Box. 'I'm home now, so . . .'

'I can't leave you now,' said Lucy. 'I promised you animal biscuits. Besides, you haven't paid for your order.'

'What order?'

'Didn't I say?' She held out the other carrier bag. It was full of ageing stock from Out-the-Back. The sun-faded box of Villagers and Townsfolk stuck out the top. 'That's why I'm here. I was coming to deliver this. Teg said you ordered it.'

'I wish he'd just leave me alone.' Ben rummaged through the bag for a minute before trying to hand it back. 'This is junk. I didn't order this.'

'He said you did.'

'I didn't.'

'Well, I can't go back without the money, can I? He'll go mental.'

'How much is it?'

'Fifty quid, he says. Special offer.'

'He'd need to give me fifty quid to take it. I don't need any hedgerows, thanks. And there's even a viaduct in here. What am I supposed to do with that?'

'I don't know. Can't your trolls live under it or something?'

'It's an accessory for a train set.'

'Don't they have trains in Battle Axe? They had trains in World War Two. For supplies and things.'

'First, no, we don't have trains. It's a fantasy game. Second, it's called Warmonger. How can you work at the Forge and not know that?'

'I didn't want to work there. I was supposed to be going to the Sun Centre, but that fell through. Then I was placed at this shoe shop in town, but the old bag who ran it wanted me to wear red, so I told her where to stick it. I don't know anything about Warmonger, and Teg doesn't want to show me.' She shrugged. 'All I do is write down numbers and make tea, anyway. My dad says it's pretty much the perfect experience of the world of work.'

'I'm sorry to hear that,' said Ben, and went to shut the door. Lucy stuck her foot inside.

'Maybe you could show me? In exchange for saving you from – what did you call them? The gorgons?'

'The Furies.' Ben screwed up his face. 'Are you going to go away if I say no?'

Lucy smiled.

'Fine,' sighed Ben. He held open the door, and Lucy ducked inside.

'Put the kettle on then,' she said.

After Lucy had drunk her tea, and shared out her biscuits, and asked him a billion questions about the Furies, and Druss, and his mother, which Ben was surprised to discover he didn't mind answering at all, they had gone upstairs. Ben got everything ready (including the appropriate codex for civil war, since he only had skeletons to battle with) while Lucy squinted at various figures through the magnifying glass. If he'd have thought about it, he'd have realized that this was the first time he'd ever had a girl in his room. In fact, it was the first time he'd had a human he wasn't related to in his room.

She was currently enamoured with a Necromancer. 'These are really good. Did you paint all these yourself?'

'Yeah. They're not as good as Tegwyn's, though. His attention to detail is amazing.'

'Yeah, right,' sniggered Lucy. 'Wait, you don't know? Teg doesn't paint all his models himself. His mum lives in a home in Denbigh. Once a week he takes a big bag of orcs round, and there's a little group of pensioners that does them for him. He only does the big showy things himself. Dragons, stuff like that.'

'Wyverns,' said Ben, quickly. He blushed, then mumbled, 'Orcs have wyverns.'

'You don't need to be embarrassed. There's no point pretending to be something you're not because you think it will make other people more comfortable.' She picked up his zombie dragon and pretended to fly it through the air, making growling noises. 'Can I have this wyvern on my side?'

'Yes,' said Ben. 'But that's a dragon.'

They played for an hour, and despite the Box burbling along impatiently in the back of his head, Ben was enjoying himself. He wanted the game to go on, so he had been playing purposefully badly, but when they came to the end of a combat phase which obliterated the last of Ben's troops Lucy put the dice down.

'I'd better be going then. Thanks for the lesson. And the tea.'

'That's all right. It was nice, you know?' He mumbled the end of the sentence into his chest, and felt his cheeks turn red.

'We can hang out again if you like. You doing anything Monday?'

'Don't think so. Gran probably wants us to visit something educational at some point, but that'll be later in the week.'

'You know the Old School Youth Centre in Towyn?'

A cautious new melody wheedled its way through the score. 'Yes?' he said tentatively.

'You should come to druidic circle. It's a lot of fun.'

'You're a druid?' said Ben.

'Yeah, didn't you know? That's how I ended up at Teg's shop. The Grand Druid sorted it out. But it's not weird or anything. Not culty weird, anyway. It's mostly nice people getting together to drink tea and talk about the nature. And magic, but you already know all about that, don't you?'

Ben sighed and shook his head. 'I can't believe I fell for that.'

'What's wrong?'

'Is that why you're being nice to me?'

'What do you mean?'

'I'm not stupid, OK?' His shoulders tightened as the music grew prickly and paranoid. 'Pretending to be interested in Warmonger. I know they sent you.'

'Who?'

'I've not been doing animal sacrifices or whatever it is they say I've been doing, OK? I just want to be left alone. Tell Tegwyn to stop ringing, tell him I'm never going back to his stupid shop, and tell him I don't want him sending his minions to my house.'

'I'm sorry,' said Lucy. Her voice was quiet, and she lowered her head. 'I didn't mean to upset you. I don't know what I said, but I'm sorry.' She picked up the bag of Villagers and Townsfolk, and left. Ben listened as she ran down the stairs. He waited for the front door to slam, then retrieved the Box from his satchel.

It brightened at his touch, and the horrible throbbing went away. His fingers tingled as he touched it, and a smile formed on his lips. He didn't need anyone else. Why would he? He had the Box. He eased the lid back, and as it yawned open, the melody exploded, and Ben felt full up. He put his hand inside the Box and rapped his knuckles on the base in time to the music.

Chapter Thirteen

The Cult of the Four Winds

That night, Ben was woken by a rustling sound, like a bird disturbed on the roost. It was followed by a horrible silence as the music of the Box stopped abruptly. In a panic, he pulled himself over to the edge of the bed to check on it. He felt like he was missing a part of him. As he fished under the bed to try and find it, an incomprehensible whispering started up in its place, and blazing angel light began to fill his room.

'Ben-the-Just?' said a deep, guttural voice. 'Are you Ben-the-Just?'

'No,' said Ben.

'Oh,' said the voice. The new angel was a hulking brute, much bigger than The Seraph. Ben wondered if his little bedroom would be big enough to hold him. He was the same shape as a bear, with broad, rounded shoulders that hunched up over his big round head. He seemed to be thinking something over, and after a slight pause he shook his wings out as if to leave. His frame made them look small, like an ostrich's.

'I'm Ben, but no one calls me Ben-the-Just.'

'Apologies. I was told you wished to be known as Just Ben. The Holy Seraph of the Strident Blasts told us not to call you Ben Robson.'

'Ben on its own is fine.'

The hulk-angel furrowed his brow. 'Shame. Ben-the-Just is a fine name. The sort of name earned in battle, and I know you have seen battle.' He rested his huge forearm on the large silver sword at his waist. The cross-guard was golden, and forged to resemble an angel's wings. 'I am The Triumph of the Skies, Lord of the Grand War, Champion of the Prime One, Second Oblate of the Cult of the Four Winds. But you can call me The Triumph. That's what the Holy Seraph of the Strident Blasts allowed, isn't it?'

'Yes. Now is there something you want? Because I'd like the music of the Box back, please.'

'Stupid primate,' rasped a sibilant new voice. Another angel shone into view, brightening the room considerably. This one was thin and rangy, with a sharp face framed by a mess of dirty black curls. He was slighter than the others, and shorter too: next to The Triumph he looked almost human-sized. He had a long quiver slung over his shoulder. 'We would leave you to your fate if the Creation was not at stake.'

'This is The Archivist of the End Times, Keeper of the Celestial Trumpet, Holder of the Key of Seals, Third Oblate of the Cult of the Four Winds,' said The Triumph. 'Don't mind him. He's not used to dealing with people. Each member of the Cult of the Four Winds has a very special skill; his doesn't lend itself to communicating with humans. Or with anyone else, if I'm honest.'

'And I suppose I call you The Archivist?'

The Archivist contemptuously broke eye contact to look at the ceiling. 'I would prefer if you did not address me at all. I am celestial, eternal, one of the Prime One's chosen. You are an evolved monkey.'

'Whatever,' said Ben. 'What do you want?'

'We need your help to rescue The Holy Seraph of the Strident Blasts,' said The Triumph.

'The Seraph is dead,' said Ben. 'The dog-demon killed him, on the Orme.'

The Archivist laughed. 'Only mortals die. There is no place for our kind in the Valley of Death.'

'Yeah? Tell that to the dog-demon. He seemed pretty dead after I shot him with the Box.'

'The Box erased that creature from Creation,' said The Triumph. 'But The Holy Seraph of the Strident Blasts still very much exists. He is trapped inside the Box, mistaken for the kind of infernal weapon it was designed to constrain.'

Ben let out a little snort of disbelief. 'The Box is empty. I can put my hand inside it.'

'This is futile,' said The Archivist. 'As I said it would be.'

The Triumph glared at him, and The Archivist shrank back a little. 'When The Adversary's Herald was erased, Ben, you became bound to the Box. It sealed the demons away, captured The Holy Seraph of the Strident Blasts, and has been working towards enslaving you ever since.'

'But I've always been bound to the Box. Ever since I was small.'

'Yes, but did it always give you the power to heal?' hissed The Archivist. 'Ever since the Orme the true power of the Box has been living inside you. How do you think you got home after the Orme? How did you recover from your injuries so quickly? How were you able to soothe the female's inflamed sebaceous glands?'

'Huh?' said Ben.

'He means Jenny's acne,' said The Triumph.

The Archivist rolled his eyes.

'How do you know about that?' said Ben 'I don't even really know about that.'

The Archivist tilted his head back with disdain. 'I have

dedicated my entire aeons-long existence to the study of the Box. Every distance it has travelled, every keeper it has known. I know every date, every number, every time it has been used. It has healed countless sick and caused plagues; it has encouraged greed, and brought blight; it has started wars, and ended them too. You have held it for fourteen years ten months two weeks six days seventeen hours and forty-' – he paused for a few seconds – 'eight minutes, and you are an insignificant blip in its long and prestigious history. Your simian brain cannot comprehend its power.'

'As I said,' shrugged The Triumph, 'his talent doesn't really lend itself to social interactions. So what do you say? Can you help us?'

Ben paused for a moment. 'No.'

'What?' said The Archivist.

'I said no. I don't want the demons back, and I like being bound to the Box. And if it gives me the power to heal sick people, I'm going to make my mum better.'

'That would not be wise,' said The Triumph. 'The Holy Seraph of the Strident Blasts has told us of your mother's condition. She believes she has met angels. Her mind must be a very fragile thing.' He shook his head sadly. 'The Box is very powerful. What if you make her worse?'

'I won't,' said Ben. 'The Box wouldn't do that to me.'

The score once more faded in, rising through the sound of the voice in the corner. Ben reached out to it. The whispering increased in intensity, and the music shrank back. Ben scowled.

'Can't you shut that noise up?'

'That is The Castellan of the Veil,' said The Archivist. 'You will show her respect.'

A new glow revealed the source of the sound: a third angel sat cross-legged on the tatty blue Garfield beanbag in the corner of the room. Her hood was draped over her head, and her arms were curled up inside her long sleeves. Her wings were raised so that the tips touched, and the light-picture her outline created made it look like she was sitting in a giant orange egg.

The whole room was now bathed in angel-light, as if they had been transported to a planet with an orange sky. It would have been quite the sight had Ben not seen so many angels appearing and disappearing that he was starting to get quite jaded about the whole thing.

'Just "The Castellan of the Veil"? That's it?'

'You would not employ her full title, even if we told it to you. Time is short, and her title is long,' said The Archivist.

'Does she have to go on like that all the time?'

'She is the only one of us who can manipulate the Veil,' said The Triumph. 'Thanks to her we are able to travel between the Worlds, and can enter your dreams like this.'

'I'm not dreaming,' said Ben. 'I'm awake.'

The Archivist let go a sarcastic snort. Ben tried to protest further, but found he could not speak. In the corner of the room, The Castellan of the Veil's covered mouth was repeating the unintelligible phrases faster and faster. Ben felt lightheaded, and the last thing he saw as his eyelids drooped shut was The Triumph and The Archivist hovering over him, their mouths moving, no sound coming out.

He experienced a sharp pain in his chest, and his eyes flicked open. The Archivist was brutally poking his ribs. The room was a little less orange now: The Castellan of the Veil could no longer be seen, but her voice continued in the dark corner.

'What?' said Ben. 'For God's sake.'

The Archivist slapped his face. 'Do not use that word, human boy, if you cannot use it properly. The Prime One is not to be called on in vain.'

'I only nodded off.'

'As we explained, you're asleep already,' said The Triumph. 'It was too much for The Castellan of the Veil to show herself at the same time as keeping us here, so she'll continue un-illuminated.'

'I'm not dreaming,' said Ben. 'I'm awake. When you slapped me, it hurt.'

'Good,' sneered The Archivist.

'Thanks to the hold the Box has on you, this is now the only way we can contact you, and it is taking an immense amount of power. If it is able to grip you any tighter, even this path will be closed to us. I beg you to reconsider, before it is too late.'

'Can you make my mum better?'

The two angels looked at each other for a moment. The Archivist's lips formed themselves into a bitter smile. The Triumph shook his head.

'I can,' said Ben.

The Archivist sprang forward, placing his hand flat on Ben's chest, pushing him back into the mattress. 'Not only is the fate of one of my kind at stake, but that of the whole Creation as well. We should let you rot, little ape,' he screeched.

Ben's instinct was to wriggle, to try and free himself, but he found he could not. A stony cold feeling had spread through his body, and now every muscle was rigid, as if frozen solid. The Castellan of the Veil was whispering louder now, and Ben's vision began to blur, switching between one version of his room with The Archivist standing over him, and one without.

The Triumph grabbed The Archivist by the scruff of his neck and jerked him away from the bed like a naughty puppy. He roughly dumped him a few feet back, and gave him a cold stare. The Archivist hissed at him resentfully. 'You dare to admonish me in front of the primate, brother?'

'He was waking up. Let me handle this.'

The coldness had abated the second The Archivist had been pulled away, as if a great stone slab had been lifted from Ben's chest. He was still shivering from the attack, but tried to disguise it. 'If you want the Box so badly, come and get it. I won't try to stop you.'

'You know we can't,' said The Triumph.

'Then you'll just have to leave me alone.' He stubbornly closed his eyes, and tried to block out the constant whispering. He reached out to the music of the Box, and the score rose to greet him. Slowly it reasserted itself, and sleep crept back in. The Castellan of the Veil started speaking faster and faster, grabbing quick breaths in between long flurries of words. The very last thing he heard was The Triumph's voice, so close to his ear that he felt its vibrations bounce around his skull.

'When the time comes that you need us – and if you are lucky, it will – go to the Druids. They will not know what to do, but they will do it anyway. Trust in the Prime One, and He shall provide.'

Chapter Fourteen

Revelation

It had taken Ben a week of nagging to be allowed back to Drylands Hall, and so it was not until the Sunday before half-term that he was able to cycle down the coast to Abergele. It had not been easy to persuade his grandmother to let him go alone, and even once she'd given in she still insisted on calling ahead to ask Pat if she would keep an eye on him, and if there would be somewhere for him to put his bike, and if she would like a batch of muffins if she made some.

When Ben finally saw how much food he had to take with him, he was glad that Djinn wouldn't be around to get at it. Alongside the muffins his grandmother had baked cakes, prepared a flask of tea and made tons of sandwiches. The satchel was so full that the Box made a slightly muffled protest at being buried under the avalanche of food.

The weather that morning was poor, and his grandmother tried to use it as a last-ditch excuse to give him a lift in the car, but he was adamant. He suspected that if she drove him, then she would find an excuse to stay. He would be going on his own, on his bike, and he didn't care about the weather. Several layers of 'waterproof' clothing later, he was finally on his way.

The upstairs corridor at Drylands Hall was dimly lit, and smelt of antiseptic and despair. Pat trundled along in front of Ben, wobbling with each step. She had been waiting for him when he arrived, a stiff hospital regulation towel in hand, and had proceeded to attack his barely wet hair before showing him to a windowless room full of bits of old junk so that he could stow his bicycle. He wondered why she didn't just leave him alone, and took out his frustrations by flicking the V's behind her back as they walked along.

When they reached the door to his mum's room, Pat clapped her hands together.

'Here we are then, just in here,' she said, and gave the door three sharp, brisk knocks, like a policeman on a dawn raid. 'Are you decent, Marie Celeste? I've got a visitor for you.' Without waiting for a reply, she turned the handle.

Mary Rose was sat in an armchair facing the window, staring at the closed curtains. She was still wearing her nightie, and the unbelted white cotton dressing gown that was issued as standard to all the inmates of Drylands Hall.

'Ooh, it's dark in here, isn't it?' said Pat, shuffling over to the curtains and pulling them open. Mary Rose looked bewildered, and squinted as light fell into the room. She looked at Ben with glassy, unrecognizing eyes, and then turned back to the window.

'Sit yourself down, there's a good boy,' said Pat, indicating the end of the bed. The mattress was lumpy and thin, and Ben could feel the springs pressing into his buttocks. 'I don't know if you'll get much out of Marie Celeste today. She's been very quiet lately. I can stay if you'd like?'

'Thanks, we'll be OK,' said Ben dismissively.

'Well, you know where I am.' She hovered in the doorway. After a few moments of awkward silence, she cleared her throat.

'Didn't your granny say something about muffins?'

'Oh yeah. Here.' He pulled a blue freezer bag out of his satchel and held out his arm. He made no attempt to move, forcing Pat to waddle back into the room. It was like throwing a sedative-filled steak to a hungry guard dog. Once she had waddled off wheezing down the corridor, he was at last alone with his mum.

He couldn't think of anything to say.

He realized that in all the years he had been visiting, it was his grandmother who had done the talking. His tie, an old one of his grandfather's, was like a noose around his neck. He worked a finger into the knot to loosen it, but it didn't make him feel any better.

Awkwardly, he leaned over and gave her a peck on the cheek. He couldn't think of anything else to do. Her eyes darted towards him, half wary, half hopeful, before they went back to the window.

'Hello, Mum.'

She turned her head slowly back towards him. A smile of recognition – or remembrance – passed over her face. She stared at him, beaming. Ben laughed nervously.

'Let's see what Gran's packed for us, shall we?'

He hoisted his satchel on to his lap and started to pull carrier bags out. As a parcel of pre-cut cake appeared Mary Rose clapped her hands together in excitement.

'Benji!' she said. 'When did you get here?'

'I came in with Pat, Mum.'

'Ugh,' said Mary Rose, pulling a face, 'she's such a minion. Did she try and steal our biscuits?'

'We haven't got any biscuits, Mum. But Gran made us sandwiches.'

'Ooooooh. Let's have breakfast in bed.'

'It's nearly lunchtime.'

'Doesn't matter.' Mary Rose clambered on to the bed and sat

111

cross-legged on top of the sheets. She patted the space in front of her, and Ben slipped his shoes off and got on the bed.

'Good. No shoes in the temple. Very important. Can I have a sandwich?'

Ben prepared a paper plate and put it down in front of her. She grabbed for it, held it at eye level, and rotated it, examining every angle. Sniffing like a pig hunting for truffles, she peeked inside before slamming it shut. She threw the plate down in front of her, crossed her arms, and stuck her tongue out in disgust.

Ben laughed. It was like watching a five-year-old.

'I hate cheese and pickle,' she said, and Ben stopped laughing. All of a sudden, she was an adult again. 'I always hated them. I used to complain all the time, but Mum always forgot. I used to just eat the bread and butter at school. You can have mine, if you like.'

'No, thanks. I hate them too. I use the clingfilm to scrape the pickle off the cheese,' he said, and started to demonstrate.

'I'll tell you what,' said Mary Rose, 'why don't we just move straight on to the cake? I won't tell if you don't.'

And so they sat, eating slices of sponge cake, talking about the weather, and schoolwork, and the best kind of biscuits to go with tea. It was everything that he wanted a visit to be. It was everything he wanted his life to be, his mum, his normal mum, living with them, their normal life. He imagined this was what it was like for the other people at school when they went home. The Box played a beautiful trill to accompany this thought, and he was reminded of what he was there to do.

'Are you all right, Benji?' said Mary Rose.

Ben took a deep breath. 'Yes, Mum,' he said, and lightly placed his hand over hers. 'This is nice, isn't it, Mum? Us being like this?'

'Yes. It is. It's a shame the minions won't let you stay longer.'

'I know, Mum. But how would you like it if you came home to live with us?'

Mary Rose bit her lower lip. 'That would be nice too. But the minions won't let me leave either. Bastards.' She quickly clamped her hand over her mouth.

'It's OK, Mum. I know that word.'

'Oh,' she said, 'well, don't use it, will you?'

'I won't,' said Ben. 'Mum, I know how to get them to let you come home.'

Mary Rose's face became stern. 'Lie about the angels, you mean? I'm not stupid, Benji. I know that's what they want, but I won't do it. I know I'm supposed to lie, but I can't.'

'It wouldn't be a lie though.'

'You sound like a minion.' Her eyes darted around the room, avoiding his gaze.

'It's true, Mum. You're very sick. You never met any angels.'

'You weren't there. No one else was there. How could you know?' She seemed distressed, as if looking for an exit. She wrung her hands.

'Because I've met them. Real angels, Mum. And they told me that they haven't been to Earth for a very long time. You couldn't have met them. You're just sick.'

Mary Rose looked unsure for a moment. Then her brows furrowed. 'Don't let anyone here catch you saying that. That's the sort of the thing gets you locked away.'

'It's true, Mum. I met four angels, and now I can make you better. I can make it so you're allowed to come home.' He reached out and took both her hands. He squeezed them to reassure her, and to stop his from shaking. He tuned into the music of the Box and searched through the score until he found the strand he needed, and let it pulse through his veins. He looked his mother in the eye, and felt his hands ignite with the healing green flames.

'Fire,' whispered Mary Rose.

'It's OK, Mum. This is something the angels showed me.' It hurt to lie to his mother, but the Box was quick to wipe away any doubt. It was a lie, yes, but the whitest one of all. 'This is going to make you better.'

'No.' There were tears in her eyes. She tried to pull away, but he tightened his grip. 'I'm confused. You're confusing me,' she said. 'This is devilry. Stop.' She started to shout, over and over: 'Stop, stop, stop.'

Ben let go. Mary Rose recoiled. The Box played a new strain, one Ben had never heard before. It was bitter, and it rang through every bit of him. He wanted to scream at her, but she looked so vulnerable that instead he took a deep breath and let it out slowly.

'I can help you,' he said.

Mary Rose shook her head. 'I don't need help.' The rhythm seemed to reassure her, so she kept doing it. 'The angels wouldn't like this. I don't know what you're mixed up in, Benji, but you have to stop. It's witchcraft.'

Ben opened his hands wide. The music was getting impatient, and his heartbeat was like a restless foot tapping along to it. He swallowed hard, and moved cautiously closer.

'Touch me and I'll scream,' she said solemnly, her eyes defiant and purposeful. 'Saint Michael the Archangel, defend us in battle. Protect us from the snares and wickedness of the devil . . .'

Ben's head throbbed. The words were like midges nipping at him. He lunged forward, and his mother caught his wrists. She squeezed them so tightly that her nails dug into his tendons, all the while repeating her prayer.

A new wave of music hit him, dangerous and vindictive.

'It's all your fault,' he said. 'Everything is all your fault. Why do you have to be like this? All I ever wanted was to be normal, but I ended up with you, and it's not fair. It's just not fair.'

Mary Rose let go, and retreated up the bed to the headboard, tangled herself up in it as if squeezing through the bars could protect her. When Ben saw how scared she looked, his hands began to shake. Before he knew it, he was crying, and he felt like a small child again.

Mary Rose slowly released her grip and crawled over to him.

'Don't cry. Please. I'm sorry.'

'I wish I'd never been born,' he spat between sobs.

'Don't say that, Benji. It's not true.'

'It is true. And don't call me Benji. I'm not four years old any more.' Tears dropped on to the paper plate beneath him, soaking the discarded sandwiches. Mary Rose enveloped him in an embrace. With her warmth around him, the sobbing juddered to a halt, and he sat there, whimpering while she whispered in his ear.

'I'm sorry. I got scared. I get confused sometimes.' Tentatively, she stroked his hair, twisting a lock of it around her finger. 'Try again.'

Ben looked up at her. She was shivering.

'Really?'

She nodded. He stretched out his hands and clamped them firmly on her head. The green light throbbed through him and into her. She gasped as the Box powered into her brain, reprogramming and reconfiguring. She jerked beneath his touch, as if he were an electric chair.

'Oh, I remember,' she cried. 'Everything is so clear now. I have been confused for so long. It was the light, it hurt my head. It stopped me remembering. Oh. You have to be careful. They are false prophets, Benji. They see everything in shades of red. They don't want to stop it. They want to let it out.'

The words continued to stream out of her, making less and less sense as she went on. As the music of the Box became more vigorous, Mary Rose's voice dampened, barely audible. Ben felt the Box coursing through every part of him. It got so that he could not see the room, or his mother; not properly. There was a part of him that was there, and part of him that was elsewhere, somewhere inside the green fire. He started to feel detached from himself, and from the situation, but he didn't mind. He felt like he was part of the Box's plan, and he liked it.

He felt a stinging pain across his face, once, twice, three times. The Box made a horrible screeching sound, and suddenly he was back in the hospital. His mother was in front of him, her hand raised ready to slap him again.

'Wake up, Benji,' she screamed.

'I'm awake . . . Mum . . . I'm here.'

Pat burst through the door in the company of two orderlies. 'What is all this racket? Oh dear. Are we having one of those days, Marie Celeste?'

'No no no no no no,' said Mary Rose. 'No. Wait. I have something I have to say. It's about the angels. I remember now. Stay away from me. Stay away.'

The orderlies crept forward. Mary Rose retreated to the headboard, her arms extended, palms out.

'Get back. I'm warning you. This is important. You have to be careful, Ben. The angels. I remember.'

The orderlies pounced. Mary Rose lashed out, nearly hitting the bigger of the two men. The other brought her down on to the mattress and held her firm as she wriggled beneath him. 'The angels. There's something I have to tell you.'

Pat quickly put an arm around Ben to usher him out while the orderlies set to work. His mother managed a final yell of '. . . the angels, Benji, don't . . .' before her voice slurred into nothing and she was out cold.

'Are you all right, love?' said Pat.

'I don't . . . yes. Yes. I think so,' said Ben.

'You haven't had much luck, have you? Let's get your things and we'll have a nice slice of cake while we wait for your granny. You're not cycling anywhere this afternoon.'

Ben's grandparents were at Drylands Hall in less than ten minutes, which was still enough time for Pat to polish off two slices of the pre-cut cake. She needn't have rushed: once Annette arrived she happily bequeathed all the uneaten food to the staff.

Ben was drained. He said little in the car, answering in monosyllables if he answered at all. His insides felt shaky. He hadn't been able to cure his Mum. If anything, he'd made her worse. At home, his grandmother put her palm across his brow, declared that he had a fever, and sent him to bed early.

When he got upstairs, the first thing he did was fish out the Grand Druid's card. Lucy had said something about half-term, and sure enough there was a meeting the next day.

The druids will not know what to do, but they will do it anyway.

Tomorrow, he would put them to the test.

Chapter Fifteen

The Salutation of the Tide

Unsurprisingly, the weather the next day was horrible. If the North Wales climate could be relied on for anything it was ruining half-term holidays. In fact, if there were anything for which North Wales could be relied on, it was ruining half-term holidays. There are only so many visits to the RSPB Visitor Centre in Betws-y-Coed a boy can take.

Dark clouds hung heavy in the sky, black and full, billowing like they had risen out of some previously undiscovered Welsh volcano. As Ben cycled along the coast road, the wind blasting him with fine sea mist, the Box made no effort to hide its glee at the awful conditions. It mocked him, as if it were saying, 'Druids? What do you think those amateurs are going to be able to do? I can control the *weather*.'

He was surprised at how many people were in the Old School Youth Centre, and how varied they were in age and appearance. Both Tegwyn and the Grand Druid were cut from a similar kind of cloth, and it was a cloth with a nice pattern on it that spelled 'Lonely Single Men'. Ben had expected a very small group of what, if you were being nice, you would call 'enthusiasts', but counted over thirty people milling around, sipping hot drinks from styrofoam cups and nibbling Rich Tea Fingers, clearly the Druid biscuit of choice.

He scanned the room for Tegwyn and the Grand Druid, or

even Lucy, but could not see them anywhere. He poured himself an orange squash from the refreshments table and took a biscuit. At the far end of the room was a small wooden stage, not unlike the one they had at school. In front of it there was a circle of plastic chairs, which the druids were beginning to gravitate towards. Ben hung back, staying near the refreshments and the drying warmth of the antique iron radiators.

The little clock that hung above the stage struck eight, and a hush descended on the circle.

The Grand Druid stepped out from the wings to a smattering of applause. He was followed by Tegwyn, who held a rickety old cassette player in one hand and a bundle of silver spray-painted twigs in the other. A piece of vaguely Celtic-sounding music blared out of the stereo. Both were dressed in long white robes, and wore curious little crowns with diamond-like gems embedded in the front. Tegwyn looked ridiculous, like an extra milling about in the background of an old sci-fi show. The Grand Druid, however, wore it particularly well. Gone was the well-meaning nerd that Ben had encountered at the Broken Forge; here was a man who was, without question, the Grand Druid. Even if he was badly shaven.

He carried a large wooden staff covered with evergreens. Pieces of fern and mistletoe enveloped his fist, making it seem as if the sceptre was growing out of him. He raised the staff off the ground, then rapped it on the floor three times. The two men walked down the steps from the stage in perfect unison, the Grand Druid striking each step with his staff. They sat down simultaneously, to the beat of the music. Tegwyn pressed stop just after the song ended, and a brief snatch of the *Star Trek* theme played just before the tape cut out.

'Righty-o,' said the Grand Druid, 'the play scheme are in soon to start setting up, so let's get cracking, shall we? Had to twist a few arms to be let in this early so we can't hang about.' He surveyed the room as he spoke, making eye contact with individual parishioners. 'So, is everyone ready? Obviously the weather is a bit . . .'

He leaned over to Tegwyn and whispered something, pointing at Ben as he did.

'Benjamino! It's a big surprise to see you here. You're very welcome, but we have to insist you sit in the circle. Helps the flow of energy in the room. It's all very technical. But if you want to stay, you'll have to join us.'

Ben nodded, and made his way to one of the two spare seats. The circle settled, and the Grand Druid cleared his throat. His casual tone disappeared, replaced by an over-earnest recitation of something he had clearly said hundreds of times before: 'Forces of nature, flow through us. Let us celebrate the nearness of the Moon . . .'

Everyone closed their eyes. Ben wondered if this was what The Triumph meant, and, determined to assist in whatever it was the druids were going to do, tried to close his eyes. He found he could not keep them shut for long. The Box kept squirming away inside his head, making it hard for him to hear, forcing his eyes open.

'Lovely,' said the Grand Druid, suddenly switching back to his conversational tone. 'Right then, let's make our way down to the seafront for the Salutation of the Tide.' The druids started to get up from their seats. The Box played a sniggering arpeggio of detuned notes, and Ben cursed under his breath.

'You're so strange,' said a voice. Ben looked up, and saw Lucy standing over him.

'I meant that as a compliment,' she said. 'Strange is interesting. I didn't expect to see you here.'

Ben blushed. 'I didn't see you come in.'

'That's because you had your eyes closed. Most of the time, anyway. I overslept and my Dad took the car so I had to walk.'

'It's good you came, Benjamino,' said the Grand Druid, as he and Tegwyn approached. 'You don't want to be messing around with that dark druidism stuff, it's bad for your aura. What made you change your mind?'

Ben thought this was probably the only time he could get away with saying 'an angel told me to do it in a dream', but chose not to.

'I just did,' he said.

'Well, I guess reasons aren't important. Will you be joining us for the Salutation of the Tide?'

'What's that?'

'Oh, just a little ceremony to welcome the sea back. We'll take a quick stroll over to the beach and say hello. It's good for the soul, the feet making contact with the water.' He pointed down, and Ben saw he wasn't wearing any shoes.

'Are you going like that?' asked Ben.

'I have to, it's part of it.'

'What if it rains?'

'Nnnn. We'll get wet,' sneered Tegwyn.

'There's no need to fear nature, Benjamino,' said the Grand Druid. 'Water is our friend.'

Yeah, thought Ben, but you're talking to someone who can't swim. 'Can I still wear my coat?' he said.

'Whatever you like, Benjamino.'

'I have to get my bike. I cycled here.'

'Of course you did,' said Tegwyn, as if that was the most obvious and inconvenient thing he could have possibly done.

The walk to the seafront was more like a procession, the Grand Druid at its head. Ben felt a bit of a wally pushing his bike in the middle of it. Clearly the druids couldn't do anything to help: the Box was as strong as ever, mocking him as he trudged around in the rain, getting funny looks from the few foolhardy dog-walkers still out in the swiftly declining weather. He gradually allowed the rest of the group to pass him by until he was at the back of the line.

'So you're into dark druidism, are you?' said Lucy. She had dropped back too, and was now walking alongside him.

Ben scowled, and Lucy gave him a friendly shove. 'Don't be like that. I was only teasing. Why do they think you're in danger of being lost to black magic then?'

Ben sighed. 'I once bought a book about the Great Orme that the Grand Druid wrote. There was all this stuff in the paper about animal sacrifice up there and so now they think I've been trying to summon my rabbit that died.'

Lucy laughed. 'No wonder you nearly took my head off. I swear I didn't know. I wouldn't have brought it up if I had. '

'I'm sorry too. I wasn't myself.' The Box played a crunching, disapproving chord. 'I shouldn't have shouted at you.'

'Too right. But I reckon I can let it go, just this once. If you explain how those Warmonger mutiny trials work again.' She linked her arm through his. 'Tegwyn and Terry take this very seriously. Most of us aren't like that. This one bloke, Frank, just comes for the free Rich Tea Fingers. I hate Rich Tea Fingers. Anyway, point is, we accept everybody as they are. Even Teg, and he's an arse. That's what our thing is about. We're sort of separatist druids.'

She smiled as if she had made a joke, and Ben chuckled along nervously, having no idea what separatist druids were. 'Our focus is on the power of the moon,' she said. 'Did you know the moon is what makes the tide go in and out?'

'Yes,' Ben lied.

'OK, so if it has that effect on the ocean, and humans are ninety per cent water, and there are seven billion people on the planet, then it stands to reason that the moon affects everything we do, doesn't it?'

It didn't sound very scientific, but as Ben was slightly in danger of falling a little bit in love with Lucy, she could have argued in favour of rebuilding the Channel Tunnel out of toilet paper and he'd have agreed that it stood to reason.

By the time they drew to a halt at the seafront the tide was so high that it was spilling on to the esplanade, as if they were standing on the rim of a giant glass of water. It was so windy that it was impossible not to be sprayed by it, but the druids seemed pleased: they let off shrill cries of delight as they were soaked by both sea and sky.

Ben looked out over the water, feeling wet and stupid. The Box was doing musical somersaults in his head, which, coupled with the choppy movement of the tide, succeeded in making him feel slightly sick.

'Are you OK?' said Lucy.

'Um . . . yeah,' said Ben, his hand over his mouth, 'I just don't like the sea very much. I live in the wrong town.'

'Don't we all? I'll hold your hand. That'll make it better, won't it?' She did, and it did. The Box grumbled a little, and Ben still felt queasy, but it wasn't half as bad as before. 'It can be quite exhilarating if you let it. Are you ready to salute the tide?'

The real answer was 'no', but Ben nodded.

'Now,' said Lucy, 'you have to scream.'

All around them delighted druids called out to the raging elements. Beside him, Lucy was shouting out gloriously long vowel sounds and laughing. She shook his hand.

'Have a go,' she said. 'It's fun.'

Ben took a deep breath and let the sound out. The Box groaned, which made him yell all the louder. He felt completely in the moment, completely alive. He released all of his fear, anger, and frustration into the wind, cast it off out to sea.

Around them, the water level began to rise, and a little ebbing and flowing puddle surrounded their feet. Ben felt dizzy, but he did not stop calling. His eyes began to go funny, and a purple-blue colour bled into his peripheral vision. He shook his head to try to clear it, but it continued to spread. He looked to Lucy for help, but she was yelling intently at the sea. He tried to speak, but found he could not: he could only make the same inarticulate noise that all of the group were making. Panicking, he pulled at Lucy's arm. All around him, the volume was decreasing: the sound of the druids' voices, the music of the Box, even his own cries were becoming more and more distant. He blinked, in a vain attempt to arrest the spread of purple-blue.

His eyes were only shut for a split second, yet when he opened them everything had changed. It was twilight. The sky was a stunning colour; shades of purple, black and blue. The sea was calm, as still as he had ever seen it, and cleaner than it had been for many, many years. Towyn's murky green waters, home to so much tourist detritus, had been somehow filtered. The moon hung high in the sky, shining big and bright. He was alone, and it was quiet.

Three orange outlines appeared on the surface of the water. The Castellan of the Veil stood perfectly still, her head bowed, flanked on either side by The Triumph and The Archivist. Their footprints made tiny ripples in the sea as they walked towards him; little waves lapped at his feet.

'Thank you for coming, Ben-the-Just,' said The Triumph. 'Do you have the Box?'

'I don't know,' said Ben, taking his bag off his back. 'Where are we?'

'Towyn,' said The Triumph.

'It's a bit too nice to be Towyn.'

'We only have until those idiot druids stop their wailing,' snapped The Archivist. 'It would be better if you kept your facile observations to yourself.'

'Quiet,' said The Triumph. 'We are still in Towyn but we are inside the Veil now. This is the only way to enter the Box safely. Are you ready?'

Ben gulped. 'I think so.'

'Good,' said The Triumph. 'Put the Box on the floor and open the lid.'

Ben did as he was told. As the lid fell back a beam of bright green light shot out of it, high into the air, like a skyscraper.

'Step towards the light,' said The Triumph.

'If I do this, will everything be OK?'

'It will release the hold the Box has on you, and it will restore The Holy Seraph of the Strident Blasts. Step towards the light.'

Ben shielded his eyes and walked towards the beam. As he drew closer, his molecules started to shift, like grains of sand moving on the whims of the tide. He was being dismantled, bit by bit, and as he slipped into the Box, he had one last thought.

'Wait. How do we get back out?' he said, but it was too late. He had been sucked into the Box.

It was dark, and it was cold. He was in a cell. He did a little exploratory crawling, patting the floor around him with his hands. It was hard stone, a little slimy. The walls were much the same.

There was the faintest trace of light. A puny yellow flame, little more than a birthday candle, flickered somewhere in the darkness. Ben crept towards it, his eyes getting used to the gloom all the time. And then the flame spoke.

'I told you no good would come of all this sending-us-to-Hell business, but no one listens to me, do they?'

Chapter Sixteen

Inside the Box

Kartofel's flame-head had burned down to barely a flicker, and the light he gave out, once capable of lighting up Ben's entire bedroom, barely illuminated the gloomy cell at all.

'You look terrible,' said Ben.

'Thanks,' said Kartofel. 'I've been chained to a wall for the last few months so I haven't been able to keep up with my beauty regime.' He tried to lift himself up, but his little talon-legs buckled under the weight of the heavy stone chain that was bolting him to the wall.

'You've been here three weeks tops,' said Ben.

'Time's different in the Box. Why do you think we want to be out all the time?'

'Where are the others?'

Kartofel chuckled. 'Now that is the only good part of this whole situation.'

A sobbing sound came from a nearby wall, two pathetic gasps.

'On the left there is what's left of Fatso. Cries himself to sleep sometimes, but mostly doesn't say a thing. Too much effort. It's brilliant.'

'I can't see him.'

'There's not much to see any more.'

'Ben?' said Djinn. His voice was reedy and thin, and took him some effort to produce. Ben crouched down next to Kartofel, and taking hold of his collar, pushed up through his legs, like he'd seen weightlifters do.

'Oi! Put me down, you cheeky—' said Kartofel, his legs wriggling in mid-air. The chain was short, and Ben was only able to shift the demon slightly, but it was enough for a little of his light to be cast on Djinn.

The difference in Djinn's appearance was drastic; he was almost completely clear, and he had lost a lot of his bulk; he looked like he had melted, his rolls of gas-fat replaced by sagging flaps of gas-skin. He squinted at the light, his eyes more used to darkness. 'H-h-have you got any food? Jus' need a whiff of something to keep me going.' He let out another pair of sobs.

'I don't,' said Ben, 'but once we're out of here, we'll go to the market. You'd like that, wouldn't you?'

'Y-y-yes,' said Djinn, with a feeble half-smile.

'Good. Where's Orff?'

'The other wall.' Djinn tried to raise his arm to point across the room. He grimaced as he did, then dropped it in exhausted defeat before it was barely off the floor.

Ben shifted Kartofel over, and found Orff crumpled in the opposite corner. He had always been thin, but now his translucent skin was stretched tight over his brittle skeleton.

'Orff?'

At the sound of Ben's voice, the demon looked up. His deep black eyes were dull and unreflective. He did not react to the light, and his head tilted as if he was trying to discover where the voice was coming from.

'He's blind,' said Ben. 'Can you hear me?'

Orff moved his beak open and shut, but no sound came out bar the clicking together of his mandibles.

'He's mute as well,' said Kartofel, 'so it's not without its benefits, this whole stuck-in-a-dungeon thing.'

'I've got to get you out of here,' said Ben. 'Have you seen The Seraph?'

'No. Should I have done?'

'He got trapped here after the demon attacked us on the Orme. I'm here to get everyone out.'

Kartofel scowled. 'Well, I reckon its fairly obvious he's not here, what with him not crying in the corner after me rearranging his face, but if you're here to get us out, you can start with this chain.'

'How?'

'I dunno. Have a look.'

The three stone links grew out of the back of the collar and into the wall. There were no lines where sections met, no cement marks. The only way it could have been possible was if the collar, the wall, and the chain had once been part of the same block, and had been carved specifically for the purpose. Ben lifted one of the links as high as he could, and let it go. It made a noise that echoed round the cell, but remained undamaged.

'I don't know if I can get it high enough to smash it,' said Ben through gritted teeth. 'It's really . . .'

'Aye, aye,' interrupted Kartofel. 'Watch out, here comes the light.'

Ben dropped the link. Poking up through a trapdoor in the floor was a green glow. It lit up the cell for the first time, revealing that the only wall that did not have a demon chained to it was in fact a massive door. It was made of the same bright red wood as the Box, and had the same four symbols carved into it. But it did not hold Ben's attention for long. As the light rose up through the floor, the shards combined to form a huge ball. Ben stared at it, enraptured. It was like being able to look into the sun without hurting your eyes; he could see the intricate details of the burning beauty of the orb, the minute nuclear reactions on its surface. Its light warmed the room, and he felt full of love, and possibility, and confidence. He could hear Kartofel trying to drag the chain away from the light, but could not turn to look.

'Oh,' he said, 'it's wonderful. You've got to see this. It's so . . . it's just . . . wow.' He had never felt anything like it. It was so positive, so inspiring that he wanted to be inside it forever. It was the smell of fresh bread, Christmas mornings, new Warmonger models. It was everything that had ever happened to him that was good.

And then it passed.

The light sank back into the trapdoor, spreading out into the cement between the flagstones. As it passed, it took with it all of the good feeling it had brought, and more besides. Ben sank to his knees, and crawled over to the trapdoor, hoping to find some residual warmth there, but the old wood and the round steel handle were icy cold.

'Oh, what's the point?' he said.

Kartofel crept slowly out from behind one of the links, which he had been using as a makeshift shield. 'Watch it, that's the light talking, that is. That's what it does. It shines, goes, and you feel rubbish.'

Ben clawed at the trapdoor. He was prepared to pull at it until his fingers were sore, if that was what it took to feel the warmth again.

'D-d-don't do it, Ben,' said Djinn. 'Down there's the Darkness.'

Ben took hold of the handle, and tugged it open. It was a strain – the door was heavy and the hinges stiff – but he succeeded in opening it. It made a loud thwomping noise as it hit the stone.

He pulled himself over to the gap, and poked his head through it.

'You don't wanna go in the Darkness,' said Kartofel. 'There's nothing there. It's just black.'

'Where else can I go?' Ben shouted. 'This is hopeless.' He rolled on to his back, and ran his hands through his hair, pulling at it. He wanted to cry, but even that seemed like a waste of time.

'It's just the light. It'll pass,' said Kartofel. 'Get over it.'

Ben lay in the dark, staring up at the ceiling. All the rubbish of the past five weeks – of the past fifteen years – played over and over in his head. He started to groan, a world-weary lament from the bottom of his soul that went on for several minutes.

'So what do you think of our pad?' said Kartofel in a gap between moans.

'Cold and depressing,' said Ben.

'Fair dos. Can't say I like it much either.'

'How do you get out? When you're not chained to the wall?'

'We open the lid, dummy. The big wooden wall.'

Ben got to his feet, and stumbled over to it. He lay against it, pressing his shoulder into the wood while he pushed with his feet. It held firm.

'It's locked.'

'Course it's locked,' said Kartofel. 'There's no music. Must be the angel. That's what happens when he's mucking about with it. No music, no exit.'

Ben slid down the wall until he was sat with his back against it. Little by little, the negative thoughts were fading away, and he started to feel less helpless.

'There's only one thing for it,' he said. 'I'm going down the hatch. The Seraph isn't here, we can't open the lid, so there's only one place left.'

'N-n-no!' said Djinn, 'N-n-no one ever returns from the Darkness.'

'How do you know?' said Ben. 'Has anyone ever gone down there?'

'Are you mental?' said Kartofel. 'It's the frickin' Darkness.'

'Right then,' said Ben. 'Here goes.'

He stared down into the Darkness. It was aptly named.

'Tch, I hope you're not going in there before you've let us out,' said Kartofel.

'I'll be back,' said Ben. He sat on the edge of the pit, his legs dangling down into the void. He closed his eyes and shuffled forward into the pitch-black hole below.

He did not fall very far, and soon felt the shock of impact as he landed on another stone floor. He opened his eyes, and then he closed them. And then he opened them again, just to be sure. It was so dark that there was no difference between the two. He started to grope around, exploring his surroundings.

'B-B-Ben?' said Djinn from above his head.

He looked up, and could just make out a small, slightly less black square in the ceiling. He reached up to touch it, and found that if he stood on his tiptoes he could grab the ledge.

'It's OK,' he said. 'I'm all right. I'm going to find The Seraph.'

'Bet you wish you had me with you now, you git!' yelled Kartofel.

With his arms out in front of him, Ben edged forward. The walls were covered in wooden panels, the same familiar texture as the Box. Wherever he was, it was narrow. He began to edge his way along, shuffling through the passage, hands pressed up against the walls as he made his way into the Darkness.

Chapter Seventeen

Into the Darkness

He did not know how long he spent walking around. He could not remember how far he had come, or how long it was since he had dropped through the hatch. It seemed like a long time. All he knew was that a moment ago he was groping along the corridor in the dark, just like the moment before that and the moment before that.

His arms and legs started to grow heavy, and he became tired of walking. His feet ached. The corridor was endless. He plodded on, feeling no variation in the wood as he stumbled along.

And then he saw it. It was a speck at first, the proverbial light at the end of the tunnel. He willed himself onward, his limbs doing their best to move as quickly as he commanded them. As he approached the light, he started to feel a little warmer, a little more hopeful. He stopped and blinked at it a few times, but the light did not stop: it kept growing as it moved towards him. He realized that it was the green light, and even as he felt it shine on him, he was aware that it could take its love away as easily as it gave it out. The thought of being stuck in the Darkness and feeling that wretched terrified him.

The light was soon strong enough to illuminate the corridor. Ben's eyes whizzed around the passage, taking in as much as he could. He saw that he had not long passed another trapdoor in the ceiling. His thoughts were like lightning: the closer the light got, the clearer he was able to think. It was no wonder that he had not found a way out of the Darkness if the exits were all up there.

He turned and ran for the gap in the ceiling. He leaped up to it, like a basketball player, and was amazed by his own athleticism. He took hold of the ledge, and pulled him himself up, popping his head into a murky grey room lit by a single candle flame.

'That was quick,' said the flame. 'Did you find the winged wally?'

Ben dropped down. He could not believe that for all the time he had spent in the dark, he had travelled so short a distance. But he could not afford to dwell on it. The green ball was still shining its way towards him, but now it was much closer. Ben ran in the opposite direction, feeling its heat on his back as he went. The radiation was feeding him, making him run faster, his confidence growing as he tore down the corridor, not daring to look back. The hotter it got, the closer it was; the closer it got, the more he believed he could outrun it.

He saw the thick oaken door too late. As each long stride brought him closer, and his stopping distance got shorter, all he could do was bring his arms up in front of his face as he hurtled into it.

To his surprise, it swung open easily, and he fell through into a large octagonal chamber with a high domed ceiling. It was lit by hundreds of candles, sitting in iron chandeliers suspended from the roof. It looked and smelt like a cathedral. He pulled up abruptly, skidding along the thick burgundy carpet as he did.

And then the light hit him at full speed.

It was the best thing that had ever happened to him. It was the best thing that had ever happened. He felt life in every part of him, in every muscle. Body and mind erupted in happiness, and positivity, and health.

And when it was gone, when the full force of the light had torn through him and moved on, then came the crash. He felt utterly alone, and all he could do was lie on the floor and wait to grow old and die.

He heard his name being called, but he felt so pathetic that he was ashamed to answer. Nevertheless, the voice continued, insistent. He managed to summon the strength from somewhere to press his palms against his ears but it didn't work very well. He wished he hadn't bothered.

'What?' he yelled. 'What do you want?'

'Ben, you must rise. Time is short.'

He thought he recognized the voice, but still didn't want to get up. He pressed his hands harder into his ears, and still he heard it: 'Ben. Ben. Ben.'

At last, the speaker got the message, and stopped. Ben breathed out, and took his hands away. As soon as he did, the voice began to sing 'Abide With Me'. Ben recognized it as another dusty old hymn from school, to be endured or ignored. It had never meant anything to him.

Until now.

The voice was so clear and beautiful that he felt full up with it. Energized, he pulled himself up off the floor, and scanned the room for the source of the voice.

'Ben,' it said. 'I am in here.' Like the dark corridor, the walls in the new room were covered in deep red wooden panels. The carpet was more like a rug, and was cut into a neat octagon in the centre of the room, an island surrounded by a moat of varnished floorboards. He could see a door in the far wall. It was small – Ben would need to duck to pass through it – with a wooden handle and a tiny letterbox window in the centre of it.

'Ben, please. We are running out of time.'

He ran towards the door and peered in through the slit. The Seraph was standing in the middle of a small room, his clothes torn, his wings in tatters.

'Open the door,' said The Seraph. 'Quickly. I am weak.'

Ben pushed hard, but it would not budge. He threw his full weight behind it, jumping at it, trying to break it down, without success.

'How do I open it?' he called out in frustration.

'Pull?' said The Seraph. Ben did so, and the door swung open easily. The floor inside was stone, but the walls and ceiling were all covered in the same wooden panelling as everywhere else.

The Seraph's face was bisected by a huge scar which ran from the back of his head, down between his eyes, and through his nose. His robes were torn open at the chest, and he was covered in claw marks. Ben threw his arms around him. The angel winced, and recoiled from the embrace. As he pulled away, embarrassed, Ben saw that The Seraph was carrying a more serious injury: what had once been his hand was now more like a paw, the fingers dissolved almost to the knuckle.

'What happened?'

'It is the wood. I cannot touch the wood. It is like the Box itself,' said The Seraph. 'I tried to open the door, and this happened. How long have I been here, in Worldly time?'

'About a month.'

'So short a time? I was afraid we had missed our chance.'

'Time is a bit funny in here, I think,' said Ben. 'I was wandering around for hours and I only moved a few steps.'

'Then we have no time to lose. I will need you to lead the way.'

Ben gulped. 'I don't know if I can. It's very dark in there.'

'I will take care of that,' said the angel, and his aura throbbed, like a light bulb warming up. 'Lead on.'

Ben stooped out of the open doorway, making sure to hold the door for The Seraph, who roared in pain as he passed through; his wings could not help but brush the frame. Once he had crossed the stone threshold, he was faced with another challenge: a wide stretch of red wooden floor between him and the carpet. He extended his wings as best he could, and hopped into the air. It was like watching a duckling learning to fly; he lacked the strength to make anything other than an extended jump. He landed in a squat at the edge of the carpet, and had to take a moment before he could stand. Ben instinctively went to help, but was waved away with a flick of the angel's withered hand.

'We must continue,' said The Seraph. 'Show me the door.'

A splash of liquid hit Ben's head. He looked up, and a few further drops hit his face. 'I think it's starting to rain,' he said as he wiped the water away. He held it out for The Seraph to see.

'Indeed,' said The Seraph. 'I assume that it was some kind of ritual that brought you here?'

'The druids. They were saluting the tide.'

'Very well. Things are about to get very wet.' As if on cue, water began to run down from the centre of the ceiling, like a tap had been turned on. 'Run to the door and hold it open. I will leap across as best I can.'

Ben nodded. There was a sudden roar, and murky green water began to cascade into the chamber, stinking of salt and sewage. In no time at all it was at knee height, and rising quickly. Ben waded through the water, and pulled the door open. The Seraph ran, and jump-flew into a roll as he dived over the wooden floor and into the Darkness. Ben dashed in after him, and slammed the door.

'What now?'

'We run,' said The Seraph. 'Where is the exit?'

'There's a hatch in the ceiling somewhere up ahead.'

'I will look out for it.' The Seraph started to run, his wings scraping against the wood panelling as he went: if it hurt, he did not show it. He did not stop. The only indication that it was affecting him at all were the floating embers of burned feathers that sprayed out behind him as he ran.

They heard a creaking sound from deep in the bowels of the blackness. It reverberated around the halls, chasing after them. The door to the octagonal chamber was getting ready to burst.

'How much further?' said The Seraph.

'I don't know,' said Ben, 'look for Kartofel's light.'

'I think I see it.'

Ben craned his head over the angel's wings, looking for the small grey square in the ceiling. The Seraph suddenly stopped, and Ben crashed into his back. It was like running into a wall: The Seraph did not move, and Ben bounced backwards.

'It is not the light we are looking for,' said The Seraph. 'It is the light of the Box, look!'

The speck had appeared on the horizon, and was shooting towards them at a tremendous pace, seemingly growing in size as it did.

'We can still reach the hatch in time,' said Ben. 'Let's go!'

The Seraph turned, and Ben saw genuine terror in his face. 'That light is the Box in its purest form. It will erase me from the Creation.'

Behind them, the creaking sound became a belch as the door splintered and vomited out torrents of water. It rushed towards them, splashing up the sides of the corridor.

'We need to go now,' yelled Ben. 'If we don't the water will push . . .'

The Seraph snatched Ben up before he could finish his sentence. He ran a few paces before diving forward, unfurling his wings as best he could. He soared towards the light, yelling out in the celestial tongue. He banked to one side, so as to avoid brushing his wings.

'There it is!' said Ben, pointing up to the square in the ceiling. The Seraph thrust Ben forward with his good arm, and he clung to the ledge, his chin resting on his folded arms as he tried to pull himself up.

'About time,' said Kartofel. 'Can we go home now?'

Ben felt the press of wings on his back. The Seraph was also dangling from the ledge. The water rushed past them, rocking them both. Ben kicked his legs, trying to find purchase to hoist himself up. His feet were starting to get warm as the green light approached: his body tingled.

'Help me,' said Ben.

'What do you want me to do? I'm chained to the wall, remember?' said Kartofel.

Ben gasped. 'I can't get up,' he called to The Seraph, but there was no reply. The angel was being overwhelmed; Ben was his only shield from the light, and the water was pushing them closer all the time. If they were to hit it, it would not be long before Ben would feel hopeless, and in all likelihood drop off the ledge into the dark water to be swept away into the bowels of the Box forever.

But first he felt a rush of positivity. The light was making him more determined, and he reached out for anything he could use to pull himself up. He pawed blindly at the floor, the water beneath drenching him, threatening to pull him away at any moment.

His hand found bone. Orff had managed to slump himself along the floor so that he was lying flat, and had kicked his legs out towards the trapdoor. Ben grabbed Orff's ankle with both hands and pulled himself up. The demon's beak groaned open in mute agony, but he did not withdraw the leg, or kick: he kept it tense, allowing Ben to scramble up through the hole in the floor.

He should have been terrified, but he had no time for that. He took hold of The Seraph's good arm and hauled him up through the gap. He heard the sound of bones cracking as the angel's wings met the resistance of the stone floor.

'We have to get out,' gasped The Seraph.

'The demons are chained,' said Ben.

'Why should that matter?' said The Seraph. 'Let us open the lid and make our escape.'

'We can't leave them here.'

'You want to free them?'

'I promised. We have to help them.'

'Very well.' The Seraph took hold of Kartofel's bonds, and dashed them against the floor, exploding the stone into fine powder. A few swift movements later, and Orff and Djinn were also free.

'Now for the lid,' said The Seraph. Together they ran at the wood, shoulder charging it. It did not move.

'It's no good,' said Kartofel, 'I told you: no music, no exit.'

Water had started bubbling up through the hatch. It was being lit from below, so that it resembled a city fountain at night. The green orb rose whole through the gap, racing to beat the water into the room. Frantic, Ben slammed himself into the lid again and again. The light expanded, steadily growing to fill the little cell.

'It's pointless,' said Kartofel.

Ben ignored him. He knew the water would soon be too high for him to keep his feet on the floor. He looked to The Seraph for help, but the angel was busy cowering from the light, laying his back flat against the wall, trying to make himself as thin as possible to avoid its reach.

'It is The Castellan of the Veil,' said The Seraph. 'There will be no music as long as she is at work. I fear we are undone.'

The ball had grown large enough to absorb the demons, sending them into spasms of delight. Ben was desperate. He looked from them to The Seraph, and an idea popped into his head. He waded over to the light as fast as he could, and let it touch his skin. Love and hope seared through him. He felt invincible. He did not want to leave the orb, but he knew what he had to do. He broke free, and splashed back over to the lid. He no longer felt invincible, but with the warming light on his back and the strength of the orb still throbbing through his muscles he pressed hard.

The lid creaked, and opened just a crack. A loud grinding sound, an irregular metallic rhythm, started up in the air. A deep bass pulse shook the room.

'It's working,' said The Seraph. 'The Castellan of the Veil will not be able to hold on for much longer. Keep going.'

Ben pushed harder, and felt the lid give a little more. His arms were on fire with the strain. The strength the light gave him began to ebb away, but as it did the music of the Box fell into a more stable rhythm. No melody was discernible, only the heavy vibrations of the rumbling bass; it was more like a great machine whirring away than actual music.

He gave the lid one last push, roaring out a mighty cry of

effort. He was drained. The power of the light deserted him, but the despair did not have chance to take hold. The lid gave way, and he fell forward, flushed through the opening by the raging water. The five of them found themselves tossed on the waves as the cell fell away. Round and round they spun, as if they were in a giant bath and the plug had just been pulled.

The next thing Ben knew, he was lying face down on the twilit beach, his lips touching gloopy wet sand. The tide was rapidly coming in, soaking his trousers and the hem of his anorak. As he staggered up, he noticed the Box was floating in the wash at his feet, nipping at his ankles as the incoming waves tossed it around. He picked it up.

'Thank you, Ben-the-Just. Today you have earned that name.' The Triumph stood at the head of the Cult of the Four Winds, his huge feet firmly planted on the surface of the water. The sea was much rougher, particularly at the feet of The Castellan of the Veil, who was whispering rapidly.

'Even if you did take your time,' said The Archivist.

'Everything is still possible because of Ben,' snapped The Seraph. 'You will show him respect.'

The Archivist hissed in disgust.

On the horizon, Ben could see that dawn was breaking quickly. The sun was rising like a balloon before his eyes, floating towards mid-morning. Everything was changing. The sea became turbulent, and dark clouds filled the sky. He tried to focus on the angels before him, but he could not make them out properly. His vision became blurred as the blue-and-purple colours of dusk receded, and the hues of the everyday world bled into view.

'What's happening?'

'The Veil is shifting. Your world is seeping back in,' said The Triumph.

Ben's eyes were fixed on the changing landscape: the water became dirtier, and more ferocious. It was raining heavily, and he could hear screams from somewhere.

'You will see us one more time, Ben Robson,' said The Seraph. 'Once more, and all this will be over. Once I have recovered, we will return. You will not need to wait long. And one more thing . . .'

Ben could no longer see the angels at all. The World was crashing in on him: real Towyn was taking the place of its Veil counterpart. He heard one more word before it kicked in completely.

'Run.'

Chapter Eighteen

Requiem

'Run!'

All Ben's senses kicked back in at once. He was cold, and wet, and there was something yanking his arm.

'Run! Ben, run! Come on!'

He was back in the real Towyn, on the seafront, and it was Lucy who was pulling him. The storm had broken. The volcanic clouds had erupted, and the wind was vigorous, and savage: it was an effort not to be thrown backwards, and simply standing was taking all his strength.

There was a flurry of hair and wobbly berobed flesh as panicking druids fled from the water's edge. Waves crashed into Ben's legs, and then retreated, ready to reach ever higher up his body on the next pass.

He was having difficulty processing what was going on. The wind tried to blow him one way, while Lucy frantically pulled him another. He lost his footing, and toppled backwards into the water, but Lucy refused to let go.

'Come on, Ben,' she said. There was fear and determination in her voice, and Ben could see why. A huge wave was building up before them, rolling high above their heads.

'I can't swim,' said Ben. All of the bravery he had found in the Box was gone. Lucy yanked him up off the floor like he was a naughty toddler, and he landed back on his feet.

The owner of a nearby restaurant stood beside her front door, beckoning the beleaguered druids inside. If she was afraid of what the sea was about to do to her livelihood, she did not show it: she stood resolute, barking orders at the incoming deluge of damp pagans.

Ben and Lucy raced inside. The door was slammed shut behind them, and seconds later the wave impacted. Water gushed through into the reception, and the woman herded them upstairs into a large function room.

Ben squelched down in the far corner, exhausted. He dropped his satchel and the demons dragged themselves out. Djinn floated aimlessly round the room, croaking out the word 'food' until his nose caught the whiff of something and he wafted over to the stairs. Kartofel and Orff both seemed to lack the energy to move, and sat quietly on the floor. Orff managed to gasp a few words about West Nile Fever, but that was all. He did not mention his ankle, which now had a large fist-shaped bruise on it where Ben had grabbed him.

The druids congregated in the middle of the room, unashamedly taking off bits of clothing and putting them on radiators. Ben had never seen so many people in underwear. He didn't know where to look.

'You need to dry out,' said Lucy. She was wearing a dressing gown, and her hair was damp. 'I grabbed you a bathrobe and a towel before they all got taken. Mrs Curry, the lady who runs this place, has given us as much as she can spare. You'll have to pass it on to someone else once your clothes are dry, but I thought it'd be nicer to have a fresh one.'

'Nnnn, how come you got a dressing gown, you little turd?' said Tegwyn, skulking over to them. 'I'm the treasurer of the Guild of North Wales Pagans, Rhyl and Towyn Branch. You're not even a druid.'

'Mrs Curry gave it to me,' said Lucy. 'She specifically said it was for Ben, since he'd fallen in the water and he was the wettest. If you don't like it, you can take it up with her.' Lucy pointed over to the woman, who was overseeing the evacuation of a large television set from the bar downstairs. She wore every one of her twenty-five years in the pub trade: they had covered her in enough tattoos to intimidate whole rugby teams. Tegwyn took one look at her and skulked off.

'I think he's upset because the sea gave him his bath a few months early,' whispered Lucy, and Ben laughed. 'When you've changed, come and sit with me, OK? I'll introduce you to some of the others. Dave's going to lead a singing session later, they're sometimes fun. Promise, OK?'

Ben nodded.

'You should probably try and call home while the phone lines are still up. Looks like we're going to be here for a while.'

As she went, the Box played faintly on in his head, half-hearted, as if it knew it had been beaten.

It was evening before he saw the demons again, having spent the afternoon with Lucy and the druids. At first he had kept quiet, but Lucy had kept encouraging him to join in, and by the time evening came he was enjoying himself so much that he was secretly disappointed when the fading light forced them to bed.

When he got back to the corner, he found his clothes – which he had left sodden on the back of a chair – completely dry and neatly folded in a pile. They were sat on top of a blanket that had not been there when he left.

'Me and ol' Creaky liberated that from Tegwyn for you. He was stockpiling all the best blankets so we waited until the caterwauling started and got you one,' said Kartofel. His flame was burning brighter than ever, and it lit the dark corner up enough for Ben to be able to see that Djinn and Orff were also looking like their old selves. 'Managed to dry your clothes as well, now that I'm firing on all cylinders again.'

'I folded them,' said Orff. 'Despite my rheumatism.'

'Have you been waiting over here all this time? On your own?' said Ben.

'Yeah, so? We're big boys, you know,' said Kartofel. 'We don't need you to amuse ourselves.'

'What Kartofel is trying to say,' said Orff, 'is that we saw you were having such an enjoyable time that we thought we would leave you to it.' The shine had returned to his eyes, and he was no longer blind, though he did mutter. 'Don't you worry about the cataracts I'm probably developing as we speak.'

'Ben! You should see the kitchen! It's massive!' said Djinn, who had turned the colour of dirty sea water. 'And there's all this food, and its all ruined anyway, so it doesn't matter if I ruin it! It smells a bit salty though. But that's fine. I like salt.'

'It's absolutely wrecked down there,' said Kartofel. 'It's amazing. I saw a shark.'

'There aren't any sharks in Towyn,' said Ben.

'I didn't say it was a real shark. It came off the wall, and now it's floating in the middle of the bar. I pulled it under the water and paddled around a bit. You should have seen Fatso's face.'

'I'm glad you're all feeling better,' said Ben, and he was surprised to realize that he meant it. 'Thanks for the blanket. And my clothes.' He hunkered down on the floor, and pulled the blanket around him. He lay his head down, and yawned. 'I'll see you all tomorrow, OK?'

'Goodnight, Ben,' said Djinn.

'Goodnight, Djinn.'

'Goodnight,' said Orff.

'G'night.'

'Don't have any really graphic nightmares about drowning or anything,' said Kartofel.

Orff coughed.

'Tch. I mean "goodnight",' said Kartofel.

Ben did not reply. He was already fast asleep.

It was days before they were finally evacuated, and they were among the best of Ben's life. The druids were all very strange, but they were also a lot of fun, and Ben loved being in their company. He got closer to Lucy, too, who told him all about their brand of druidism, and asked him loads more questions about Warmonger. He even started to enjoy the demons' antics. Particularly when they teamed up to annoy Tegwyn.

When they finally left, it was through the window rather than the front door, winched down to a waiting lifeboat to be taken to a community centre on the dry side of town. On the way there they got to see the extent of the flooding. There were more boats on the streets than cars, and most houses they passed were abandoned. The only other people they saw were journalists, who had swarmed into the area like mosquitoes. They were even filmed as they docked at the community centre.

Ben's grandparents were waiting for them. Ben leaped out of the boat, excited to introduce them to his new friend, his first one ever. But as he ran towards them, he did not get the welcome he expected. They both looked tired, and sombre, and his grandmother looked so much older than she had on Sunday night. They must have been so worried, he thought, and started to feel a little guilty for all the fun he'd been having. He bounded up to his grandmother and wrapped his arms around her.

She started to sob. She seemed so frail that he relaxed his grip a little. He looked to his grandad, who stepped in to separate them.

'We need to go inside, Ben,' he said. 'We've got some bad news.'

As he was led away from the main hall and into a small side office, the Box played an insidious, spidery little tune.

In the end it was his grandad who told him. Every time his grandmother tried, the tears would start and the words would stop. When he had finished, his grandad sat back in the overused plastic chair, his arms dangling down by his sides like a boxer between rounds in a fight he knows he has already lost.

Ben sat perfectly still, staring at his grandparents. They were on one side of the desk, he on the other.

Nobody spoke.

Maybe if nobody spoke, it wouldn't be true.

His grandmother began to sob again, and in her grief shuffled round the desk on her knees. She pawed at his hair, and tried to wrap his head in her arms. Ben knew he was supposed to be feeling something other than embarrassment, but nothing came.

'I want to be on my own, Gran.' The words tumbled out of his mouth.

She stopped snivelling. 'Pardon?'

'I need to be on my own.'

She buried her head in his shoulder, weeping. His grandad rose, gently draped his arms around her, and ushered her out of the room.

It still hadn't sunk in. He heard the lid of the Box swing open, and Orff popped his head out of the satchel, blinking at the new surroundings.

'I think I might have malaria.'

Ben could not make sense of what his grandad had told him, could not understand how it could be right. He shook his head.

'Ben?' said Orff. The lid opened again, and Kartofel and Djinn burst out.

'What's going on?' said Djinn. 'Is Ben OK?'

'I don't know,' said Orff.

'Perhaps he's been possessed or something,' said Kartofel. 'We've not had any weird stuff happen to us for a few days, so we're probably due.'

There was a timid knock at the door, and when Ben did not answer it was followed by a meek turn of the handle. It inched open, and Lucy stuck her head through.

'I wondered where you were hiding,' she said. 'Someone said they saw you come in here. When am I going to meet your gran then?'

Ben slowly turned his head to face her. A little half-sob escaped his throat.

'What is it?' she said, pulling a chair round to his side of the table. 'Is something the matter?'

'It's my mum,' he said. He opened and closed his mouth, struggling to find the words, not quite believing them himself. 'She's gone. She died. On Tuesday night.'

The noise he made next was barely human, dredged up from

deep inside him. It continued even as Lucy put her arm round him and drew him close.

The funeral was held at the end of March, delayed by both the floods and the inquest. Ben's grandmother had insisted on a Catholic burial, with accompanying Mass, because 'it was what Mary Rose would have wanted'.

The huge church was cold and draughty, lacking as it was in congregation: the funeral party consisted of Ben, his grandparents, Lucy, and Pat. Ben's grandmother held his hand tightly throughout, sometimes squeezing so hard that it hurt his fingers. As the decrepit Irish priest mumbled his way through the service, Lucy leaned forward and placed a reassuring hand on his shoulder.

They were met at the church door by the demons, who were lined up to form a guard of honour. Djinn and Orff had their heads bowed, and Kartofel – who lacked the necessary joints to bow – had toned his flame down for the occasion. Ben felt a lump form in his throat at the sight of them.

There was no wake, much to Pat's disappointment. She had made a great show of how upset she was, complete with handkerchief eye-dabbing, and kept saying what a beautiful and fitting service it had been (the only word of it Ben had understood was 'Amen'). It was only after the third or fourth 'thanks for coming' that she got the message and flounced off, disappointed that there would be no cake.

The cemetery was quiet. They were the only living souls there.

The demons were present at the graveside, but they did not cause trouble. They observed the silences, and they paid their respects, just like the rest of the family. As the coffin was lowered into the grave, it struck Ben that for better or worse that is what they were. Family.

As they walked back to the car, Ben noticed that they were no longer alone. A veiled woman, dressed entirely in black, was kneeling at a moss-covered memorial. They walked past in silence, her whispered prayers the only sound.

Ben stopped. She was speaking a language both completely familiar and utterly alien to him. The language of the angels. He turned to look, and as he did the woman rose from the gravestone and walked away.

'I think I need a moment on my own before we go,' he said.

Ben's grandmother looked to his grandad, and then nodded. Lucy stepped forward, and took his hand.

'Take your time,' she said.

'I will. Thanks for coming. I didn't have anyone else to ask and—'

Lucy put a finger to his lips. 'That's what friends are for. We'll see you back at the car.'

Ben waited until they were far enough away, and then headed after the woman.

'Where are we going?' said Djinn.

'That woman,' said Ben. 'She was speaking the angel language.'

'Oh well, let's follow her, then. Following angels has worked really well for us so far,' said Kartofel.

'We're going after her whether you like it or not,' said Ben. 'You can walk, or you can go in the Box. It's up to you.'

'All right, all right. Touchy.'

They stalked through the plots after the woman in black, down a tree-lined grass path to the far end of the cemetery. Once they were close enough, Ben reached out a hand to tap her on the shoulder. She spun round, still whispering. Two massive wings unfurled from inside her robe as if they were on springs.

'It *is* you,' said Ben.

'Great,' said Kartofel. 'Another heavenly halfwit.'

The Castellan of the Veil spat out a few words in a sudden rush of intensity. A gust of wind whipped across the graveyard, sending Kartofel tumbling backwards into a headstone.

'All right, keep your halo on,' he said.

'We are sorry for your loss,' said The Seraph. He still bore the scars of Llety'r Filiast, and his wings were frayed at the edges, but he looked much healthier than he had in Veil Towyn. He was flanked by the rest of the Cult of the Four Winds. 'And we are also sorry to be coming to you today, of all days, but it is time. You must come with us.'

The Seraph held out his good hand. Ben looked from the demons, the sorry ragtag band that had been following him around all his life, to the imposing majesty of the Cult of the Four Winds, and back again.

'No,' he said. 'I can't.'

The Seraph's eyes flicked over to The Triumph.

'Why are we even asking him?' said The Archivist. 'We are celestial. We should just snatch him up where he stands.'

'That is not the way we do things,' said The Seraph. 'We have discussed this.'

'I grow tired of kowtowing to the boy when everything is at stake.'

'It is because of him that everything is still possible,' said The Seraph. 'Ben, this is the last thing we will ask. It is the best chance for us to prevent The Adversary from unleashing the Horsemen of the Apocalypse. Don't you want to help? Don't you want to be free?'

Ben shook his head. 'The Adversary hasn't bothered me since the Orme. But every time you get involved, it just makes things worse. I was better off before, when it was just me and my demons and my mum was still alive. I don't want to hurt anyone, I don't want to go back in the Box, and I don't want to cause any more damage. Do you know how many houses were destroyed in the flood?'

'Two thousand seven hundred and eighty-four,' said The Archivist without missing a beat. 'It is nothing compared to the enormity of what we are trying to achieve. It is not such a big number.'

'I don't care.'

'Nothing will go wrong this time,' said The Seraph. 'We will take you to the nearest sacred place, somewhere the Box lay hidden for centuries. It is a fortress from where we will be able to resist any attack, even if The Adversary sends legions of demons. This is our last chance.'

'I can't. Not today. I'm sorry.'

The Archivist clicked his tongue. 'He is just like his mother. A coward.'

'Hold your tongue,' said The Seraph.

'What did you say about my mum?' Ben squared up to The Archivist, jutting his chest out and tilting his head up.

'Only the truth. If you were all she had to be proud of, it is little wonder she resorted to the highest blasphemy.'

Ben launched himself at the angel, hammering punches on to his hard chest. The Archivist laughed, and swatted Ben away with a flick of his hand.

'That's enough,' said The Seraph. 'Forgive The Archivist of the End Times, Ben. He will be dealt with later.'

'Today, I want to be with my family,' said Ben. He looked at the demons. 'All of them.'

Djinn clapped his hands in joy, and wisped himself once round the gathering. The Seraph sighed. 'Then we have no choice. I wish it did not have to be this way.'

He raised his arm as if he was about to take an oath, and then let it fall. The Castellan of the Veil's voice increased in volume, and the celestial words became clearer, more distinct.

The Box cut out completely, and Ben's vision blurred. The blue and purple colours of the Veil spread across his eyes like ink shot out into water.

Four gusts of wind swept in from each of the points of the compass. Air whirled around them, and Ben felt himself lifted off his feet. He tried to struggle, but the gusts kept him immobile: all he could do was shout pointlessly into the winds until he dropped, gasping, on to the grass, the strange colours of the Veil slowly receding.

Twenty minutes after Ben had left, with his grandfather barely able to hide his impatience, Lucy went to look for him. She walked through the same archway of trees that Ben had disappeared down, but as she got further down the path, and the memorials became progressively less loved, she thought that it was a strange route to take. If anything, it was away from his mother's plot.

As she trod through the overgrown area, she did not notice the folded and flat patch of grass that had not been there twenty-five minutes ago. She walked straight through it, and on to the very rear of the grounds, before making a wide circle back towards the spot where she had left Ben's grandparents.

The cemetery was deserted. Ben was nowhere to be found.

Chapter Nineteen

The Beginning of the End

'Get up,' said The Seraph.

The dark blues and purples slowly faded, revealing the dull greens and muddy browns of a riverbank. In front of them was an old concentric castle, half ruined. The Seraph strode up the bank towards it.

'Where are we?' said Ben.

'Rhuddlan Castle,' said The Archivist. 'The Box lay here for a time. This is the nearest sacred ground we could come to. Thanks to you, Llety'r Filiast is compromised.'

'Yeah, I remember this place,' said Kartofel. 'We came here on a school trip. There was a bloke who showed us how they made swords. Hit himself in the face with a wooden one by accident. Great day out.'

'Take us back or I'll start walking,' said Ben.

'You cannot,' said The Seraph. 'The Castellan of the Veil is containing us in this place. Nothing can get in, and nothing can get out. All of this will soon be over, Ben, particularly if you cooperate.'

The Seraph led them up a gnarled misshapen path and into the castle. In the main courtyard there was a round hole in the floor covered by a heavy iron safety grate. It looked like it may once have been a well, or else some sort of medieval toilet. It certainly looked deep and dark enough.

The Triumph reached down and pulled the bars up with one

hand. Pieces of masonry and sods of earth came away as he casually threw it behind him. The Castellan of the Veil stepped into the void, and gently glided down the shaft. Once she had landed safely, The Seraph followed.

The demons peered over the edge. It was so deep that the angel-light could barely be seen from the top.

'I hope we're not going down there,' said Djinn. 'It's scary. And I don't like the way it smells.'

'I could do myself a serious injury with a fall like that,' said Orff. 'We don't all have wings, you know.'

'You do not have a choice,' said The Archivist as he swung his legs over the hole. He dropped down the well quickly, leaving it to the last minute to unfurl his wings.

'Looks like you need a lift,' said The Triumph, wrapping a large arm around Ben's waist and carrying him to the edge of the well.

'Hang on, hang on,' said Kartofel. 'At least let us get in the Box first.'

The Triumph stepped forward, and they fell down the shaft, air whooshing through Ben's hair as they rushed towards the floor. It was a little bit scary, but Ben never felt in danger: The Triumph was more graceful than his size suggested, and he controlled their fall superbly. The demons, however, did not have it so easy. The stretching began almost immediately, and the strangled noise it made – a mixture of the Box's music and the demons' screams – was like a key being slowly scraped down a guitar string.

They landed in a large round chamber with a domed ceiling, lit in campfire warmth by angel-light. The Triumph gently placed Ben on the muddy stone floor, and the demons sprang out of the Box.

'There was no need for that,' said Kartofel.

'I think I might vomit,' said Orff.

'Quiet,' said The Seraph. He moved to the centre of the room, directly underneath the tiny speck of daylight that was being cast into the chamber. He hunched down and placed his hand on the floor, a rectangle of fizzing orange light forming beneath his fingers. He pressed down, and the stone gave way, leaving a Box-shaped hole in the ground.

Once it was done, he moved to the edge of the chamber, and the rest of the Cult of the Four Winds did the same, positioning themselves so they formed a cross with the hole at the centre. Each then carved one of the symbols from the Box's lid into the floor, and stood on it. The Seraph wiped the dirt from his hands and turned to face the room.

'Everything is prepared. Ben, take the Box and place it in the recess.'

'No,' said Ben. 'You brought me here when I didn't want to come. You took me away from my family. From my mum's grave. Why should I help you?'

The Archivist swooped forward and grabbed the back of Ben's head, lacing his fingers through his hair and squeezing his skull. He forced Ben forward into the centre of the chamber, stripped the satchel from his back, and upturned it. The Box clattered on to the flagstones.

'Do as you are bid,' said The Archivist. Ben felt a chill grow in the back of his head. It was like his brain was being turned to ice, and The Archivist was intending to make a slush puppy out of it.

'Ben!' whimpered Djinn, swooping forward. The Seraph rose his arm and splayed his fingers. Djinn's collar throbbed, and he froze. The Seraph turned his attention to Kartofel and Orff, lighting their collars and keeping them still.

Ben scrabbled for the Box, desperate to make the cold go away. Once he had his hand on it, The Archivist released him, and his head returned to normal.

'I hate you,' he said.

'Once again, I am sorry for the methods we must employ,' said The Seraph. 'This will go easier if you cooperate. Place the Box in the recess.'

It slotted in easily, as if it had always sat there. It fit so perfectly that removing it would not be possible; the gaps between floor and Box were so minute that there was no space for fingers to lever it out.

'Everything is prepared,' said The Seraph. 'Let us begin.' He opened his arms wide, and raised them above his head. His wings extended to their full span, and he began to sing a note in a perfect clear baritone. One by one, the others joined him, each taking a different octave, from The Triumph's rich bass to The Castellan of the Veil's ringing soprano. Their auras shone as bright as ever, and as they each extended their wings the tips touched, sealing everyone in a giant ring of orange light.

It was one of the most beautiful things Ben had ever seen. A single tear ran down his cheek as the music of the Box harmonized with the angels' rapturous soaring melodies. A thin green light started to creep out of the tiny crack between Box and floor, slowly pushing up towards the daylight like a budding flower.

As it grew, the music became more impatient, eager to have the light bursting out of it. There was a slight tremor in the earth, and when Ben looked down at the Box he saw that it was shaking, wriggling to be free of the hole, wanting its lid open. The more it struggled, the more violent the trembling ground became, until hairline cracks appeared all around the edges of the Box. Within seconds they had spread to cover the floor like ivy.

'The moment is upon us,' said The Seraph. 'Let us have the first four Strident Blasts!'

The Archivist took the drawstring quiver from his back and carefully drew out a long silver trumpet. It reflected the light in the chamber, causing such a glare that Ben had to turn away. The Archivist raised the instrument to his lips, and blew a loud bass blast. The ground, and the Box, replied with a rumble of their own. The Archivist blew again, and again, each time matched by a heavier, more intense tremor than the last. As the fourth and final blast echoed around the chamber, The Seraph addressed the Cult in elated, breathless tones.

'We have waited a long time for this day, my friends. Today, we launch a new Creation, one with the Prime One at its head. Today, He returns. Today, we use chaos to purge chaos, and so bring Everlasting Order!'

The light tore through the lid of the Box, shooting up the well shaft like a geyser and out into the sky above. Ben was thrown backwards into the wall, and moments later he felt the impact as the same thing happened to angel and demon alike. The demons' collars exploded in a puff of fine powder, dirt and stone rained down from the ceiling, and the light expanded until it filled the chamber in a blinding flash.

Everything stopped, and the chamber was thrown into complete silence, and total darkness. Even the light of the angels was extinguished.

Groggily, Ben got to his feet. It was even quiet in his head. The music of the Box was gone, and he knew that this time it would not be coming back. As he stumbled over the intricate web of cracks, he heard the rustle of wings. The Seraph throbbed back into light, followed by each of the other angels until the chamber was once again lit by a warm glow.

There was a large smoking crater in the middle of the room, in the centre of which lay the charred remains of the Box. Four figures were gathered around it. The first was an old crone with wild grey hair and a stooped and twisted physique. She was bound up like a pharaoh, and insects swarmed all over her, burrowing in and out of her bandages. Next to her was a grotesquely fat bald man wearing nothing but a lionskin loincloth. He had a bloody sack slung around his shoulder, from which he produced a constant stream of food. Crumbs and splashes of gravy flew everywhere, splattering on the black-clad paper-white young woman with pale green hair nearby. She gave the fat man a deathly glare. He wiped his mouth and mumbled an apology.

The quartet was completed by a big man with bulging muscles. He wore a strange jumble of armour, and had a variety of weapons hanging from his waist. If there was any doubt as to who they were, it was dispelled by the fact that each was on horseback.

The Four Horsemen of the Apocalypse were free, and they did not look happy.

'Angels,' snarled Famine. 'And demons, too.'

War drew a large curved sword. 'You dare to imprison us? We who are so much more powerful than you? We who are infinite?' He advanced on The Archivist, who shrank back, his arm outstretched in horror.

'I have cancerssss and sssstrokesss and blightsssss burssssting to be releasssssed,' said Pestilence, exhaling a wave of dead mouse breath that turned Djinn yellow. 'Perhapssss I could have a demon or an angel to practisssss on?'

'There are plenty to go round,' said Death. 'It has been so long since we were last sentient.'

'I want to start with this one,' said War, raising his blade to The Archivist.

'Wait,' said The Seraph. 'My lords and ladies, please.' He got down on his knees, and bowed his head.

'You think kneeling will save you?' laughed Death. She bunched her fist, and a black scythe grew out of it, glowing.

'No, milady,' said The Seraph. 'We know this humble act cannot even begin to make amends. But we ask your forgiveness. We were led astray by The Adversary, who convinced us you needed to be stopped. We have rued that day, the last day of the Grand War, ever since. We wish to aid you in your work.'

'What?' said Ben.

'We have released you because it is our wish that you are successful. The Grand War should have brought the Apocalypse. We should not have stopped you. We are sorry, and are now your humble servants.'

'Excuse me, but I think Ben just said "what?"' said Kartofel.

'Silence, demon,' said The Archivist.

'What are you doing?' asked Ben.

'What we have been working towards for millennia,' said The Seraph. 'The Apocalypse.'

'But . . . you said . . . Why?'

'Do you know what the word "apocalypse" means, little ape?' scoffed The Archivist.

'Does it mean "all angels are idiots"?' said Kartofel.

'It means "the Coming of God". The aeons we have spent waiting for Him are at an end. He will finally show himself, and purge the Creation of the sin of free will. There will be everlasting order, and all the infidels will be put to the sword.'

'I like swords,' said War. 'And axes. I'm going to put something to the axe as well.'

'Of course, my lord,' said The Seraph. 'We intend to present you with the greatest army ever assembled. You may do with them as you wish.'

'You will not try to stop us?' said Death.

'No, milady,' said The Seraph. 'The opposite. We will aid your work in every way we can. This is our gift to you, my lords and ladies. Go forth and destroy.'

War chuckled. 'I like the sound of that.'

'Yesss,' said Pestilence. 'Oh, my lovely ssssicknesssss. All that perfect health out there, jusssst waiting to be corrupted.'

'And all that hunger,' said Famine. 'And all that gluttony. I shall enjoy that, I shall.'

Famine pulled his reins, and his horse reared up with a terrible whinnying. Its heavy hoofs drummed down on the stone, and Famine geed it on, circling the chamber. As he passed Pestilence, she urged her horse to join him. War and Death soon followed, and all four became a blur, a macabre carousel, racing round and round until there was a whoosh of air, and they were gone.

'We've won,' said The Triumph. 'We've won! The Apocalypse is here!'

'Not quite, brother,' said The Seraph. His lips were set in a sly smile. 'We are close, but there is still much to do. For one, you still have an army to raise. Let us leave this place, and make the necessary preparations. Sister?'

The Castellan of the Veil turned to face the wall, and laid her hands on the bricks. The stone shimmered, and The Triumph charged towards it. He dived into it headfirst, passing through as if it were a hologram.

'What about us?' said Ben. 'You can't leave us down here.'

'What would be the point of removing you?' said The Archivist. 'This world is ending. It is all one to us where you die.'

'Please try to understand, Ben,' said The Seraph. 'It was inevitable that this should occur, for it was written, prophesied by the Box itself. If it is any consolation, your name will be writ large in the new Creation. We could not have achieved this without you.'

'But I don't want it,' said Ben.

The Seraph shrugged. 'Then this is the right place for you.' He beat his wings, hovering momentarily, before plunging into the wall. One by one the others followed, leaving little ripples in the rock as they became submerged. Once they were gone, the disturbance in the wall subsided, and it became still, like it had never been anything other than cold hard stone.

Chapter Twenty

The Valley of Death

The only light now came from Kartofel, save the blip of daylight that could still be seen far above their heads.

'What an ignoble way to end,' said Orff. 'I just want to say, gentlemen, that apart from the terrible physical agony I have endured the entire time I have known you, it has been a pleasure.'

'And I just want to say that as far as things stand, I've won the Apocalypse,' said Kartofel. 'I said no good would come of this angel business, so I get bragging rights for the rest of our lives. Short as they're likely to be.'

Djinn whimpered.

'Stop scaring him, Kartofel,' said Ben.

'I'm just being realistic.'

'That's not helpful.' Ben looked around the room. The walls were slimy and smooth, and curved up towards the entrance to the shaft. 'We have to try and get out.'

'What for? So we can face the Apocalypse in the middle of a ruined castle instead of at the bottom of a well in the middle of a ruined castle?' said Kartofel. 'It's not like we can stop it, is it? We're bound to you, and you're hardly the saving-the-world type, are you?'

'I don't know if that's true,' said Orff.

'Oh yeah, he's a proper action hero,' said Kartofel.

'I mean the part about us being bound. Our collars are gone. The Box appears to be burned out. Perhaps we're free.'

'I can't hear the music any more,' said Ben.

'I don't see how that helps,' said Kartofel. 'So we won't get stretched if we climb out. But how can any of us climb out anyway? The ceiling is round.'

'Can't you try?' said Ben.

'I can't hang upside down, can I? I'm not a bloomin' spider. Why can't Chunk go? He floats, doesn't he?'

'That's rather a good point,' said Orff, turning expectantly to Djinn.

'Do you think you could?' said Ben.

'I don't know,' said Djinn. 'It's a long way. What if I get tired?'

'Just imagine there's cake at the top,' snorted Kartofel.

'Shut up, you,' said Djinn.

'Actually, that's not a bad idea,' said Ben. 'Maybe if you pretend there's bacon, and mustard, and jam tarts waiting for you, you won't think so much about how high it is. Imagine cheesecake.'

'And fish and chips,' said Orff.

'Really?' said Djinn.

'And carrot cake.'

'Yeah, and that other stuff you like,' said Kartofel. 'That orangey-pink stuff that looks like pigeon vomit.'

'Taramasalata?' said Djinn, hopefully.

'If it helps,' said Ben.

'OK,' said Djinn. 'Here goes . . .'

He started to expand, his form getting more and more transparent as he grew. Before long, he was at the entrance to the shaft, and he began to twist himself through it, moving slowly upward like the world's laziest tornado.

'I'm doing it,' he said through snatched breaths. 'I'm doing it! Hahahahaha!'

His laughter echoed down the shaft as he got further away. And then it stopped abruptly. There was whoosh of air and Djinn shot back down the tunnel, a panicked look on his face.

'Ben,' he said. 'Ben. It's that thing. It's back!'

'What thing? What happened?'

'From the train. It's waiting at the top.'

'Watch yer heads,' shouted a voice from the top of the well. It was a little slushy, but it had more of a gruff bark to it than the demon from the Orme. The speck of light at the top of the shaft was momentarily blotted out, and a clanking noise followed as something was thrown down to them. A few echoey crashes later, and a chain ladder unfurled in front of them.

'Hop on,' said the voice.

Ben put his foot on the first rung.

'Don't do it,' said Djinn. 'It's the dog thing. Honest.'

'Whatever it is, it's better than being stuck in a hole as the world ends,' said Ben.

'Aren't you forgetting something?' said Kartofel. 'How are we going to get out? It's not like we'll get stretched, and I can't climb up a rope ladder. I doubt the old geezer can either.'

'Labyrinthitis,' said Orff.

'I tell you what, lads,' shouted the voice. 'Sound carries well from down there. I can hear every word. Don't worry about climbing. Just hold on, and we'll take care of the rest.'

'That settles it,' said Ben. 'Let's go.'

He climbed a few rungs, and Orff clung on below him. Djinn wrapped himself around the ladder between Ben and Orff, and finally Kartofel clawed his way on to the bottom rung.

'We're ready,' shouted Ben.

'Right y'are,' said the voice, and the ladder began to retract at a steady pace. It took much longer to get to the top than it did to get down, but before long Ben was clambering over the lip of the well. There were large cracks in the ground from the earthquake, and several pieces of the castle wall had fallen down.

The ladder was long, and trailed out of the main courtyard. Even as Kartofel clambered over the top of the well, it was still being pulled away by some unseen creature.

'Hello?' said Ben. 'We're out?'

A small head in an ill-fitting helmet of Norman design poked out from around the wall. The ladder stopped moving, and sure enough the dog-demon padded in wearing chain mail.

'See?' said Djinn, wisping behind Ben. 'I told you.'

'Oh no, that weren't me, lad,' said the demon. He chewed constantly between sentences, only stopping to speak. 'That were me brother Squat. I'm Neil, Captain of the Chaotic Guard.' He took his helmet off, and bowed his head. 'When the trumpets started blaring, His Nibs said I had to fetch yer.'

'Who's His Nibs?' said Ben.

'His most Chaotic Majesty, the King of the Underworld. Anyway, we'd better do one, what with all the apocalypses.' He turned on his heels, and scampered back outside.

'What do you reckon?' said Kartofel.

'I don't trust him,' said Djinn.

'I don't think we have a choice,' said Ben. 'We can't stay here.'

Neil stuck his head back through the entrance. 'Come on, we haven't got all chuffin' day.'

There was a giant green-and-yellow stegosaurus waiting outside the castle, peacefully drinking from the River Clwyd. It had a small saddle around its neck, and a bit in its mouth. Further up its spine, spaced out between its plates, there were four other saddles, each a different shape and size. Neil hurriedly finished winding the ladder back up and tucked it into his saddlebags.

'All aboard. Stedge here is going to take us home. I know she looks fierce, but she's right gentle really.'

They approached the creature with caution, Orff muttering something about salmonella under his breath. One of the saddles had eight pommels, and was obviously meant for Kartofel, who clambered on to it. There was a particularly large saddle towards the tail, which was taken by Djinn, and Orff and Ben settled into the remaining standard ones. Stedge huffed as they got on, and Ben could feel her massive lungs working, moving his legs up and down. Once Neil was mounted, she lumbered forward, lazily splashing into the river and then stomping out of it as easily as if it were a puddle.

'She takes a while to rev up,' said Neil as he patted Stedge's flanks. 'Sixty-five million years young, that's what we say, hey, girl?'

They blundered on through a succession of fields, gradually picking up speed as they went. Most of the buildings they passed had been reduced to rubble in the earthquake, and thick black smoke rose from those that weren't. The once-green fields were now brown and dying, and the only living creatures were swarms of black insects.

'This is horrible,' said Ben.

'Aye,' said Neil. 'Horsemen's first stop it was, reckon they went a bit overboard. You should see the streets. Fightin' and car crashes everywhere. We got stuck in a tailback just outside of Rhosesmor on the way in. Ooh, Veil's coming up now, so everyone hold on tight.'

'What if you haven't got opposable thumbs?' said Kartofel.

Neil kicked his heels into Stedge's flanks, and she immediately surged forward, giving Kartofel his answer: you fall off. Ben managed to grab him as he tumbled, and held him firmly in the saddle. In the now fast-approaching distance, Ben saw the smouldering remains of the A525. There was a massive pile of cars stacked up in the middle of it, blocking their way. Stedge headed straight for it, and Neil made no effort to steer her away.

'This is where it gets a bit hairy,' he said, kicking his heels. 'Go on, girl, you can do it.'

Stedge roared, and Ben closed his eyes just as they were about to crash through the metal mountain. His ears popped, and when he opened his eyes again, the Rhuddlan countryside had been reset. The pile of cars had gone, and they were racing through a genteel twilight world, untouched by the Apocalypse. They tore through this Veil version of North Wales until Ben's ears popped again, and all was instantly grey.

He looked back at the road that had been luscious grass a moment ago, and saw only monotone gravel wasteland, as if they had always been travelling along this path. The abrupt change of terrain did not seem to faze Stedge, and she thundered on until they came to a steep hill, shrouded in thick mist.

Ben could no longer see more than a few feet ahead, and the journey suddenly became a slog. The never-ending incline caused Stedge to slow to a plod, and the unsteady ride made his saddle even less comfortable than before. He began to hear whispers as he passed through the fog, little snatches of gossip commenting on him, and on the demons, adding to his general sense of discomfort and disorientation:

'Who's this?'

'Dunno.'

'Someone should tell someone.'

'Who?'

'Dunno. You?'

'Why tell me? I already know.'

'No, you should tell someone.'

'Who?'

'Dunno. The Queen? It's the kind of thing I'd want to know about if I was her.'

'That one don't look normal.'

'Neither does the lizard.'

'I meant the lizard, but now you come to mention it . . .'

On it went, until they reached the summit. The mist was thinner there, and Ben could see that the road twisted down into a valley. The opposite ridge was clearly visible, but the contents of the valley itself were unknowable, hidden by an even thicker mist than the one they had just come through.

'What is this place?' said Ben.

'The Afterworld,' said Neil. 'Purgatory, some call it. Ones that do are normally the most put out to end up here. It's where all the dead come, after they die. That's what the mists are.'

Ben shivered. 'So when we walk through the fog, we're walking through people?'

'I hadn't thought of it like that, like, but aye. Suppose we are.'

'That doesn't sound very hygienic,' said Orff.

'Oh, little bit of a death stroll never did nobody any harm,' said Neil. 'We just have to pass through the Valley of Death, and then we can cross the Veil on the other side, get ourselves home.'

'The Valley of Death?' said Djinn. 'I don't like the sound of that.'

'You're not alive, idiot. Why would it bother you?' said Kartofel.

'It sounds scary.'

'Oh, there's no need to be scared, lad,' said Neil. 'They can't hurt you. It's only cos there's so many of them makes the journey slow. Stedge doesn't see too good in the fog.'

Before them, the mist began to part, forming a clear path.

'Err . . . that doesn't usually happen,' said Neil with a forced grin. 'Still, I'm sure it's nothing to worry about . . .'

Stedge rumbled on, occasionally turning her head as if she sought to move away, but the corridor of fog was so thick on either side that she had no choice but to follow the path the mists were making. They were led down to the valley floor, where they caught sight of a lone figure on a horse wearing a long black hooded robe. The mist parted around it, making a clearing. As Stedge drew to a halt, the figure pulled back the hood to reveal a black crown atop a head of pale green hair.

'Well, well, well. Trespassers, is it?' said Death. 'Is this how things are in my kingdom now? Is it a thoroughfare for impudent demons?'

Neil dismounted, and gave a little bow. 'Sorry about that, m'lady. We were just on our way to the Underworld. I've got papers, signed by The Opposition himself.' He rummaged around in his saddlebags. 'I can show you if you wait a sec . . .'

'I'm sure that won't be necessary,' said Death. 'So all the little demons are returning home in time for our lovely Apocalypse, are they? You don't want to stay in the World and watch the show? How atypical.'

'That is well demonist,' said Kartofel. 'We're not all obsessed with destruction, you know.'

'You are,' said Djinn.

'She doesn't know that, though, does she? She can't go around making assumptions about people. It's not right.'

Death bent down and looked straight into Kartofel's eyes, which shut him up immediately. She then did the same for Djinn, and Orff, before moving on to Ben. He felt a numbness inside his head, as if parts of his brain were dying just from having looked at her.

'And what's this? You dare to bring a living being into my realm? An actual breathing human? Tell me, demon, why shouldn't I have my mists lead you round and round in circles until your mount drops dead and this little human starves to death?'

'Err . . . well, to be honest, your deathliness, I wasn't really expecting to see you here. I'm sorry, like, err . . .'

'I'm the keeper of the Box,' said Ben. 'And you should let us pass. You'd still be in there if it wasn't for us.'

The mists began to whisper excitedly. Neil bowed even deeper than he had before, so that his nose was almost touching gravel. 'Err . . . I'm sorry, your most morbidness, please forgive us, the boy's never been out of the World. We're not trying to offend you, honest we're not.'

Death laughed, and the mists stopped their chatter. 'No offence was taken, little demon. So the human thinks he is owed a favour, does he? Tell me, boy, what is your name?'

'Ben Robson.'

'I shall remember that, you can be sure,' said Death. 'Very well then, Ben Robson. I will grant you and your party passage through my kingdom. You may take your leave.'

'What, really?' said Neil. 'Crikey. Thanks very much, like. Consider us your servants.'

'I have servants aplenty, demon, and many more on their way.'

The mists parted in front of them once more, and Neil

tipped his helmet in Death's direction.

'See, nothing to worry about,' he said.

'Gladiators!' shouted Death.

Individual figures of fog stepped out of the mists. Formidable men and women with shields, battle axes, and helmets formed in front of their eyes. Djinn whimpered as they passed a particularly tall and rugged woman with a large trident in her hand.

'Are you ready for some sport?' shouted Death.

The gladiator mists roared in agreement.

'Very well. On my count, you may pursue our visitors. Are you ready?'

The gladiators roared again. Ben turned round in horror. 'But you said you would grant us passage.'

'I never said *safe* passage,' laughed Death. 'I shall give you to the count of ten. One . . .'

The gladiators started to bash their spirit weapons together, which made a strange whispery whistling noise, like wind through autumn trees. Neil whipped the reins, kicked his heels, and Stedge lurched into action. 'Right. Best hold on tight again.'

The dinosaur took the bank at speed. Mists parted and then reformed in front of them, causing Stedge to move in a zigzag to be able to see. Behind them, Death reached 'five', then shouted, 'Go!'

The whistling noise became deafening. Behind them, every gladiator that had ever lived – and since 'gladiator' was not a profession that encouraged longevity there were quite a lot of them – stormed up the hill behind them. They did not suffer the same impairment as Stedge when moving through the mists, and so they were very quickly upon them. They pressed against the dinosaur's haunches, slowing her progress and throwing her off balance. Ben kicked out, and managed to make a little space around him, but the press of mists was soon irresistible, and they were penned in.

'What do we do now?' said Kartofel. He was waving his head around, which seemed to be working: the gladiators dodged out of his way. Even Djinn was getting in on the act, wisping around the mists so that they turned away in confusion.

'How am I supposed to know that?' said Neil.

'I thought you were the Captain of the Guard,' said Orff.

'Yeah, but I've not been chased by ghost gladiators before either. It's normally a nice day out, this is.'

'Kartofel,' said Ben, 'get down to the tail and dig your claws in. I've got an idea. Neil, how fast can we circle round?'

'I dunno. Pretty quickly if she puts her mind to it. We'll have a go, like.'

'Good. We're going to try and make some space.'

Neil pulled the reins to the left. Stedge swerved, and her tail flicked round in a wide arc. The mists sprang back, clearing the way and making it easier for Stedge to see.

'It's working,' said Ben. 'Keep going round until I say, then charge forward, OK?'

'Right y'are,' said Neil.

They spun round, forcing the mists further back, until Ben judged that they were facing the right way. He yelled 'now!', Neil brought the reins centre, and Stedge pounded up the hill. Before long they reached the top, the thick greys became wispy whites, and they were free to continue on their journey.

The sound of Death's laughter boomed out from the valley floor, echoing all around. It continued to ring in Ben's ears long after it died out.

Chapter Twenty-One

'Abandon Hype, All Ye Who Enter Here'

The mist lifted, and all was clear. Stedge built up speed into what might be called a gallop in anything other than a stegosaurus, and they were away, off down a long straight road that stretched out to the horizon, bordered on either side by vast barren mudflats. Ben did not need to be told that they were on the road to Hell, because it was literally paved with good intentions. Clearly The Adversary had a sense of humour, for he had erected a walk of fame made of hundreds of thousands of sandstone slabs, each one carved with a different message: 'I WAS ONLY TRYING TO HELP' read one. 'I NEVER MEANT TO HURT HER' was another. 'IT WAS AN ACCIDENT' appeared frequently.

Eventually they came to a set of iron gates emblazoned with a giant yin-yang symbol. Above them, in the style of a Hollywood studio lot, was a rainbow-shaped sign that read 'PANDÆMONIUM'. The walls on either side stretched as far as could be seen in both directions. 'Going-round-the-back' did not appear to be an option.

'Are we nearly there yet?' said Djinn.

Neil dismounted, and tied Stedge to a nearby stake. He walked up to the gates and raised his paw, but before he could knock the doors swung open with a loud crunching groan. As they filed through, Ben noticed that someone had stuck a laminated sheet of A4 paper to one of the doors. The tape was old and crinkly, and only by some strange alchemy did it manage to hold the sign up at all. It read:

ABANDON HYPE, ALL YE WHO ENTER HERE!

They passed into a wide courtyard, and were greeted by the overpowering stench of incense. The floor was dotted with small pots of burning patchouli oil and joss sticks, and the walkway – a deep-pile black carpet – was lined with large, pungent potted plants with strange jagged leaves. The walls were painted orange, badly, and there were a number of cushions strewn around, all of them embroidered with sequins in psychedelic patterns.

At the end of the carpet was a purple and yellow door with a vintage poster advertising a music festival pinned to it. Neil knocked, and a voice beckoned them in.

The walls of the next room were covered with doors of all shapes and sizes, from the too-small-to-fit-through to the ridiculously unusable, positioned halfway up the wall or diagonally across the ceiling. Sitting in the lotus position at the far end of the room, wearing a yellow smoking jacket and purple silk pyjamas, was a long-haired man with ash-grey skin. His eyes were closed, and he was emitting a low hum. Neil coughed, and the man's eyes flicked open, revealing the same red irises and white pupils as the angels.

'Ah, Captain,' said the man. 'Welcome back. And you managed to retrieve our friends. Well done.'

Neil bowed, and turned to Ben and the demons, back straight, chest out. 'May I present His Most Chaotic Majesty, The Opposition,' he barked. 'King of the Underworld and All Other Mythical Variants Thereof.'

'The Opposition?' said Ben. 'Not The Adversary?'

The Opposition gave a weary sigh, and rolled his eyes. 'That's what the angels insist on calling me. I prefer "The Opposition". Much more dignified. And much more accurate. I'm very grateful for your assistance, Captain, but I'm sure you have other things to do. Defences to prepare, demons of lesser rank to bawl at, that sort of thing?'

'Yessir, right you are, sir,' said Neil, saluting. The Opposition returned it, and the dog-demon exited through a cat flap in the far corner.

'Now,' said The Opposition, 'would you all like some tea? We have so much to discuss.' He clapped his hands, and Neil reappeared, dressed in a butler's uniform and carrying a silver platter with four handleless cups and a square teapot on it.

'How did you get changed so fast?' said Djinn.

'Oh, this isn't Neil,' said The Opposition, taking a cup. 'This is Crouch, his brother.'

The butler distributed cups to each of the demons, and then finally to Ben. He placed the tray under his arm, and bowed, but as he turned to leave a snake tail slithered down from under his jacket. It hissed, and tried to strike out at Ben, but was pulled away by the retreating motion of its owner.

'Please excuse Crouch's lack of courtesy,' said The Opposition. 'He took Squat's erasure quite hard. I suppose we all did, in our way. He was a very popular little demon. I assume he fought bravely at the Battle of the Orme?'

'He tried to kill me,' said Ben.

'Oh, I rather doubt that. Considering I sent him to protect you.'

'I find that hard to believe,' said Ben.

'Really? Even after he saved you when you tried to throw the Box into the sea? You do realize you could have died? Squat was your guardian demon. He'd been watching over you ever since the Box took you up.'

'If that's true, then why didn't he tell me?'

'Oh, anyone with half a brain would have. But that was always Squat's problem. He only had one third of a brain. You see, he and his brothers weren't always three. They used to be one, but mealtimes got so tiresome that I was forced to perform a bit of DIY surgery. Now they are three of the most loyal demons in all of Pandemonium, maybe the whole of the Underworld. What do you think of it so far, by the way?'

'What, Hell?' said Ben.

'Ach, "Hell" has such negative connotations. I prefer "the Underworld", but there you go. Do you like it?'

'I wasn't expecting quite so many scatter cushions.'

'No. No. Why would you? Millennia of propaganda to overcome. It's not at all easy.' The Opposition ruefully rubbed his hand along the side of his face, lost in reverie. 'Anyway. Speaking of loyal demons, allow me to welcome you back, Ichthor, Thrichthlor and Mnemnor. My old friends.'

'Eh?' said Kartofel.

'I think he's talking to us,' said Orff.

'You must be round the twist, fella. I have literally been living in a Box for the last Mammon-knows-how-many years,' said Kartofel. 'I've never been here before.'

'Ah, classic Mnemnor. Always with a ready quip.'

Kartofel looked up at Ben. 'Can't believe we had to go through all those gladiators for this.'

'What's going on, Ben?' said Djinn. 'I don't understand.'

'I think there's been a bit of a mix-up,' said Ben. 'These are the demons that have been trapped in the Box.'

'I know,' said The Opposition.

'They're called Orff, Djinn and Kartofel.'

The Opposition laughed. 'Really?'

'Yes,' said Orff.

'This isn't some elaborate Thrichthlor prank?'

'And which of us, pray tell, is supposed to be Thrichthlor?'

'You are.'

'Well, I've never been so insulted . . . Pranks! In my condition.'

'Can this really be true? Friends, do you not remember? Well, this is priceless. I had not expected this. It appears exposure to either the Box or the World has given you all a little amnesia. I suppose it has been rather a long time. Djinn, Kartofel and Orff. Wherever did you get those names? Assuming you're Djinn, Ichthor, I can see where that might come from. But Orff? That's just bizarre. And Kartofel? Ha! You are aware that "kartofel" is the word for "potato" in several European languages?'

Djinn giggled.

'Shut it,' said Kartofel.

'No, you shut it,' said Djinn, still giggling. 'Spud.'

Kartofel growled.

'I will explain,' said The Opposition. 'But first: this is a vintage green tea, brewed in Ancient China. If I am to tell the whole story of the Box and how you came to be in it, a gentle tea such as this is the perfect accompaniment.'

'I can't drink anything,' said Djinn, glumly. 'Or eat anything.'

'Whatever gave you that idea?' said The Opposition. 'Maybe that's true in the World, but not here.'

Djinn tentatively clasped his fingers around the cup, and tried to lift it. He was so surprised when it rose that he clapped his hands together in excitement, and sloshed tea all over Kartofel. Steadying the cup, he drank, turning a dark green colour as he did.

'You see?' said The Opposition. 'And I think I have one of your special straws here somewhere, Mnemnor.' He reached inside his jacket and produced what looked like a bendy straw, except it was solid shining silver. He popped it in Kartofel's mug.

Ben drank. It was indeed a lovely tea. The Opposition gestured for them all to sit, and they did, pulling up scatter cushions where necessary. 'The first thing you need to know about this story is that it is very old. Impossibly, amazingly old. Really, it is the only story ever told: good versus evil, if you want to be coarse about it. I don't, but if you do, then be my guest. I prefer to say it is a story of night and day. You need one to have the other, and there is plenty to commend either of them. Consider the barn owl, or the bat. To them, is it not daylight that is to be feared? So let us think of things in shades of grey. A kind of grey miasma, which has been around for as long as time itself.

'Now in this pool of grey, there are various shades, but broadly they can be called Light Greys or Dark Greys. One day, the Light Greys got to thinking that they'd rather not have the Dark Greys living with them, near them, or even around them, and that the best thing would probably be to give the Dark Greys the boot so they could live in a nice clean Light Grey heaven. And so they embarked on a . . . let's call it a crusade.' He rolled the word around his mouth, savouring the emphasis. 'The Light Greys soon found, like every crusader ever since, that those they sought to oppress weren't going to go down without a fight. And so there was an almighty battle, a Grand War, which lasted until every world was so full of death and war and famine and pestilence that each of those things was made flesh and set about destroying the universe.

'Now at this point, both sides realized that there was little to gain and too much to lose and so the Head of the Light Greys, who had started the whole thing because he got it into his head that a magic invisible being called the Prime One wanted him to, and the Head of the Dark Greys, a poor unfortunate victim who simply wanted to get on with his existence without worrying what an imaginary sky giant thought, sat down together – it may help you to imagine a tent in the middle of some battlefield somewhere – and they made an alliance. The war against the Horsemen raged for a few aeons more, until all four were captured, and the question of what to do with them arose.

'Now, bitter old enemies being what they are, namely old and bitter, neither had much trust for the other. So they came up with a foolproof way to avoid the future complete and utter destruction of everything, and that was to create something that could cause the future complete and utter destruction of everything, but only if both sides agreed to use it. And so the Light Greys, because they were good carpenters – I hope I am not being too oblique with my analogies here – carved a Box, and they sent it to the Dark Greys, who were good blacksmiths, to forge clasps and hinges for it. Then they met up in that little tent – a theoretical tent, of course, but let's for argument's sake say that it was pitched in what was at the time a tropical paradise on the equator but would eventually become a dreary seaside resort on the North Wales coast – and they left it there.'

'Wait. You left the Four Horsemen of the Apocalypse lying around Llandudno?' said Kartofel.

'It seemed like a good compromise at the time. Besides, I didn't leave it unguarded. Unbeknownst to the other side, I sneaked three of my most trusted and powerful demons inside to act as jailers.'

'There are other demons in the Box?' said Djinn.

'I think he's talking about us,' said Orff.

'You're crackers,' said Kartofel. 'Either that, or you have some seriously weak demons knocking around. These two are the least powerful people I know. And I know Ben.'

'Thanks, Kartofel.'

'Jus' bein' honest.'

'Yes, well, how was I to know you'd forget everything? Incidentally, now that you are free of the collars, you might find you have slightly wider parameters when it comes to power. Anyway, an uneasy peace was reached, and the Box was hidden in plain sight, with Mankind. Oh, I forgot. There's another group stuck in the middle of the Light Greys and the Dark Greys. Let's call them the Foggy Morning Emulsion Greys, shall we? And so the whole grey miasma went about its business as before. There's been the odd diplomatic incident every now and again, but generally it's worked.'

'Until now,' said Ben.

'Yes. Well, that's down to something no one could have predicted. Over the years, the Box grew a sort of consciousness. It became aware of its own power, and so it reached out to those who could help fulfil its potential. Various religions, cults, sects got their hands on it, and believing it to be a totem or a relic or an ark of whatever heavenly body they were chancing their arms with that century, they worshipped it. Legends built up around it, humans lusted after it, and occasionally some of the more ambitious ones worked out how to use it to their own ends:

to win wars, cripple enemies, amass power.'

'But you said both sides would need to agree to be able to use it,' said Ben.

'And what do you think those Foggy Morning Greys are made of exactly? What is Man but Order and Chaos combined? So the Box made its way around the World, causing trouble, changing things, sending out visions of how it could one day be used. Some of the people who received these messages – prophets, artists, priests – wrote them down, and they came to the attention of someone who was prepared to make them happen. Specifically, an angel who thought he could use the Apocalypse to provoke the Prime One into showing himself, since no one in existence had ever seen him. I contend that is because he does not exist. They say it is because he will only show himself when the Worlds end. I will leave you to choose which sounds more likely.

'Once they had decided on their course of action, they needed a willing human they could manipulate into handling the Box for them. Someone young and vulnerable and alone who would willingly swallow their half-truths, and could easily be overlooked or forgotten.'

Ben's head sank. 'Me.'

'Not you, no. Your mother. Didn't you ever wonder where you got the Box from? They visited her before you were born, took her to where the Box was hidden, and had her retrieve it. They needed a child to be bound to the Box from birth, for the ritual to work. By the time your mother found out what they wanted it was too late. They filled her head with their light, and put her on the road to the asylum. Didn't you ever consider that she might have been telling the truth about the angels, once they started meddling?'

'They told me . . .' began Ben, before stopping himself. He shook his head. 'I've been so stupid.'

'Not stupid, no. Just human. There is a difference, though you'd not know it, the number of people who watch *EastEnders*. Try not to blame yourself. They have been planning this a long time.'

Ben closed his eyes. A tear dropped onto his cheek.

'It's all right, Ben,' said Djinn. 'We're not going to let them get away with it.'

'Certainly not,' said Orff.

'Now *that* I can get behind,' said Kartofel. 'Although, if everyone had listened to me at the start . . .'

'Let's bash them!' said Djinn, his fists in the air.

A strong sustained trumpet blast rang out, shaking the room. Djinn dashed behind Ben, cowering.

'W-w-what was that?'

'The Fifth Strident Blast,' said The Opposition. 'The angels are in the Afterworld, marshalling their army of zealots and martyrs. They will sound the trumpet twice more: the Sixth Blast will set off a devastating string of natural disasters on Earth, and the Seventh will bring down the Veil. The Worlds will collapse in on each other. They'll be expecting their Prime One to show up before that happens though.'

'We can't let them do this,' said Ben. 'It's not fair. Can't you do anything? Send some demons or something?'

'As it happens, I can, yes. Or rather, I am in the process of doing it. Who better to prevent the next blasts than the four newest knights of the Underworld? Ichthor, Thrichthlor, Mnemnor, and their friend Ben Robson, Keeper of the Box.'

'What do you expect us to be able to do?' said Orff. 'I have terrible trouble with my joints.'

'I expect you to ride out to stop them, and save all the Worlds. What could be better than that?'

'Not getting saddle sores?' mumbled Orff, rubbing his thighs.

'I'm not going anywhere else on that bloomin' dinosaur,' said Kartofel. 'I had to dig in something rotten to stay on.'

'No, of course not. I have your old mounts ready for you. And something special for you, Ben. But first, there is the formality of the ceremony.' He clapped his hands, and Crouch entered with a sword resting on a burgundy cushion. 'Now, gentlemen, if I could ask you to bend the knee, we can get this started.'

'I haven't got any knees,' said Djinn.

'Then hover lower,' said The Opposition. 'My spine is aeons old and I'm not stretching up. I'm going to dub thee.'

They knelt, and The Opposition lightly tapped each of them on the shoulders before returning the blade to Crouch. 'I expect you'll find the angels in Rhuddlan Castle. The Sixth and Seventh Blasts need to be performed in the World, on sacred ground. Now if you would be so kind as to follow me through to the stables, we can see you mounted.'

The Opposition nodded at Crouch, who scampered over to a large wooden stable door and pushed it open. A horrible earthy smell wafted into the room, accompanied by the noise of hundreds of different animals.

'Come along,' said The Opposition as he passed through the door. 'Not only would the Apocalypse really ruin my dinner plans, this door is allowing in both a draught and the smell of horse manure. I do like to keep this room aligned aromatically.'

Chapter Twenty-Two

The Augean Stables

The Opposition coughed, and a rotund, hunchbacked demon with a toad's head, horns, and one arm hobbled out of a nearby stall. His left horn had been snapped off, and had a jagged edge instead of a point.

'Master Opposition sir, I didn't think we'd be seeing you today,' he said. 'And what's this? Curse my eyes, if it isn't Masters Thrichthlor, Ichthor and Mnemnor. It's been many a day since I've clapped eyes on you, sirs, make no mistakes.'

'Unfortunately, our friends have been away too long, Drablow,' said The Opposition. 'They don't quite remember the Underworld, so you'll have to forgive them if they don't recognize you. They need to be reacquainted with their old steeds. I was hoping you could help?'

'Don't remember?' said Drablow. 'Don't remember? Well I never. I tell you now, they haven't forgotten you. Practically pining away, they are. They'll be so pleased to see you back.'

'Quite,' said The Opposition. 'So where to first?'

'Biochem, I reckons, sir. Simplest route round.'

Drablow took them through an empty pen and up a small staircase. He stopped outside a heavy white door and punched a code into a nearby keypad. The door opened with a *pfft* sound, and they went through to a very white, very quiet room. On either side there were large white pens, each protected by a keypad door, and each with a window so that the occupant could be observed from outside. However, each pen they passed was empty. They came to a door about halfway into the room, and Drablow punched a code in.

'This be you, Master Thrichthlor.'

They entered the pen, and found that it too was empty.

'There appears to be nothing here,' said Orff.

'I wouldn't be too sure about that,' said Drablow, and suddenly Orff was raised off the floor. The air beneath him turned a lilac colour, and for a moment it looked like he was sitting on a cloud. It wobbled, and shifted, and then took on the rough shape of a large hyena.

'Legion here is a colony of a thousand viruses,' said The Opposition. 'It can reform to take any shape you desire, depending on circumstance. You will find riding it as gentle as riding air, since that is essentially what you will be doing.'

'How is it?' said Ben.

'I . . . I don't know how to say this, but . . . it's *comfortable*?' said Orff. 'Is this what that word means?' Legion changed form, becoming an elephant, raising Orff even higher into the air. He made a dry and dusty groaning noise. Ben thought might it have even been a chuckle.

'We should let them get reacquainted. Or acquainted. I'm still not entirely sure how all of that works,' said The Opposition. 'Where next?'

'Walk this way,' said Drablow as he hobbled to the end of the corridor and jerked his way up a metal staircase.

'If I walked like he did,' said Kartofel, 'I would never ever say that.'

The staircase led up to a large trapdoor in the ceiling. Drablow pushed it open with his hump, and they came into a large aviary.

It was full of different types of birds, all seemingly content to roost on perches behind the huge chicken-wire enclosures. A few of them bristled as the group walked past, and a goose laid a golden egg, but otherwise they were unhindered. At the far end of the loft, Drablow unhitched a door.

A giant yellow head with a long sharp beak poked out, and then quickly poked back in again. Drablow turned to Djinn and smiled. 'That's a good sign, Master Ichthor sir. Alf has been a little shy these past few millennia, since you been gone.'

'Is that mine?' said Djinn. 'He looks big.'

'Oh, he is indeed. But he wouldn't hurt a soul. Not unless you wanted him to. Shall we go in?'

Djinn looked nervously at Ben, who nodded. Drablow ducked in through the door, and Djinn followed. Ben lifted it a little higher to allow Orff and The Opposition in, and then entered himself.

Inside was a huge gannet, so big that if Djinn had weighed as much as he looked like he weighed, the bird would still have had little trouble transporting him. When he saw Djinn, he flapped his wings excitedly.

'Is he going to eat me?' said Djinn.

'He eats a lot, certainly. You should see the piles of bills,' sniggered The Opposition. 'He's rather fond of duck.'

'Oh, you've nothing to fear from Alf, Master Ichthor,' said Drablow. 'He's very excited to see you.'

'It's OK, Djinn,' said Ben. 'You can pet him.'

Djinn reached out a hand, ready to retract it at any moment. He made contact with Alf's chest, and smiled. 'He's really soft.'

'You can get on,' said Drablow. 'He don't bite. Not demons, anyway.' Alf sat down, forcing everyone else to take a swift step backwards. Djinn ran his fingers up through Alf's feathers, floating higher up his body until he was on his back. He threw his arms around the gannet's neck, and buried his face in his ruff.

'It's lovely,' said Djinn.

'Heartwarming,' said The Opposition. 'But I was planning on finishing my book before the world ends, so let's push on. Where next?'

'Unicorn enclosure, I reckons,' said Drablow.

'Unicorn enclosure?' said Kartofel. 'Unicorn enclosure? I hope that's what you're giving him. I can't be seen on a flippin' unicorn. I've got my reputation to think about.'

Drablow led them through another hatch and down to a secluded area, which Ben guessed was somewhere to the rear of the stables. They passed no more pens, and heard no more noises until they came to a large round area. The words 'BEE WHERE: UNICORN INNCLOSER PEN' were daubed on the thick gates in dripping red paint. An impatient stamping of hoofs filled the air, followed by a terrible whinnying. Drablow pressed his remaining shoulder into one of the gates and with some effort pushed it open.

They quickly learned that actual unicorns bear as much resemblance to their fictional counterparts as the average online profile does to the person creating it. The enclosure was full of creatures with hideous rhino horns growing out of their muzzles, terrible red eyes, lank dead hair and thick carthorse legs. They snorted angrily as they stomped around.

'Woah,' said Kartofel. 'Unicorns have had a bad press. Which one's mine then? The big mean one, I hope, with the sharp teeth.'

'Not quite, no,' said The Opposition as Drablow made his way to the back of the enclosure. 'Though Talullah can be something of a handful. Or armful, if you will.'

Drablow returned holding a long set of reins. The other unicorns immediately stopped, and backed into the edges of the pen. He gave a fierce pull and from out of the shadows trotted the smallest, most placid unicorn you could possibly imagine. It had a long fringe that covered its eyes, and couldn't have been much taller than Kartofel himself.

'What's this?' said Kartofel. 'Is this some sort of joke?'

'This be Talullah,' said Drablow. 'Purebred Shetland Unicorn, last of her kind. Many a day she and ye would rampage round the plains of Gehenna, Master Mnemnor. She's a fiery one all right.' The hunchback waved his flapping empty sleeve at Kartofel. 'It's fair to say she's missed you something dear. Don't take kind to anyone else. Getting her saddled was a hell of a chore.'

'The name's Kartofel, pal. And I don't want this. I want one of them big ones. I can't go fighting angels on that.'

'Right you are, Master Mne – Kartofel,' said Drablow. 'She'll be right glum to know it. There won't be much sleep for any of the others tonight. Walk on, Talullah.'

Drablow pulled the reins. Talullah reared up on her hind legs, and neighed. Thick black smoke streamed from her nostrils, and a blast of fire belched out of her mouth. She craned her neck forward, chomped off the hunchback's other arm, and quickly wolfed it down her throat.

'Woah,' said Kartofel.

'I-I-I told you she was fiery,' said Drablow, black blood dripping on to the floor.

Talullah trotted over to Kartofel and nuzzled his head, somehow managing to lick his face. He gave a lopsided grin. She buried her nose under his claws and then threw her head back so that he was flung into the air. He landed squarely in the saddle.

'I'll take her,' said Kartofel.

'Y-y-yes, Master Mnemnor,' said Drablow.

'Oh dear,' said The Opposition. 'Did it take you long to grow that arm back?'

'J-j-just a couple of years, sir.'

'I suppose you better report to Doctor Phlegethon, Drablow. I can take it from here.'

'A h-h-hundred thousand thanks, your majesty.' Drablow hobbled back down the corridor, leaving a spotty trail in his wake. The Opposition led Ben out of the unicorn enclosure, and shut the gates behind them. Ben heard Kartofel saying, 'Oo's a good girl then? Oo's a good girl?' as they walked round the exterior of the enclosure to a portcullis in the back wall. The Opposition threw a lever, and with a great crunching of gears the iron gate rose.

'This is where we part, for now at least,' said The Opposition. 'I have an apocalypse to prepare for. Should you be unsuccessful, of course. You will find your mount tethered outside. The others will join you in due course. Best of luck.'

Ben stepped through the archway, and the portcullis began its clanging descent behind him.

He was back outside the walls of Pandemonium. To his left, some way along the wall, he could see the Road of Good Intentions. Stedge was no longer tethered outside the main gates, and in her place was a large four-legged creature. It was nearly as tall as he was, and at least twice as long. It was covered in soft grey fur, and on its back was a red leather saddle. Its head was protected by a matching mask which accentuated its huge black eyes and flat front teeth: there were holes for its whiskers, and long ears flopped down on either side of its head. It did not seem to be very agile: an assumption proved true when it made an odd grunting sound before lumbering to one side, as if trying to ignore him.

Ben stuck out a hand to stroke the creature, and as soon he touched the fur he knew it was angora. There was something familiar about it, something that he couldn't quite place, but the more he stroked it the better he felt. It was somehow reassuring.

'You remember Druss, don't you, Benji?'

The creature bristled as Ben turned to face his mother. She was a mist, of course, but otherwise she looked just the same. He threw his arms around her, but did not pass through like the mists they had encountered before. Not that she was solid: it was like hugging a cloud.

'I'm sorry,' he said.

'Oh Benji, what have you got to be sorry for?'

'I'm sorry we didn't believe you. About the angels. The Opposition told me,' he sobbed.

'It's OK,' she whispered, her face close to his ear. 'There were days I didn't believe it. I was so confused for so long. It's not easy, living halfway between the imaginary and the real. But then you came, and you cured me, and everything was clear again. It was wonderful.'

Ben stopped crying, and pulled away from her. 'I don't understand,' he said. 'Then why did you do it? If you were better? Why did you leave?'

'I didn't. How could I ever leave you?' She took his face in both hands, and traced the tracks of his tears with her thumbs. The droplets became part of her mist as she touched them. 'It wasn't me. It was the angels. They knew you had healed me, and they knew I would warn you, so they came on the night of the flood, and they took me to the roof . . .'

Ben threw his arms around her and held her tightly. He didn't ever want to let go. She enveloped him in her mist. His shoulders heaved in sobs, but as she held tighter he felt her reassuring warmth cover him, and his breathing slowed.

'Why don't you say hello to Druss? Druss always made you happy, didn't he?' She guided his hand to Druss's haunches. The familiar smell of the rabbit filled his nose, and he buried his face in the fur. He was more like a great bear than a rabbit.

'The Opposition said you were going to stop the angels.'

'I'm going to try,' said Ben. 'But it's just me and the demons. I don't know if that's enough.'

'A strong heart is enough, and you have the strongest.' Mary Rose smiled, and planted a kiss on his cheek. 'Mum and Dad did a good job with you.' She bit her ghost lip, fighting back tears that could never come. Ben put his arm around her.

'There's no point getting upset about it,' she said, pulling away. 'The others will be here soon.' She bent down and made a stirrup out of her hands. Ben put his foot into it, and she boosted him on to Druss's back.

'Be careful,' she said. 'Save the world for me, OK?'

There was a loud cawing noise, and the sound of hoofs on sandstone. A cloud of dust gathered a few hundred metres further along the wall, gaining pace as it moved towards them. Ben coughed, and turned his face away. Three mounted figures rode out of the dust.

'It's the demons,' said Ben. He turned back to his mother, but she had already gone, faded into the dusty shroud that surrounded them.

'Wotcha,' said Kartofel. 'You ready?'

'Yes,' said Ben firmly. 'Are you?'

'Are you joking? I've been waiting an eternity for this.'

'Djinn? Orff?'

'I feel . . . *well*?' said Orff. 'Not being in pain comes with a whole new vocabulary, doesn't it?'

'I'm going to bash them, Ben,' said Djinn.

'Then let's go.' Ben leaned forward and patted Druss's flanks. 'OK,' he whispered. 'Let's just try and keep up with the others.' He was about to dig his heels into Druss's sides, when the rabbit bolted. Caught unaware, he had just enough time to grasp the pommel as they shot off down the Road of Good Intentions.

'Oi, wait for us,' yelled Kartofel, but Ben didn't hear him. They were already too far away.

Chapter Twenty-Three

The Fifth Strident Blast

Death laughed.

She had watched with a smile as her gladiators had pursued the demons and their boy, and as their dinosaur madly spun around, desperate to get away, she found she could no longer contain the joy she felt. All the time she had been locked away she had been powerless. Now she was back she felt all the death coursing through her. The other Horsemen were sending her new mists by the millisecond, and she was starting to feel absolute again, as she should.

Ever since she had returned, the valley had been full of whispers as to what her coming meant. All human death was there, so there were as many opinions as there were spirits. Were there a fifth horseman, one named Rumour, he would have found no better playground than the Afterworld at that precise moment. The mists swirled around, overlapping, passing through each other, making her beautiful frosty fog thicker than ever. All those voices, all those souls, and they all belonged to her.

And then they were spontaneously silent.

Death turned to the ridge that the demons had fled over, wondering if perhaps they had been foolish enough to return, and saw that instead the mists were all looking in the opposite direction, towards the border with the World. She turned round, and in the distance, high above the slopes, she saw four orange shapes in the sky. Angels. They hovered down to the valley floor, and the mists parted as each set softly down.

'We are seeing a lot of tourists today, aren't we?' said Death. 'I thought you weren't going to interfere?'

'We said we weren't going to stop you,' said the scrawniest of the four. 'We fully intend to interfere.'

'Forgive him, Lady Death,' said the angel with the deformed hand. 'He meant no disrespect.'

'Really? Then assure him that I will mean no disrespect when I have you chased out of my kingdom. My gladiators have just enjoyed some sport. Perhaps I will exercise my Maccabees next.'

'I'm sure that won't be necessary, my lady.' The angel with the deformed hand made a deep bow. 'We have come to aid you in bringing about the Apocalypse. We have come to raise an army.'

'Then you are in the wrong place. There is no army to be had here. Only my mists.'

'They are not yours,' hissed the scrawny angel. 'All things were created by the Prime One. All things belong to him.'

'Brother,' warned the deformed angel.

'We are wasting time,' said the scrawny one. 'And I do not care to hear these blasphemies.'

'Then do not listen.' The deformed angel turned to Death. 'Apologies, my lady. Allow me to explain. We have come to this place for the souls of the martyrs and the zealots, the faithful and the righteous, to resurrect them in service of the Prime One.'

The mists erupted in excited chatter. Death's head swam with the noise and the movement around her, as if the tumult in the fog was clouding her own mind. She raised her arm, expecting instant silence, but it took several minutes for the whispers to quieten. She felt her fists ball involuntarily.

'This is my kingdom, and these mists are mine. It does not suit me to give them to you. I prefer instead to grow stronger as the other Horsemen fill my valley. I do not need your help.'

'You misunderstand, my lady,' said the angel. 'We are here to do the Prime One's work, and to recruit the righteous into his army. It is vital to the Apocalypse.'

'I refuse permission,' said Death.

The angel sighed. 'Then, my lady, we do not seek it. Brother?'

The largest of the group rose into the sky and addressed the mists, letting his voice ring out for all to hear. 'Comrades! The Prime One has had many forms. Most of you know Him, even if you don't know that name. He is Odin, and he is Zeus. He is Pangu, and Coatlicue. He is Mbombo. He is a God of many names, and a God of many parts. Those of you who were zealous, and true to Him in life, you martyrs, you brave men and women the heathen dared call extremists: your reward is coming. We will resurrect you. You will live again, incorruptible and undefiled!'

A muttering spread through the mists. There were little pockets of chanted prayers and religious slogans, but mostly the mood was one of discontent and doubt.

'What about the rest of us?' shouted a mist. 'What if you wasn't zealous, but still believed?'

'Yeah,' said another. 'What happens to people who went to temple nearly every week, but missed some weeks due to other commitments?'

'I donated some clothes to the Salvation Army once,' said one.

'I used to listen to *Thought for the Day* religiously.'

'I was an agnostic in life, but now you've turned up I feel a bit of a wally. What about me?'

'The Prime One is still your Creator, and He loves you,' said the big angel, and the mists fell silent once more. 'But there is no place in the new Creation for naysayers. Those of you were atheists, agnostics, heathens, idolaters, infidels: you will remain mists, to suffer this world for eternity. But those of you who believed in any of His aspects, knew Him by any of His names, you will be forgiven your little lapses, provided you join us. We will remove all doubt, we will fill you with zealous fire, and you will live again! Cast off the shackles of Death! Rise, and be resurrected!'

He drew his sword, and thrust it high in the air. The blade burst into flames. 'What say you?'

A cheer rose, one more deafening than any crowd had ever made before. The scrawny angel took the quiver from his back, produced a silver trumpet, and raised it to his lips.

'Stop!' yelled Death. Her voice passed through every mist in the Afterworld, bringing them to perfect stillness. The fog hung in the air, frozen in position. 'Do you think you can take what is mine so easily? I control these mists. I say where they go and what they do. I am Death, of the Four Horsemen. Who are you, who are so arrogant?'

'This is not arrogance,' hissed the scrawny angel. 'It is righteousness.'

'The others shall hear of this,' said Death. 'Then let us see what becomes of your apocalypse.'

'My lady, they have already heard,' said the angel with the deformed hand. 'As I said, we have come here to help.'

There was a wave of movement through the suspended mists, a rolling white froth, like spray on an incoming tide. Frozen mists were thrown into the air and then fell back down again, and the sound of horses' hoofs heralded the coming of the other Horsemen. They entered the clearing and dismounted.

'I don't understand,' said Death. 'You know of this insolence?'

'We are part of it,' said War. 'The last battle is coming, and we will be at the head of it. It will be the ultimate war, and I have been promised the ultimate army to fight it.'

'But these are mine,' said Death.

'And who gave them to you? Who delivered them, but sickness, and conflict, and greed? They are as much ours as yours, and we want to fight.'

'Then I will stand against you.'

'I was hoping you'd say that,' said War, drawing two large cannons from holsters on his belt. Death felt her scythe grow in her hand, and immediately moved into a fighting stance.

Pestilence's jaw fell open, and she emitted a horrible screech. Death twisted to avoid the plague that streamed out, and at the same time swung the scythe in Famine's direction, striking him in the knees. The glutton folded, and fell. Death ran towards him, and leaped up, forcing his head down to the floor, using his body as a platform from which to strike at War, who fired both barrels. Death dodged the first, but the second cannonball grazed her shoulder and threw her off balance. She toppled from Famine's back, and landed face down. Seconds later she felt the weight of War's boot on the back of her neck, then the clutch of Famine and Pestilence on her wrists and ankles.

'You should leave the fighting to me,' said War. He turned to the angels. 'Are you going to blow this horn or not?'

'With pleasure,' said the scrawny one. He blew hard into his trumpet, and a single note rang out. It sustained for a few minutes, and then died out. An eerie silence filled the valley.

And then the cries started.

At first Death thought they were cries of pain: all around, unfrozen mists began to writhe and struggle, but in their contorted faces she saw only joy. Those affected were becoming more defined, more individual, until they could be clearly distinguished from those who were not. Nearby, a young girl was sculpted out of the fog. Red flesh sprouted all over her body, and she became completely solid. New hair and skin formed over it, followed by the stiff black fabric of her clothing. Her new eyes flicked open, but they were not the same eyes she had in life. They were milky grey swirls, tiny galaxies set in bloodshot space. She moved her head round, as if trying to see.

Death wriggled beneath War's boot, trying to get up. She pulled her arms, hoping to break free of Pestilence and Famine, but both held fast.

She yelled another polyphonic command to her subjects, but only the unchanged mists froze. The fleshy horde continued to stumble around in blinded confusion and wonder, arms outstretched.

'They are eternal now,' said the angel with the deformed hand. 'They are neither living nor dead, and so your powers will no longer work. They serve a higher power.'

War lifted his foot, and took a step back. Famine and Pestilence let go, and Death leaped to her feet. 'You've blinded them.'

'They do not need to see,' said the scrawny angel. 'We have given them unwavering, certain faith. See how they are ready for war!'

The army pressed forward, and Death found herself in the middle of a seething mass of flesh and prayers. All rational thought had been taken from them, and even the most gentle and moderate believer in the most obscure deity had been transformed into a zealous fanatic. The odour of rotting meat was all-pervading. There were too many bodies for the valley to hold, and Death was soon overwhelmed, drowning – or at least what she imagined drowning was like, having only ever been present for the end before – in a sea of mouldy cadavers. She was pulled to the ground, and the horde trampled over her.

The hooded angel started to screech at the top of her voice, repeating the same unintelligible phrase over and over again until there was a deafening boom and the army, the Horsemen, and the angels disappeared.

Death rolled on to her back. There were hardly any mists left at all, and those who remained were spread thin across the vastness of her once-full valley. Her crown lay crumpled by her side, and there on the stony ground she understood the desperation of the dead: she knew what it meant to be powerless.

The demons and their steeds had caught up to Ben and Druss just as they reached the Veil, and so they all crossed into the Afterworld together. Even at the very top of the ridge, where the mists had been the thinnest, there was a marked difference in the amount of fog, and it didn't get any thicker as they rode into the valley.

What was left parted at the bottom to reveal the figure of Death hunched over, sitting on the ground. Her clothes were torn, and her china-white face was splattered with mud. She raised her head as they approached, and then sneered when she recognized them.

'Have you come to gloat?' she said.

'No,' said Ben. 'We're on our way to stop the angels from tearing down the Veil and destroying the Worlds.'

'We may not have come to gloat,' said Orff. 'But can't we take the opportunity now that it's presented itself?'

'Orff!' said Ben.

'Well, I'm sorry Ben, but last time we were here she was very inhospitable. That terrible lizard had no idea of passenger comfort. It's played havoc with my hips.'

'Perhaps we could gloat a little?' said Djinn.

'Nobody's doing any gloating, OK?' He turned back to Death. 'What happened?'

'The others,' said Death. 'They came with the angels and turned my mists into these horrible blinded creatures, half dead and half living. I had no dominion over them. They trampled me. I felt what I think might be called pain.'

Kartofel sniggered. Ben shot him a look.

'Still now I feel it, not just in my body but in my head as well. I do not feel myself, and everything seems to be darkness.'

'It sounds like we feel after the light,' said Djinn. 'It's not nice.'

'No, it is not,' said Death. 'And now all I want to do is sit here.' She threw her crumpled crown across the valley, wincing as she did.

'Can you stand?' said Ben, offering his hand. Death frowned at it.

'Please,' he said. 'We're trying to stop the angels. We could use your help.'

She took it, and pulled herself up. As she did he shivered, though he tried to hide it. 'How many mists have you got left?'

'I don't know. A few hundred thousand, maybe. A lot of atheists and agnostics. A few druids, some heathens. A lot of angry ex-nuns who were forced into convents.'

'Nuns?' said Kartofel.

'Ex-nuns,' said Death. 'And since they did nothing but fight their entire lives, you should be glad they're on your side.'

'Good,' said Ben. 'If we can't stop the angels, the Afterworld will need to be ready.'

'What for?' said Death.

'War.'

Chapter Twenty-Four

The Coming of God

They crept up to the well in Rhuddlan Castle in silence, which was quite impressive for a party that included a giant rabbit and a feral unicorn. They needn't have bothered: the sound of the angels' voices echoed up the shaft, drowning out any noise they made.

'. . . the Zealous Army of Martyrs?'

'Billeted in the Veil. Their numbers grow with every death.'

'Excellent. And the Horsemen?'

'War has assumed command, and is preparing for battle.'

'Then I see no reason for delay.'

'How are we gonna get in?' whispered Kartofel. 'It's not like we've brought a ladder. Jabba's bird isn't going to fit down the hole, and I'll bet the bunny's too fat for it too.'

Druss snorted, and a gust of air blew through Kartofel's flames, knocking him off Talullah. Ben stifled a laugh.

'We'll have to leave the animals here, that's for sure. Maybe Djinn . . .'

A trumpet rang out. The skies darkened, the earth shook beneath their feet, and what was left of the castle walls began to crumble. There was a horrible screeching noise, like the world was being ripped apart, and meteors appeared in the sky, hurtling towards Earth.

'The Sixth Strident Blast!' said Ben.

A massive crack opened up in the ground, and the ceiling of the chamber stared to collapse beneath their feet. Loose earth cascaded into the hole like a waterfall, and they had little choice but to sink with it.

'I guess that answers the question of how we get down,' said Kartofel.

The trumpet died out, the tremor came to a stop, and the chamber beneath Rhuddlan Castle was no more, mostly because Rhuddlan Castle was no more. In its place was a massive earthen bowl, the burned-out Box at its centre. The Seraph smiled.

'We wondered what had happened to you,' he said. 'We expected to find corpses.'

'We know everything,' said Ben.

'I doubt that,' said The Seraph. 'Only the Prime One is all-knowing. But I assume from the colourful steeds you have acquired that you met The Adversary, and he told you of the travesty that ended the Grand War. Much good may it do you. The Sixth Blast has been blown. Natural disasters are striking the globe. Soon all life will be wiped out, and the Prime One's army will be unstoppable. And once we blow the Seventh Blast, He will return to lead them.'

'Not if we can help it,' said Djinn, doing an admirable impression of bravery.

'Really? Three worn-out demons and a teenage boy, so easy to defeat that all it takes is a flick of my wrist?' The Seraph thrust his hand out in front of him, his fingers popping and fizzing with amber light.

Djinn winced. When nothing happened, he slowly opened one eye, and then another. He looked at the other demons, and saw that they weren't suffering either. Kartofel scuttled over to The Seraph.

'Is that supposed to be doing something?'

The Seraph snarled, an intense expression of hatred on his face.

He moved his hand so that it was directed at Kartofel alone, but still nothing happened.

'Nah, it's not working,' said Kartofel, turning to the others. 'It's not working.'

The Seraph growled, and lunged forward. He raised Kartofel into the air with both hands, and started to squeeze his palms together.

'You may have found a way to deflect our powers, demon,' said The Seraph, his face tense with the strain. 'But you are not immune to pain.'

Kartofel yowled. His flame flared up, growing until it was as tall and wide as The Seraph, who staggered back in shock. Kartofel shunted his head forward, and The Seraph was immediately consumed by fire. He dropped Kartofel, and then threw himself on the floor, rolling around to put the flames out.

'That is so cool,' said Kartofel. 'I am even more awesome than I first thought.'

Across the room, The Castellan of the Veil threw a punch at Djinn. As if by instinct, his gassy body separated to allow her fist through, then closed up around it, sealing it inside. With a look of determination on his face and a totally unnecessary arm gesture that would have made Superman proud, he wisped upward, dragging the angel with him.

At the same time, The Triumph charged towards Orff. Startled, he raised his arms and Legion dived in front of him, transforming into a snarling purple bear as he did. Orff took a step forward, and so did Legion. They lunged for The Triumph, who dug his feet in, refusing to be pushed back. They grappled, The Triumph wincing as Legion roared filthy contagious breath in his face until his legs buckled, and he was forced to his knees.

In the confusion, Ben ran for The Archivist, who had been

viewing the attacks with a look of horror. Ben wrapped his whole body around the trumpet, hoping that gravity would help him pull it from The Archivist's hand, but as he dangled there, something impacted hard into his side, and he fell awkwardly, skidding across the floor. Suddenly the sky was alive with colour, and The Triumph, The Seraph and The Archivist were all shielding their eyes.

A black robe lay on the floor directly underneath Djinn. The Castellan of the Veil glided down from the ceiling, naked. Unlike the other angels, her skin was not midnight black but diamond, and she refracted tiny spears of rainbow light as if she were a prism. Ben could not move, and it appeared the demons were similarly afflicted, skewered to the spot by the light.

She spoke. It was the first time Ben had heard a human language from her. Her voice was pure, and clear, and high enough to shatter glass.

'I am the Castellan of the Veil, Majestic Herald of the End Times, Usher of the New Kingdom, Bailiff of the Court of the Celestium Majora, Harbinger of the Apocalypse, Speaker of the Celestial Parliament, Duchess of the Heavenly Host, Most Reverend Bride of the Prime One and the Ultimate Oblate of the Cult of the Four Winds. And I say: "Enough!"'

'Yes!' cried The Seraph. 'Yes! Brother, sound the Seventh Blast! Behold the Prime One!'

The Archivist strode over to Ben, and easily slid the trumpet out of his paralysed grip. He blew forcefully into the mouthpiece, and a fanfare echoed around the crater, repeating over and over, as if it would sound for all time.

Once The Archivist's breath was exhausted, and the last of it passed through the trumpet, it split, and it was discarded it as if it were scrap. The fanfare, with its perpetual echo, was now the only sound. The constant repetition made it far from triumphant, and it took on a taunting tone. The angels looked to one another. Every second brought more hope and less expectation.

'Where is He?' said The Triumph. 'Why hasn't He come?'

'I don't know,' said The Seraph, turning to The Archivist. 'Brother, you must have done something wrong.'

'I have trained every day since the end of the Grand War for this task,' said The Archivist. 'If there is a fault here, I think we all know where it lies.'

'I don't care for your tone,' said The Seraph.

'I have never cared for yours. All this time, you have pushed us into your plans, had us to pander to children. And what is the great revelation the sacrifices you have asked of us has brought? That the Prime One is not coming.'

'Is this true?' said The Triumph. The Seraph looked worried.

'Of course it is true,' said The Archivist. 'Of course He is not coming. All eternity, with no word from Him? He abandoned us long ago.'

'Recant that,' said The Seraph, his voice rising as he spoke.

'You are a fool,' said The Archivist. 'You are not worthy of the name angel.'

The Seraph sprang at him, his good hand balled into a fist. The Archivist sidestepped, then quickly turned to attack. The Seraph levered him over his shoulder, and they brawled messily on the floor.

'Wait!' said The Castellan of the Veil. 'I can feel something.'

'What is it, sister?' said The Seraph hopefully. 'Is it the Prime One?'

'No.' Her body juddered, and she let out an ecstatic moan. 'The Veil is cracking. Tiny hairline fractures, but I can feel every one. Oh! The End Times are upon us! The Veil will fall!'

'Do you see what you've done?' said Ben. 'You have to stop it.'

The Seraph's face dropped. The Prime One was not coming. He had brought about the end of Creation. He shook his head. 'It cannot be stopped. The Worlds are ending. If the Veil is cracking . . . the Prime . . . it cannot be stopped.'

'Why would you want it stopped?' said The Archivist. 'The plan has not changed. The Prime One may not be here, but there is no reason we cannot seize Creation in his name. This is our chance. We will march on Hell, crush The Adversary, and remake the Creation. A new angelic age will begin!'

'No,' said The Seraph. 'Enough.'

'I have had enough of you telling me "enough", Brother.' The Archivist lunged for the warped shell of the Box, wrenching it up from the floor. Smoke rose from his palms, and he cried out in pain and effort. He twisted his upper body and slammed the Box into the side of The Seraph's head. It slid through like boiling water over snow.

The Seraph's headless body juddered for a moment, then exploded in a blinding orange flash.

The Archivist threw the Box on the floor, and turned to the other angels. 'What say you?'

'The Angelic Age,' said The Castellan of the Veil.

The Triumph stared at the spot that was so recently The Seraph. 'Brother?'

The Triumph nodded dumbly.

'Good,' said The Archivist. 'Now for Armageddon.'

The Castellan of the Veil picked up her cloak and wrapped it around herself. The last of the rainbow javelins shot through Ben, but before he could move again The Castellan of the Veil had spoken, and the Cult of the Winds were gone.

Chapter Twenty-Five

The Last Battle

Walking through the cemetery was the last thing Lucy remembered clearly. After that, she mostly remembered lots of water, and the confusion as it reared up in front of her, impossibly massive, and so far inland. What a pity, she thought. So soon after the last flood, when we were just getting back on our feet. And as the absurdity of that thought hit her, so did the wave. Suddenly she was trying to swim, and there were dislodged tombstones floating in the water, slamming into each other, and then into her, and then she was dead, and in a strange version of Rhyl town centre without any litter or dog dirt or tourists.

She found herself at the back of a long queue, most of whom had suffered horrible injuries: there was a man with a road sign sticking out of his chest, and a woman in a hard hat who was so pierced with nails that she looked like a hedgehog. Everybody seemed slightly out of focus. Lucy brought a hand up to her face and saw that she was too. In front of her were three younger girls with pale skin and blue lips.

'Here, Jen, what's going on?' said one. She had a hard face, and greasy blonde hair.

'Dunno, Sal,' said Jen. 'I think we might be in Heaven or something.'

'Looks like Rhyl to me, Jen. A rubbish Rhyl, without a shopping centre or a Greggs or anything else good.'

The third girl, a slight redhead, laughed nervously.

'Maybe it's not Heaven then. Maybe this is the queue to get into Heaven,' said Jen.

'Do you think we'll get in?' said Sal.

'Course. We're under eighteen. They got to let you in if you're under eighteen. It's the law. We're definitely dead though, because I remember the big wave round the back of the cinema and I can't swim.'

'Oh,' said Lucy. 'I think I drowned too. I was at the cemetery, and now I'm here.'

The girls stopped talking and looked Lucy up and down. The redhead giggled.

'Oh my God. Are you, like, talking to me?' said Jen. 'She is, isn't she?'

'That is well embarrassing,' said Sal. 'Are you some sort of emo or something then?'

'No. I'm Lucy. It's nice to meet you.' She extended her hand.

'Loser,' snorted Jen, and turned round. 'So what do you reckon Heaven will be like? I bet everyone gets a boyfriend as soon as they get there. And an iPad.'

Death gathered her mists into legions and platoons. She could not quite believe she was doing it. She was usually the result of fighting, not the cause of it. This was War's area of expertise. But when she started to think about her fellow Horsemen she got angry, and decided that anger was probably all you needed for a war. Then she looked at her sorry bunch of mists, and thought: anger, and someone else to fight for you.

Although the death rate had rocketed, very few of the freshly killed were coming to the Afterworld. The Apocalypse was doing very little for the recruitment of new atheists, and the ones that did turn up were hardly spoiling for a fight. It seemed that the most bloodthirsty and fervent army of all time would be facing the kind of people you would want on a protest march, but who would not have been much use at, say, the Somme. Unless some poems needed writing.

Death lined her army up on the ridge nearest to the Underworld. She was not sure where the war would be coming from, but she knew that waiting for it at the bottom of a valley was probably not that smart. She had hoped that they would not be needed, but when the Seventh Blast sounded, she knew it would not be long before the demons and their boy returned. She mounted her horse, and turned to address her troops.

'It seems that you were right all along, all you naysayers. There is no Prime One.' This got a massive cheer, and Death felt an uncharacteristic shiver of excitement pass through her. 'This is not the Apocalypse. It is a coup, engineered by extremists. And now their army is coming here to end us, and if they are successful they will go on to destroy everything in existence.'

This didn't get a cheer, and Death suddenly felt a little less confident, which was also a new sensation for her. If she had one characteristic, it was certainty. 'I don't want you to think that we don't have a chance though, even if we are just mists and they are flesh and angry and are filled with a supernatural zeal for ending mists who disagree with them.'

The mists seemed even less happy at this. Afraid that she might be losing them, she thought back to all those noble last words that had been uttered over the years, and saw a way through. Rhetoric, that was the trick, which in her mind just meant more exclamation marks. 'I say that being mist is your greatest advantage! You can move in ways they cannot! They cannot hurt you, because you are already dead! And best of all, you can do this!'

She raised one clenched fist in the air. Her scythe appeared, and a huge roar of excitement blasted back at her. 'Think of a weapon, and the fog will reform to place it in your hand!'

The mists cheered. Exclamation marks, thought Death. That's all it is.

As the mists excitedly tried out their previously unknown talent for making weapons appear – she saw one man manifest a tank, which immediately squished him – the demons and their boy appeared on the opposite ridge.

'You failed,' said Death once they were in earshot. It was a statement rather than a question.

'Yeah, well, you did a great job of holding on to all the dead, didn't you?' said Kartofel.

'At least I have an army,' said Death. 'What about you?'

'Call that an army?'

'They're ready,' said Death. 'See how they eat out of my hand!' She turned back to her troops, and gestured for silence. 'And now we will show them what it means to mess with the Dead!' she yelled, raising her scythe in the air, expecting another roar.

A worried murmur passed through the crowd. The mists fidgeted nervously. Some of them looked away. Kartofel cackled.

A crazed ululating battle cry rang out, and they turned to see what had worried the mists. War was standing on the other side of the valley, drenched in blood, his eyes the only specks of white on his whole body. As the battle cry died out, he cackled with glee. 'Here we come! The last battle! The ultimate army! The greatest war of all time! Awesome!'

'What a wally,' said Kartofel.

'That much we can agree on,' said Death.

The heads of the Zealous Army of Martyrs appeared over the crest of the hill, stretched out over the length of the horizon: it was not possible to look on them all at once, for they were wider than any one field of vision, and this was just their front line. The air filled with a rumble of undead feet.

The Afterworld army immediately broke ranks, becoming a shapeless fog so thick that it became hard to see anything at all.

'Fall in! Stay in ranks! The only chance we have is if we stay in ranks!' Death bawled. 'We're here to defend this world, and defend it we will!'

The mists settled instantly, reformed, and once again became organized into rows. Death folded her arms and looked at Kartofel.

'Fair dos,' he muttered. 'So what's the plan?'

'We let them pour into the valley,' said Death. 'They'll have to climb the slope to get at us, and hopefully that will tire them out.'

'Have we got a better plan? One that doesn't rely on zombies getting tired?'

'I think that's a good plan,' said Ben. 'I'll go back to Pandemonium. Hopefully The Opposition can send reinforcements.'

'What about us?' said Djinn. 'Can't we come?'

'No. You three will need to fight. If they push us back to the Veil, the mists won't be able to pass it. We'll be penned in. We need to hold the ridge.'

On the other side of the valley, War had watched the chaos in the opposing army with a hungry smile. Then he watched Death pull them back into order incredibly quickly, which ruined the moment for him a little bit. She wasn't supposed to be going off organizing armies. That was his job. She was supposed to clean up after him.

Fair enough, he had sort of betrayed her, but that didn't give her the right to start fighting wars. He responded with a bloodcurdling cry (although his opponents had no blood to curdle).

'CHAAAAAAAARRRRRRGE!'

Lucy and the girls had progressed to the head of the queue. An old man with a bulbous nose, a bushy white beard and a bald head was sat at a small writing desk. He wore a black suit with a high white collar and was using a quill to check off names on a long scroll. On either side of him were a number of zombie clerics, each one representing a different religion.

'Good afternoon,' said the man as the three girls stepped forward. 'My name is Charles, and I am the Classification Officer for this ward. Ahead of you are two choices: eternal paradise, or an existence of everlasting worry and doubt. Should you choose eternal paradise, there are representatives of your chosen religion on hand to discuss your onward journey according to belief system, whether that involves absolving you of your sins, some sort of trial, or paying the ferryman. If the latter is applicable we have a variety of attractive loan packages.' He dunked the quill in his inkwell and held it over the parchment. 'Now, do you believe in an all-powerful Creator or Creators, whatever name you know Him, Her or Them by?'

'I've got a cross, if that's any good,' said Jen. 'It's more of a fashion thing though . . .'

'Fear not. You shall be filled with a complimentary blinding righteous zeal on recruitment. What say you? Paradise, or barren waste ground of tormented souls?'

'Paradise,' said Jen.

'Paradise,' said Sal.

The redhead sniggered.

'Three for paradise,' said Jen.

'Step to the right, please, good ladies. Welcome to the Zealous Army of the Martyrs. May the Prime One or Ones go with you, depending on your personal faith journey.'

'Army?' said Sal. 'What d'you mean, army?'

The girls were ushered to one side by a smiling undead priest, and led away. Charles made a note on the scroll, and beckoned Lucy forward.

'Good afternoon. My name is Charles and I am—'

'Oh yes,' said Lucy. 'I heard you tell those girls. I'm Lucy.'

Charles looked down at the scroll. 'I know. What say you?'

'Well, I have a few questions first . . .'

Charles slapped his head and ran his hand slowly down his face. 'Another one for the waste ground of tormented souls,' he shouted. Lucy opened her mouth to protest, but before she could say a word there was a soft popping noise, and she was gone.

Ben tore back through the ranks, bursting through gaps and leaping over heads. As they neared the Veil, he looked back over his shoulder and saw just how vast the angels' army was. And although the horde charging towards the relatively thin band of fog was scary, there was a small part of him that couldn't help seeing an army of ghosts about to battle an army of zombies without thinking it was kind of cool. If only Tegwyn could see me now, he thought. And then another thought hit him: he probably can.

Lucy had become a creature of fog. And somehow she had ended up shoulder to shoulder with fog versions of the Grand Druid, and flippin' Tegwyn Price. And then, in the distance, she had seen an army of zombies and before she knew it she was holding a long green staff in her hand, and she realized that she was in a war.

She looked around her and saw that her fellow fog-druids were also equipped with inexplicable weapons. Tegwyn was armed with a long bronze shield emblazoned with an eagle's head, and the Grand Druid had somehow gained a green wizard's hat. Everywhere she looked new fog-people were materializing, and they had weapons too: spatulas, hedge trimmers, shovels. One small boy was armed with a barbarian's club, his older sister with just a cloak. Confusion reigned, and as Lucy looked out over the fog she could see panic lapping over the army, breezing backwards through the ranks. She looked at her fellow warriors, and their massively inappropriate weapons, and could not help but think that perhaps panic was the most sensible option.

In the heart of the disarray, a young woman with pale green hair and a horse to match raised her arm, and the rippling waves of panic that were thrusting up towards them suddenly stopped. The fog-people in front of them refocused, and began to steel themselves behind the girl on the horse.

'Nnnn,' said Tegwyn, 'I don't believe it.'

'What?' said the Grand Druid.

'We're just going to wait for them to charge, are we? It doesn't make sense. Whoever that silly girl on the horse is, she doesn't know what she's doing.'

'I'm sure she's doing her best, Teg. It's not an easy situation, obviously for anyone. It's caught us all a bit unawares, hasn't it? One minute you're reading up about pagan birthing rituals, the next you're dead and preparing to fight in a battle loosely based on Judeo-Christian myth. I checked the woodland auguries just this morning and they didn't say anything about this.'

Tegwyn screwed up his face in annoyance.

'You think you can do better, do you?' said Lucy.

'We need experience,' said Tegwyn. 'Since there don't appear to be any genuine warmagi here, we'll have to pass to the artillery phase. Strategy, that's ninety per cent of what war is.'

'Oh, shut up, Tegwyn,' said Lucy.

'Nnnn,' said Tegwyn, and muttered something extremely sexist under his breath.

A grey blur suddenly leaped over their heads, shaking the ground as it landed. They all looked behind them in time to see a massive furry creature dash away with a teenage boy on its back.

'What was that?' said the Grand Druid.

'This is going to sound weird,' said Lucy, 'but it looked a bit like Ben Robson riding a giant rabbit.'

'Nnnn,' said Tegwyn. 'As if.'

The Martyrs had slammed into the Afterworld army with zeal, ripping and tearing at the mists until they evaporated in an anti-climactic hiss of steam. Death barked out orders quickly and often, hoping to distract her troops from any shock they might feel at seeing that they could be torn apart so easily.

Fortunately, the martyrs were not that hard to kill either. Their bodies were already decaying, and so it was easy to separate them from their heads. Death was enjoying that part of it, swooping her scythe around in wide circles, beheading zealots. The only trouble was that they were outnumbered, that and the fact that for every mist killed the air became heavy with steam. Not only did it make it hard for her to see, it also condensed whenever it touched her skin. Soon she was dripping in a sweat of departed spirits, and the

218

wetter she got, the further back they were pushed, closer and closer to the edge of the Afterworld.

'Nnnn, I've had enough of this,' said Tegwyn as he narrowly missed being evaporated by a Saracen. 'I'm going to the front. If this was Warmonger she'd be facing a mutiny trial by now. We need to attack their flanks.'

'What flanks?' said Lucy as she shoved the end of her staff into a Vestal Virgin's eye. 'They're everywhere.'

'I wouldn't expect you to understand. You're not a gamer,' said Tegwyn.

'Actually, I know exactly what you're talking about. You take the number of casualties in an engagement by and subtract it from the army's loyalty score. Then, using three dice, you have to roll equal or less than that number to avoid your army running away. Somehow I don't think that applies here.'

'Nnnn,' said Tegwyn. He ducked a blow from a passing Zulu warrior and made a dash for it. Before long he was recklessly running over the terrain, dodging blows from mist-thirsty zealots.

Lucy sighed. 'There's always some idiot who wants to copy what they've read in a book or played in some game somewhere, isn't there? I suppose we'd better go after him.'

'Idiot, Lucy? That's a bit strong, isn't it?' said the Grand Druid. 'I know Teg can be a bit, well . . .' He was interrupted by a martyr dressed completely in tartan waving a mace in his direction. Without thinking, Lucy thrust her staff upward at a sharp angle, and took the martyr's head clean off.

'Let's worry about being polite after the war, shall we?'

*

There was one small part of the Afterworld where the Martyrs were making no progress at all. No matter how many of them charged up the hill, they could not press beyond what was now technically the Afterworld front line, although line is a very strong word for three demons fighting more or less back-to-back. They were so successful, in fact, that their opponents had started to swerve away from them, which says a lot for blind faith: when it meets an obstacle it does tend to find a tricksy way round it.

'This is rather fun,' said Orff, as Legion turned into a rhinoceros and skewered four marauding monks on its horn. Then it changed into a thousand wasps, dumping the four bodies unceremoniously on the floor while simultaneously attacking a whole group of Teutonic Knights.

Alf swooped his head forward and gulped down several attackers in one go, making a little runway for Djinn to wisp into. He expanded his girth to absorb six Aztec priests, then contracted suddenly, knocking them together so that bits of them fell off.

'Told you so,' said Kartofel as Talullah incinerated a whole platoon of Spanish Inquisitors. 'All those years of whining. All you needed was a little bit of healthy destruction. Does you the world of good.'

Death pulled hard on the horse's reins, and swung the scythe round. A row of rotting cavaliers were sliced in half just before they could lunge at the group of mists fighting nearest to her. The horse reared up, and they changed direction, heading for the next closest band of mists in peril.

'Nnnn, you there,' yelled a voice from behind her. She lopped off the heads of a couple of Spartans and turned to see a mist scrambling toward her carrying nothing but a shield. Behind him, doing an excellent job of preventing his evaporation, were two more: a young woman with a long staff, and a portly man in a wizard's hat. 'Nnnn. What do you think you're playing at? We should be in retreat, or else we should be turning!'

Death's brow furrowed. An axe thudded into her thigh, as if she were a ham on a butcher's block. The sound she made was more out of shock than pain. Her attacker, a stern fat-faced little man, was clumsy: he had a crazed look of righteous indignation on his face, but he lacked experience. He frantically yanked at his axe, trying to dislodge it.

Death swore. (She had quite an impressive vocabulary of swear words, thanks to her presence at the scene of so many accidents.) The man put his foot against her horse's flank and pulled with all his strength. She felt herself begin to topple, and before she knew it she had let go of her scythe and was on the ground. She landed on top of her attacker, pressing the axe deeper into her thigh. She flailed at the man, only stopping when she was sure he wouldn't be able to axe anybody ever again.

'And now you've gone and lost your horse,' said the mist with the shield. 'That's like losing a standard bearer. Shoddy.'

'Excuse him,' said the young woman. 'He's a sexist idiot. I think you're doing a great job. Cool hair, by the way.'

'Are you trying to lose us the war?' yelled Death. She yanked the axe from her thigh, and it came away cleanly. The indentation (for 'wound' seemed too grand a name) fizzed a little. Steam rose from it, and it was healed.

A zealot wearing a Welsh Guards uniform blundered out of the mist. Death swung the axe in an upward curve, literally disarming him before felling him as she brought it down.

'What do you say to that then, Teg?' said the mist with the staff.

'Nnnn, I could do that if I had an axe,' said Teg.

'You could have,' said Death. 'Think of it, and it will be in your hand. Don't you know anything?' She demonstrated by making a new scythe appear.

Teg's shield reformed itself into a huge axe, and he promptly fell over from the weight of it. The mist with the staff started to laugh, and even Death allowed herself a smile. It was a moment soon cut short, for a mob of angry villagers and townsfolk charged out of the fog. A man in dungarees and a straw hat thrust his pitchfork at them. Death dodged it, and instead the blow stabbed Teg in the backside, and with a steamy *fsst* he was gone.

Death called out for her horse. The mist with the staff had now become the mist with the spear, and her companion had gained a bow. The three of them stood back to back as the villagers circled them, farming implements jabbing out of the steam. They were surrounded.

Their enemies did not get much time to sport with them, however. There was a great beating of wings, and the gas demon and his gannet landed in the middle of the circle and gobbled down the front row of attackers. Seconds later, the other two demons joined them, and they had enough breathing space to rejoin the main army.

Heartened, Death cried out, 'Let's show them what we are made of!'

Nearby, a philosopher was evaporated by an angry conquistador.

'I think they already know,' said Kartofel.

Chapter Twenty-Six

The War Games

Ben wasted no time tethering Druss and dashed towards the gates of Pandemonium. He raised his hand, expecting the door to swing open as it had done for Neil, and when it didn't he knocked. When there was no reply, he followed up with a series of loud raps, building in intensity until he was pounding his fist on the door, making an ominous gong sound.

Druss, who had been sitting patiently on the soft earthen wasteland, stirred. He sat up on his hind legs and tilted his head forward, his ears raised. He twitched his nose, scraped a paw across his face twice in quick succession, and began to stamp rhythmically with his left hind leg. The ground shook, and the walls of Pandemonium soon followed.

It was not long before a little head popped over the wall about fifty metres from the gates. 'Oi,' it said. 'Shut that chuffin' rabbit up, will yer?'

'Neil?' said Ben.

'Eh up, Ben. You all right?'

'Not really. I need to see The Opposition.'

'Ooh, I don't know about that. Don't you know there's a war on?'

'That's why I'm here. It's urgent.'

'Makes sense, I suppose. Hang on a mo.' Neil's head disappeared, his chain mail clanking as he went. A good while later a hidden door swung out of the wall, and Neil reappeared.

'Come on then, I haven't got all chuffin' day.'

Ben ducked inside, and Neil pulled the door shut with a sharp tug.

They walked down a humid dark corridor full of glistening cobwebs. The further they went the hotter it got, until it opened out on to a massive warehouse.

On every spare bit of floor there was a piece of machinery working at full pelt, ranging from huge looms to tiny clockwork contraptions. Around each machine worked a number of demons: two gorillas with goats' legs worked a furnace one-third their size, while dozens of penguin-grasshopper hybrids with eyepatches on fell over each other trying to work a single crane.

'I suppose all this chaos is how Pandemonium gets its name,' said Ben.

'Oh no, not at all. Would've thought an educated bloke like yerself would know that. Gets its name from an old poem by some bloke called Milton Johns. His Nibs liked it so much he nicked it. Used to be called Lxtyplxc before that, but no one could say it.'

Neil scampered past busy demons and even busier machines. The heat was intense, and in the few minutes they had spent crossing the factory floor Ben was able to watch the sweat patch on the back of Neil's tunic grow.

At the opposite end of the room was a metal staircase leading up to a gantry, at the end of which was a wooden door with glass panels. The top panel had 'PROPRIETOR' painted on in gold letters. Halfway down was a small brass knocker in the shape of a dog's paw. It was too low for Ben, but the perfect height for Neil, who rapped on it three times. A tired voice beckoned them to enter.

The Opposition was pacing along the wall, his hands clasped

behind his back. He was wearing a general's uniform in the classic style, with one exception: it was purple tie-dye. Ben saw a flash of worry in his face, one that was soon choked away with a warm smile.

'Ah, Ben. It seems we're in a bit of a pickle. They blew the Sixth and Seventh Strident Blasts.'

The office door rattled as it closed, and Neil stood to attention beside Ben, his chest out.

'Oh, hello, Captain. At ease. How are things at the foundry? Ben, would you like some tea?' The Opposition clapped his hands before either of them could answer, and a small door opened. Crouch entered, carrying the tea things on a silver platter. Neil cursed under his breath (Ben caught the word 'chuffing') and gave a low growl. Crouch unloaded the tray and left, his snake tail hissing at Neil, who erupted in uncontrolled yelping.

'Come now, Captain,' said The Opposition. 'The Foundry?'

'Oh yessir, sorry, sir,' said Neil sheepishly. 'Foundry's running at full capacity, sir. All claws, paws, hoofs and wings to the pump, sir.'

'Very good. And the army?'

'All the armies of Hell are primed and awaiting yer orders, sir. Except the ones without weapons yet, foundry's working on that. And the Dis Fusiliers, but you know what chuffin' lazy bar stools they are down there, pardon my Aramaic, sir.'

The Opposition rolled his eyes. 'Please don't call it Hell, Captain. You know I can't abide that word. I've told you countless times before. That will be all. Dismissed.'

'Yessir, thank you, sir,' barked Neil, and saluted. The Opposition lazily returned the gesture, and Neil exited through yet another door.

'So, Ben, I assume that the Prime One did not make an appearance?'

'No, he didn't.'

'Indeed. How did the angels take it?'

'They don't care. They're going to attack anyway.'

'How predictable of them. Speaking of attacking, what do you think of the uniform? Khaki isn't my thing, but I'm not entirely convinced this is either.' He turned side on, as if admiring the cut in a mirror.

'Erm . . . it's very nice?' said Ben. 'Look, I'm sorry but maybe we should focus on the war? There's an army of ghosts between them and you, but they're massively outnumbered.'

The Opposition brought a cup to his lips and sipped slowly. 'Quite. Any suggestions?'

'Take the fight to them. We need reinforcements, and you've got an army.'

The Opposition drained his cup and put it down. 'The problem with that is the Veil has already begun to crack. And the most important thing about the Veil is that it's not just a barrier keeping the worlds apart: it's also the glue that holds them together. Now what do you suppose will happen if an army is marched through it?'

'An army is coming through it one way or another. At least if it's yours then we've got a chance.'

'Well, yes. When you put it like that, I suppose you have a point. This whole business requires something of a tactical mind, and I, well, I made Neil Captain of the Guards. That, and this outfit, should tell you how suited I am to military thinking. Which is why I am happy to cede all my armies directly to you.'

'Me?' said Ben.

'Why not? You know a thing or two about war games, don't you? Squat used to tell me all about something called War Monster in his reports. He was rather enthusiastic.'

'Warmonger. But that's done with dice, and a tape measure, and miniatures. And not when the existence of everything everywhere is at stake.'

'True, but I expect the principle is much the same. Someone somewhere nonchalantly pushes the pieces around, and somewhere else some poor group of grunts dies.'

The edge of the Veil was a disconcerting place. Light refracted in strange ways, and a constantly evolving stream of colour filled the vision: reds, oranges and yellows collided and morphed into blues, indigos, violets.

The movements of both armies were severely restricted. Combatants would turn to the left and find themselves unable to move, an unseen barricade blocking their way. A turn to the right, and all would be well again. It was as if the battle had entered an invisible labyrinth. They did not know it, but they were fighting inside the Veil, slipping in and out of the imperceptible cracks that the Seventh Strident Blast had made.

Death and the demons had the advantage of their mounts, all of which could pass through the Veil unhindered, but even they were restricted by the horde of cadavers, so densely packed that even Legion was finding it difficult to take shape. And with still more zealots flooding up the hill, eager to join the melee, it appeared that it would not be long before they were overwhelmed.

Ben and The Opposition shook hands.

'I think you might have use of that metaphorical tent of mine,' said The Opposition. 'A literal metaphorical tent.'

'We need someone to deliver our terms,' said Ben.

'Of course,' said The Opposition, making a little humming noise as he mulled it over. He did not have long to think about it before the glass-panelled door shot open, and Neil came hurtling through.

'Sorry to interrupt sir I've a scout just back from the rim of Hell of the Underworld I mean sorry sir and he says that the mists have been pushed to the outer rim sir and that the angels are coming.'

'Sir Ben has assumed command of all our armies, Captain,' said The Opposition, fluttering a hand in Ben's direction. 'Tell him.'

Neil turned to Ben, and took a deep breath. 'Sorry to interrupt sir but I've a scout just back from the rim—'

'Just obey his orders as if they were my own, Captain.'

'Right y'are, sir,' he said, and again turned to Ben, this time standing to attention. 'Awaiting yer orders, sir.'

'Right. Orders. Yes . . . I think you should prepare the armies, and we'll ride out to the Veil as soon as they're ready. If that's all right with you.'

'Sir, yessir.'

'Erm . . . dismissed?' said Ben, returning Neil's salute. The dog-demon turned on his heels, and scampered out.

'So the battle of Armageddon is to be fought on Good Intentions,' said The Opposition, sniggering slightly. Ben did not laugh along. He felt a bit sick.

'You'll be fine. Cheer up! It's not the end of the world. Ha! Now, about that emissary . . .' The Opposition clapped his hands, and Crouch came in through one of the doors.

'Ah, Crouch. How would you like to be made an Ambassador?'

Three of the angels appeared in the sky, high above the advancing army. Their orange auras turned pink, then purple, then blue in the light of the Veil.

'Push through!' screamed the scrawny one. 'Tear it down! We will march on Hell! We will execute The Adversary at the gates of Pandemonium! The angelic age will begin!'

A cheer rose in the ranks of the Zealous Army, and there was a sudden surge forward. All around, Death saw mists being pressed together, forced into an ill-defined grey mass. The tide of bodies swept her away from the demons, and the girl with the spear and her companion disappeared, lost in the fog.

Everything began to shake. The revolving rainbow of colour shimmered and bled into one twilight-purple shade. Pressed bodies spilt on to the floor, and the ground groaned under the weight of them.

And then all Hell broke loose.

The boy and his rabbit burst through the Veil and landed square in the middle of a legion of undead monks. The rabbit bit and kicked at them before zipping forward unexpectedly. It swerved, trampled three angry-looking teenage girls, and then shot off into the distance.

Behind them, with banners unfurled and blades drawn, was what could just as well be called a menagerie as an army. It was led by a little dog-demon riding a velociraptor, and included minotaurs, harpies, cockatrices and kittens.

The demons' war drums started to pound, and Death saw confusion and horror on the faces of her opponents. Freed from the constraints of the Veil and bolstered by reinforcements, the mists set about their work with a new vigour.

In the chaos, no one noticed the grand canvas tent that had appeared exactly in middle of the valley, as if it had always been there. Nor did they notice the squealing demon in a butler's uniform soaring over the heads of both armies, deep into enemy territory.

Crouch was used to indignity. The Opposition had a flair for doing things the wrong way round (which secretly annoyed him, as he was the kind of demon that liked things to be *just so*) and therefore it was no surprise to him that his new role as Ambassador for the Underworld would involve being catapulted behind enemy lines to deliver terms of engagement. He didn't protest – he was nothing if not loyal – and just got on with the job of being flung through the air really quickly.

He landed at the back of the Army of Martyrs. The last few soldiers, a platoon of diademed clerics, were about to charge into the valley when one of them spotted him, picked him up by the scruff of his neck, and took him protesting and squirming all the way to where the Cult of the Winds and the Three Horsemen of the Apocalypse were surveying the battle.

'There's ssssso little for ussss to do here. It'ssss really dull,' moaned Pestilence. 'I'm redyoossssed to growing cancerssss in my fingerssss for fun.'

'We don't need you,' said The Archivist, exasperated. 'You don't have to be here.'

'We dessssstroy the world for you and now you can't wait to get rid of ussss,' she said. 'It'ssss not like there'ssss anything to infect out there. That'ssss the problem with epic battlessss between sssssupernatural beingsss. No place for disseassessss. If thissss was happening on Earth, I'd have cholera, gangrene, trench foot to play with. Jusssssst look at poor Famine, he'ssss wasssssting away.'

'As long as there's canapés,' said Famine, stuffing his face with a handful of vol-au-vents, 'I don't really mind what we do.'

'Shut it, you two,' said War. He had been talking over the finer points of his strategy – keep killing them until they're all dead – with The Triumph, and had to break off the conversation to silence the others. 'I'm working. Can't you see that this is my masterpiece?'

It was into this argument that one of the clerics brought Crouch.

'Pardon me, Monsignor,' said the cleric, 'but I found this infernal creature behind our lines.'

'And?' said The Archivist. 'What do you want me to do about it, Rodrigo? If he's a spy, put him to the sword.'

'Oh, I do hope that won't be necessary,' said Crouch, still squirming under the clerics's grip. 'As I was trying to explain to this gentleman, I am an envoy from His Most Chaotic Majesty the King of the Underworld, The Opposition.'

'Ha,' said The Archivist, 'is he surrendering already?'

'No, sir, he is not.'

'Then I don't see what he needs to send an envoy for. Dispose of him, Rodrigo.'

'Monsignor.'

'Please,' said Crouch hurriedly, 'I have been sent to deliver the terms of engagement, and to settle the articles of war.'

'I don't think we'll be needing them,' sneered The Archivist. 'Erase him.'

The cleric tightened his grip on Crouch's neck and, holding him at arm's length, made to leave.

'No,' said War. 'We're going to do this properly. I'm not having anyone saying I cheated afterwards, all right? We settle the rules of engagement. Put him down.'

Rodrigo looked from War to The Archivist. The angel nodded, and Rodrigo dropped Crouch on the floor.

'Give us your terms,' said War.

Crouch cleared his throat. 'In the first instance, His Most Chaotic Majesty wishes it known that he has ceded control of all the Infernal Armies to Sir Benjamin Gabriel Robson, who will conduct this campaign on his behalf. Also, Lady Death has ceded her armies to the same gentleman.'

'Stupid cow,' muttered War. 'Fine. Tell them that I conduct this campaign on behalf of . . .' He turned to The Archivist. 'What are you called again?'

'The Archivist of the End Times, Veteran of the Trumpet of Seals, Prime Oblate of the Cult of the Winds, Celestial Lord of the Skies,' said The Archivist.

'Just say "The Archivist",' said War. 'What else?'

'In the second instance, Sir Ben would like to decide this battle in a more ordered manner.'

War grunted. 'What's that supposed to mean?'

'He would like to issue a challenge. He has erected a tent in No Demon's Land, and wishes to finish this battle on the tabletop, using the current edition of the *Warmonger* rulebook.'

'No,' said The Archivist, 'absolutely not.'

'I'm sorry, sir,' said Crouch, 'but I thought that Lord War was conducting this campaign. Perhaps I should be presenting our terms to you, instead?'

'Don't you dare,' said War. 'Tell him that it's a tempting offer, but one I'll pass on. I'm having far too much fun flinging undead soldiers at him to bother with action figures and bits of paper.'

Crouch bowed his head. 'Lady Death advised as much, sir. She said that in the unlikely event the angels let you, you would probably shy away from it. She said to say that you were fine at bashing people around the head, not so good at using your own.'

'What?' said War. 'What? The cheeky – doesn't she remember all those great classics? The Thirty Years War? The Hundred Years War? World War Two, the greatest sequel ever made? I can't believe she thinks a little boy can beat War in a war game.'

'Forgive me, m'lord,' said Crouch, 'but Lady Death suggested that your best work was behind you, and that gone were the days when a strategic victory was a thing of pride. She said you prefer the "cannon fodder" approach nowadays. She said to mention the Somme.'

'That was the first attempt at a World War. It doesn't count.'

'My lord, surely you are not considering taking up this ridiculous challenge—' began The Archivist.

The Horseman roared in response. 'Why? Don't you think I'll win? I'm War. I always win. Tell this "Ben" that we accept his challenge. I'll show him a thing or two.'

'Lord War, please—'

'Are you saying I don't know how to beat a teenage boy?'

'Of course not, my lord,' said The Archivist.

'Then that settles it. Someone fling this little cur back over to their side. Tell your master that we will meet him at his tent, and that he can look forward to being instructed in the Art of War.'

Little cur, thought Crouch. If that hadn't gone so well, I would be rather insulted.

And so the major players in the Apocalypse gathered together around a scale model of the terrain that lay between the gates of

Pandemonium and the far edge of the Valley of Death. Miniatures depicting the two armies had been set out exactly as they were on the battlefield, the ordered rows hardly doing justice to the bloody brawl that was taking place around them.

Ben stood before the game board, dice in hand. At the opposite end, War sat sprawled in a throne made of skulls, licking his lips in anticipation. Behind him stood the angels, and beyond them Famine and Pestilence were lazily sprawled out on giant sequinned cushions.

So this is the way the world ends, thought Ben. Not with a bang, or a whimper, but with the roll of the dice. He cupped his hands and rattled them around before throwing them out on to the little silver tray.

Amongst the jumble of dice, in a neat little row, were three sixes.

The battle of Armageddon had begun.

Chapter Twenty-Seven

The End Times

Armageddon turned out to be something of an anticlimax. This was because although War was the living embodiment of every conflict in history, he had not grown up studying the *Warmonger* rulebook.

The moment Ben pushed his first regiment into position on the board, the indiscriminate brawling at the edge of the Veil stopped, and a sort of psychic ripple passed through the ranks of the Afterworld army. Demon and mist alike suddenly (and quite inexplicably to them) became well-drilled soldiers. They moved with purpose through the Martyrs' ranks, and for a moment even succeeded in pushing them back. Old ladies armed with tuning forks and china plates felled rampaging Vikings, and a gaggle of poets armed only with their quills took out a number of swordsmen. However, the same discipline was instilled in their opponents once War had taken his turn, and the scrappy carnage became a proper battle.

They traded blows equally through the first few turns, and ground gained was lost a roll later. But Ben was soon using his experience to employ a strategy of divide and conquer, cutting off large swathes of War's forces and then overwhelming them with ease.

There was a final roll, a brief skirmish, and the last of War's regiments were removed from the board. The result had been beyond doubt for some time, but War had insisted on fighting down to the last figure. He took his first defeat with uncharacteristic good grace, in that he only smashed his own chair into toothpicks and didn't upend the table. He cut a large hole in the side of the tent with his broadsword, and then left on horseback. Famine and Pestilence sloped off after him, dejected.

Once they were gone, Neil poked his head through the hole, followed by a minotaur carrying a large wooden hammer. 'Sir, the Second Antenoran Guard have the tent surrounded, as per yer orders, sir.'

'Thank you, Captain,' said Ben.

'Do you think this over?' rasped The Archivist. 'It is not. Sister?'

The Castellan of the Veil emitted a high-pitched scream, and all three angels extended their wings. They lit up, and an inky black slit appeared in the air.

'We are veterans of the Grand War,' said The Archivist. 'Did you really expect us to yield because a teenage boy won a board game?'

'Yes,' said Neil. 'Fred?'

The minotaur lowed, and then quickly swung the hammer round. The Castellan of the Veil crumpled, and the gap in the air closed up immediately. Fred hoisted her round his shoulders, grabbed the other two angels by the scruff of their necks and dragged them out, Neil yapping excitedly behind them.

They were bound in chains and taken straight to Pandemonium through the cheering ranks of the mists. As they passed into the Underworld, Neil made sure to point out the newest addition to the Road of Good Intentions, which had been laid right at the edge of the Veil:

I WILL DESTROY ALL CREATION IN ORDER TO PROVE THE EXISTENCE OF GOD

As the demons and mists celebrated their victory in what must have surely been the only joyous scenes to ever take place in the Valley of Death, there was one combatant who was not joining in the fun. Ben sat in the tent on his own, the remains of the greatest Warmonger victory of all time in front of him. He was glad that they had won, of course, but when he looked at the massive piles of discarded figures it made him realize that not only was his own world destroyed, he was also the last person alive to mourn it. Everyone else, everyone he had ever met, was either ghost or zombie.

The tent flap rustled, and Death entered. Her clothes were grubby and torn, and her hair was matted with martyr blood and dirt, but she looked about as radiant it was possible for the personification of mortality to be.

'Am I disturbing you?' she said.

'Not really,' said Ben.

'I just wanted to thank you. I don't know what I'd've done if the other Horsemen would've won.'

'That's all right. What will happen to them?'

'Oh, there will still be conflicts, and hunger, and disease, and death. None of it stopped when we were locked in the Box. It won't stop now that we're out.'

'But if there aren't any people, and the world is destroyed, won't it stop anyway?'

'I don't know. Everything is dead now, and I'm still here.'

'Everything except me,' said Ben.

Neil ducked under the tent flap, followed by the demons.

'Permission to speak, sir.'

'You don't have to ask permission,' said Ben. 'And you definitely don't need to call me "sir" any more.'

'Right you are, sir. I mean Ben. Sorry, sir. Ben.'

'Did you have something you wanted to say?'

'What? Oh yeah. I've been rushed off my chuffin' feet today, I don't mind telling you. Don't know whether I'm coming or going. His Nibs has sent me to invite you lot to dinner. Says he wants to talk about the future. He's in a funny mood if you ask me.'

'Can we go? Can we?' said Djinn. 'All this fighting has made me hungry.'

'You were hungry before,' said Kartofel.

'Even hungrier, then.'

'Maybe you'll get your answers there,' said Death.

'I guess this is goodbye, then,' said Ben. He shook her hand, and tried to smile even as the hairs on the back of his neck stood on end. 'It was nice to meet you.'

'Oh, it's never goodbye with me,' said Death. 'I'll be seeing you again, that's for sure.'

If the hairs on the back of his neck could have risen any higher, they would have.

The Opposition's office had been remodelled as a dining room, with a low Japanese-style table set out for five. The Opposition beckoned for them to sit, and they did: Ben and Orff cross-legged, Djinn hovering as low as possible, Kartofel for once at a table that was just the right size for him.

Once the meal was over, and Crouch had taken away the empty plates (it took several overloaded trips to clear Djinn's dishes), they retired to a set of high-backed leather chairs that had been positioned next to an open fire at the other end of the room. They settled down, and soon lapsed into an awkward silence, punctuated only by the occasional sigh from The Opposition.

'Erm . . . Neil said you wanted to talk about the future?' said Ben.

'What? Did he?' said The Opposition. 'Oh.' He turned to look into the fire, and a few more minutes passed in silence. Ben pushed his chair back.

'Maybe we should go,' he said.

'Really?' said The Opposition. 'Where to?'

'I was going to ask you that, but you don't seem to be in the mood for company.'

'No. No. I don't suppose I am. Or ever will be again.'

'Why not?' said Kartofel. 'We saved the whole world. We're heroes. And you were proved right. When I'm proved right, which is all the time, I feel awesome.'

'Indeed, friend Mnemnor. But do you really think it worth going to war to prove oneself right? Actually, don't answer that. I know you too well.'

'But . . . you won,' said Ben.

'Oh, this was never about winning. It never has been. They were trying to convert me to their way of thinking, not the other way round. I was quite happy to leave them to their delusions, if it gave them comfort. I just didn't want my existence dictated by it.'

'Then why are you sad?' said Djinn.

'Because, good sweet Ichthor, I do not know how I will fill the endless restless days ahead. Doubt has been removed. There is no Prime One. The problem with defining yourself as The Opposition is that one day you may have nothing to oppose.'

'Then why don't you help rebuild the Creation?' said Ben.

'It can hardly be called the Creation if no one created it, now, can it?' The Opposition smiled. 'No, I have no desire to replace one deity with another. Besides, it cannot be rebuilt.' The Opposition clapped his hands, and a door that looked like something you might find on a submarine creaked open. Crouch waddled out in a radiation suit, carrying something at arm's length with a pair of tongs. He dropped it at Ben's feet, bowed, and left the way he came.

'The Veil is still in a perilous state. That didn't change because we won the war. It could still collapse, and the Worlds could still crush each other.'

Ben looked down at the object. It was burned, misshapen, and had a large splinterous hole in the lid, but he knew it right away. It was the Box.

'I had Crouch retrieve it,' said The Opposition.

'Why?' Ben ran his hand over the lid. A few of the burned black splinters crumbled, and he could see through to the empty interior. It did not react at all.

'Why don't you open it? In case there's something left at the bottom there?'

The hinges were bent out of shape, and the lid was stiff. As Ben prised it open, it emitted a very dim green glow.

'Perhaps you would do well to remember back to when the Box had hold of you. It had a certain restorative power, did it not? Remember that I had a hand in its creation. I could not very well let it out with the power to destroy if it did not also have the power to heal. Balance in all things.'

'And this will fix the Veil?'

'And more besides. It will also restore the worlds to their preapocalyptic state. Everything will be as it was. Simply ride through the Worlds, et voila! All the people and animals et cetera et cetera will be restored to life.'

'Even my mum?'

'Ah,' said The Opposition. 'No. I'm sorry. Everything that lived before the Horsemen were released. But be assured, I will keep an eye on your mother. For one thing, someone will need to look after Druss when he returns. I assume you don't have the room for a giant rabbit at your house?'

Ben shook his head. The dull green light from the Box started to bleed into the corner of his vision, reaching out to him. He looked straight into the heart of it, and it shone a little brighter as he did. His mood lifted as he thought of all the people he would restore, and he smiled.

At last, he understood the light's power; why it had tormented the demons, and why it was the only thing left in the Box after the apocalypse had been let loose.

He knew what the green light was.

It was Hope.

The four of them rode out over the plains of the Underworld. The Box brilliantly lit up the Veil as they passed through it, instantly revealing and then healing all the scars in the glue of the Worlds. They sprinted through the Afterworld and the light of the Box shone on both martyr and mist, wheedling out all those who had been alive before the Horsemen were freed, returning them to life.

They pressed on to the World, and saw natural disasters reverse before their eyes. Meteors hurtled back through space, lava seeped into the Earth's crust, and tectonic plates rubbed and shifted back into position. For the people, it was as if they had all blinked, all at once; for in that second between darkness and light each of them had died and been resurrected without knowing.

And once everything was restored, Ben and the demons headed back to the cemetery, and dismounted.

'What now then?' said Kartofel.

'We say goodbye,' said Ben. He put his arms around Druss's neck, and cuddled him tightly. Druss twitched his nose three times, then nuzzled Ben's body with his head.

'You can go now. Mum's going to look after you.' He ran his fingers through Druss's fur one last time, and then patted his haunches. 'Thank you.'

The rabbit tore off, and disappeared in a purple fizz.

'Do we all have to do that?' said Djinn. 'Because I think Alf would be upset if I sent him back.'

'No,' said Ben. 'You can go too.'

'What's that supposed to mean?' said Kartofel.

'There's no more Box. You don't have collars any more. You can do whatever you want.'

'I've always been able to do whatever I want. What you on about?'

'I think,' said Orff, 'that Ben is trying to tell us something.'

'I'm confused,' said Djinn.

'We have to say goodbye,' said Orff.

'Oh.'

'But . . .' said Kartofel. 'But you said we can go wherever we want.'

'Just not here,' said Orff.

Ben nodded. 'I'm sorry.'

'We quite understand,' said Orff. He remounted Legion, who

had taken the form of a donkey. Four small patches of grass turned brown beneath his hoofs.

'Where are you going?' said Djinn.

'I'm not sure,' said Orff. 'Perhaps back to the Underworld. I think Legion would like to see Drablow again.'

'That sounds nice,' said Djinn. 'Can we come?'

'I can't believe you two are seriously entertaining this,' said Kartofel. 'We can't split up now. It's not right.'

'Oh, but it is,' said Orff. 'Good luck, Ben. Perhaps we will meet again, next time the Worlds need saving. Goodbye.' He dug his heels into Legion's sides, and the cloud became a leopard. It sprinted away, with Orff holding on tight. Djinn mounted Alf, and they leaped into the air.

'Bye, Ben,' said Djinn as they flew off. 'We love you!'

'Big soft idiot,' said Kartofel. 'Now them two have gone, perhaps we can have some proper adventures. I understand you not wanting to say while those two were around, but it's all right if I stay, isn't it? Your old pal Kartofel.'

'No,' said Ben.

Kartofel sniffed. Little clouds of steam rose from his eyes, as if he was a boiling kettle. He turned away from Ben and scurried over to Talullah. 'I didn't want to stay anyway,' he muttered. 'I was only asking to be nice.' He clambered into the saddle and Talullah whinnied. 'Let's go somewhere they care about us, hey girl?'

'Good luck,' said Ben but they had already disappeared into the Veil.

He walked through the cemetery, ready for his last goodbye. On the way he picked a few wild flowers and made a posy. He came to his mother's plot, and set them down on the earthen mound.

'I love you,' he said. 'And I won't forget you.'

He wiped a tear from his eye, walked back to the place the angels had snatched him, and sat down to wait.

For her.

Lucy blinked. She had forgotten, for the briefest moment, where she was, and the sudden realization that she was in a particularly unloved part of the cemetery made her shudder. It occurred to her that it would have been a strange route for Ben to take to visit his mother's plot, which was when she remembered what she was doing. She was looking for Ben, yes, her friend Ben. And then she thought, How long have I been here, walking through this place? An inexplicable wave of panic crashed over her, and she felt as if she was about to drown.

'Lucy,' said a voice from behind her. It jolted her from the woozy feeling and anchored her to the present. For the briefest moment she thought that she recognized it, but there was something in it that jarred her. She turned round to face it, and there was Ben. And although he had been gone less than half an hour, it was as if he had completely changed. He didn't look any different, but there was a sort of invisible definition to him now. He still had the same vulnerability, the same thing that had made her want to take him under her wing in the first place, but it was no longer pathetic and helpless. There was, she was a little surprised to find out, something even a little *attractive* about him now.

'Hi, uhh, we were wondering where you went, because if you're ready we can go but if you're not you know you can take as much time as you want, you know, if you want to.' She winced inwardly. Get a hold of yourself, she thought. This is Ben. Little Nerdy Ben.

Little Nerdy Ben held out his hand, and she took it. 'I'm ready,' he said, and as her palm slipped inside his, he was no longer Little Nerdy Ben but somehow Her Ben. His hand was warm and dry, and she felt safe.

As they started to walk away, she realized he was missing something. Perhaps that was why he seemed different. He was always carrying that satchel around with him, wasn't he? He'd even taken it to his mother's graveside.

'Wait,' she said, and looked back over her shoulder. 'You forgot—'

'I left it somewhere. I don't think I'll be needing it any more,' said Ben. 'It doesn't matter. Don't worry about it,' and she didn't. He was right. It didn't matter.

They walked back to the car through the rows of head-stones – facing away as if death was turning its back on the pair of them – and off into a lovely spring day in a quiet, forgotten, and somehow not-quite-as-bad-as-it-had-once-seemed seaside resort on the North Wales coast.

Epilogue

Deus Ex Machina

In the far reaches of space, so far from Earth as to be inconceivable to the human mind, there is a planet. It is a barren lump, little more than a piece of rock orbiting far from the nearest star. It is a deeply cold and dark place, totally uninhabitable by any creature anywhere in the universe. It is useless, a cosmic afterthought, a piece of space debris eternally rotating around a distant and indifferent sun.

Around that planet orbits a satellite, but it is not made of rock, like our own moon. This satellite is no accident, no wanderer that happened to be hurtling through space until it collided with the orbital pull of the planet below. This satellite is made of metal. It is a bright, white, pristine, twenty-faced shape that remains immune to cosmic rays and asteroids: it does not, and never will, have a scratch on it.

Inside this satellite is a single room. And inside that room – also white, also pristine – is a computer. It is the fastest, largest, most powerful computer ever built, and its sole job, the sole task of this machine that is so powerful that it needs an entire planetary satellite to house it, is to run one program.

This program is called 'TERRA'.

There are many screens, and buttons, and levers, all easily accessible from the single red leather stool in the centre of the room. On the largest screen, which is as big as one wall, runs a series of words and numbers; green characters on a black background, like the most primitive home computer. And hidden within these symbols, these constantly moving, constantly changing, constantly updating figures, is everything that has ever happened as it is happening, including the events set down in this book, and the writing of this book, and now, as your eyes pass over these words, the reading of this book.

And as strange as this is, there is something stranger still about this satellite, something that can only be seen if the writing on one of its twenty faces happens to catch what little light the distant sun provides. For emblazoned on that icosahedron high in orbit around a dead and forgotten world, are these words:

PRIME 1.0

Acknowledgements

A book isn't just the work of one person, but then neither is a writer. So I need to thank Mum and Dad first of all: not just for the lifetime of unconditional love and support, but also for moving to North Wales when I was four. Luckily they took me with them, and *The Box of Demons* is the result.

Alex read and reread the manuscript nearly as many times as I did, was right about most things along the way and nudged me in the direction of the Write Now! competition. It's thanks to him that you're holding this book at all.

Lynne was always on hand for advice and support and having things she told me pilfered and put into the dreams of rabbits.

Sylwia had the most difficult job of all: she had to live with me while I grumped around going on about angels and castles and monsters and whatever else popped into my head. *Kocham cię, kochanie moje.*

I'd also like to mention all the people who took the time to plough through early drafts and were nice enough to offer encouragement: Philip Benjamin, Emily Butterfield, Morven Christie, Linda Gale, fish & chip consultants Silv and Sarah del Prete, and the Rowleys, who sent me a lovely email when (unbeknown to them) I needed it most. Druss's revenge is for them.

I want to thank Nancy Miles for her faith in me; Chris Riddell for making the characters look better than I imagined them; my brilliant editor, Rachel Petty, for coming up with loads of brilliant ideas that have made the book brillianter (she wasn't allowed to edit that sentence), and the judges of the Write Now! Prize for choosing *The Box of Demons* as their winner.

I'd like to finish by recognizing all the booksellers and librarians out there, fighting the good fight and putting the right stories into the hands of the people who want to read them. I've been bowled over by their passion, their support and above all their kindness towards me. But since they're probably too busy finding awesome new books to bother reading these acknowledgements, will you do me a favour?

Next time you see one, thank them for me.